"We leave in the mor

"What about us?" Pri

"I informed the Queste... ...cess Lahoree would wish to keep her pet toads safely in the wagon, and they were not to be disturbed."

"*Pet toad?* I'm a princess!" Princess cried.

"And I, wise master—though I'm certain you had excellent reasons for doing as you did—am a handsome prince," added Handsome.

"My dears," said the wizard. "We must be realistic about the dangers that surround us on all sides. Surely you are aware of how valuable you are. Certain powerful spells require an enchanted toad as a key ingredient, and there are sorcerers and necromancers who would go to any lengths to acquire one."

"What spells, learned master?" Handsome asked after a brief apprehensive pause.

"Chiefly spells for reanimating the dead."

"And what role does the toad . . . play?"

Kedrigern averted his eyes and looked uncomfortable. "A very nasty one. It is always fatal, and quite unpleasantly so . . ."

John Morressy
The Questing
of Kedrigern

ACE BOOKS, NEW YORK

For Ed Ferman,
A Wizard's Best Friend

Portions of this book have appeared, in somewhat different
form, in *The Magazine of Fantasy and Science Fiction.*

This book is an Ace
original edition, and has
never been previously published.

THE QUESTING OF KEDRIGERN

An Ace Book/published by arrangement with
the author

PRINTING HISTORY
Ace edition/August 1987

ISBN: 0-441-69721-6

Ace Books are published by The Berkley Publishing Group,
200 Madison Avenue, New York, NY 10016.
The name "Ace" and the "A" logo are trademarks
belonging to Charter Communications, Inc.
PRINTED IN THE UNITED STATES OF AMERICA

10 9 8 7 6 5 4 3 2 1

Of bodies chang'd to various forms, I sing. . . .
—JOHN DRYDEN

⋯⊰ One ⊱⋯

for old times' sake

KEDRIGERN AWOKE TO a glorious golden morning. The air was bright as crystal and heady as wine, with a gentle reminder of the turning season in its mild and not unpleasant touch of chill. He breathed deeply, stretched luxuriously, and without turning, looked out in benevolence at the innocent pale sky. This was a day to be enjoyed; a day for a picnic, or a long walk in the woods, amid the reds and golds and tawny browns of autumn. Princess would enjoy such a day, he thought, and this day would be theirs: no work, no worry, no spells, just a pleasant holiday for the two of them.

He turned, to wake her gently, and found her already awake, propped up against her pillow. The little green book of vocabulary-building exercises that had been her constant study in recent months lay face down on the coverlet, beneath her folded hands. She was looking thoughtfully out the far window.

"Good morning, my dear," said Kedrigern, laying his hand on hers. "Lovely morning, isn't it?"

"Yes, lovely," she said, without shifting her eyes.

"A perfect day for a picnic, I was thinking. We could have Spot make up a basket, and go to the top of the mountain for the day. Magnificent prospects from up there."

"I thought you had work to do."

"Nothing pressing," he said, pushing himself up into a sitting position at her side. "It's much too nice a day to spend

1

in my study when we might be on Silent Thunder Peak, just the two of us, with the world at our feet."

"Yes," said Princess, and sighed.

"Is everything all right, my dear? You sound less than delighted."

"Oh, no, Keddie, everything is fine. It's lovely up there this time of year, and I do enjoy picnics. Very nice of you to think of it. Only . . ."

"Only . . . ?"

"Only every time we go anywhere, or do anything, it's always just the two of us. Aren't we ever going to have company, callers, visitors, or guests? Won't we ever do any traveling, journeying, or wayfaring, or go on a tour, quest, or pilgrimage?"

"Of course we'll entertain, my dear. We've already invited Bess to dinner twice."

"But she didn't come either time."

"And we took that long trip to Castle Grodzik."

"That was a business trip, Keddie."

"Well . . . yes, I suppose it was. But it *was* a trip. You can't say I never take you anywhere."

"We returned from Castle Grodzik weeks and weeks ago, Keddie, and we haven't gone anywhere since then, and no one's come here except people to see you on business."

Kedrigern shook his head bemusedly and scratched his chin. "Has it really been that long?"

"Yes," said Princess emphatically.

"I lose track of time when I'm busy."

"You haven't been that busy, Keddie."

"I haven't, have I? Well, I lose track of time when I'm not busy, too. But truthfully, my dear, I've been thinking of taking a little trip to some new place where we might meet interesting people, see new things, enjoy a complete change of scene. Something like that would do us both a lot of good."

"Keddie, what a nice surprise! When are we leaving?" said Princess, at once lively and animated.

"Oh, I thought . . . the summer is a good time to travel. The roads are—"

"The summer? *Next* summer?"

"That's right, my dear. We'll have plenty of time to plan our trip, and make some—"

"Keddie, it's autumn. It's *early* autumn. Summer has just ended. You're asking me to wait a year."

"Not quite a year. Hardly more than a half a year, actually. And this way, everything will be leisurely and unhurried."

Princess fixed him with her blue eyes. Her sweet voice was decidedly chilly as she said, "Keddie, for an unknown number of years I sat on a lily pad in a bog. I went nowhere, saw no one, and did nothing. My life was leisurely and unhurried, and I hated every minute of it. You restored me to my human form, married me in honorable fashion, and brought me to this small but charming cottage remote from the stress, struggle, and turmoil of the world. I now look and speak like my former self, I have a gorgeous wardrobe, and have taught Spot how to prepare and serve exquisite dinners. And still I go nowhere, see no one, and do nothing. I might as well have remained a toad."

The room was silent as Kedrigern drew a succession of deep slow breaths and nodded his head. "You'd rather not wait until summer," he said at last.

"I would not."

"I understand, my dear. I really do. But spring is a bad time to travel, and winter is worse."

"We can go now. Autumn is a lovely time to travel, and you're not busy. It's the perfect chance to get away, Keddie."

"But I can't just *go*. It's true I don't have pressing business, but I do have a few small matters. . . . And something could turn up at any moment."

Princess took his hand. "Do you really want to stay here all winter?" He looked at her uncertainly, and she went on, "Wouldn't it be nice to get away from the cold, and the snow, and the barbarians? We could go south, where there are no blizzards, and the days are long and sunny and warm, and people sing, and smile, and drink wine."

"I've never been south," Kedrigern admitted thoughtfully.

"You could gather fresh herbs. There are herbs in the south that don't grow here. They could open up a whole new field for you."

"I've always liked working with herbs. It's a good clean kind of magic. Nice for cooking, too. But what would *you* do, my dear?"

"For one thing, I'd stay warm. I could sit under the fruit trees during the heat of the day and work on my vocabulary and my spelling. I have dozens of spells I want to practice. Evenings we would entertain. Oh, Keddie, let's do it! You can settle everything here in a few weeks, and we'll spend the whole winter in the sun. What a wonderful idea!'' she said, throwing her arms around his neck and kissing him enthusiastically.

By afternoon, Kedrigern had convinced himself that going south for the winter actually was a wonderful idea, and wondered why it had never occurred to him before. He reclined on a cushioned bench in his front yard, sheltered from the breeze. A book lay at his side. His face was upturned to the autumn sun; his eyes were closed; a sleepy half-smile was on his face. Fall had always been his favorite season, marred only by the inescapable arrival of winter, his least favorite season. Now, by the simple expedient of going south late in the fall, he could enjoy his pleasure to the full and escape his displeasure completely. True, it required travel; but one could not expect to get one's way without paying the price, as he had, on occasion, reminded a client.

A soft fluttering of wings broke his reverie. He opened his eyes a slit and saw, to his surprise, a pair of white doves hovering in the air just beyond the foot of the bench. In their beaks they held a broad golden ribbon. He raised a hand slowly, so as not to frighten the timid birds, and rubbed his eyes. Something was written on the ribbon. Shielding his vision from the glare of the descending sun, Kedrigern read the message printed in great scarlet letters:

WIZCON WELCOMES WONDERFUL WISE WIZARDS.

The doves abruptly wheeled and flew off, trailing their message, and Kedrigern watched, smiling. A soft footfall made him turn, and he saw Princess standing close by. In one hand was her vocabulary book; the other was raised in a picturesque gesture, shading her eyes as she peered after the doves.

''What was that about, Keddie?'' she asked.

''Just a reminder about Wizcon, my dear. The committee is promoting it very aggressively.''

''Hadn't you planned on attending?''

''Not exactly planned, no. I had thought of it, but it was all very indefinite. It's out of the question now.''

"But shouldn't you go to such things? I'm sure they're a great help to you professionally. If you really think you should go, we can always leave for the south a bit later."

"No, my dear. Wizcon has its attractions, but I'd rather be seated by your side on a sunny terrace, looking out over the sea and drinking good red wine, than putting up with noise and crowds."

She laid her hand on his shoulder. "As long as it's your choice, election, and volition, Keddie, that's fine. But I'm sure you'd enjoy seeing some of your old friends, companions, consociates, colleagues, and mates, and hearing what they're all doing, and learning of new developments in the profession. It's thoughtful of you to pass it up for my sake, but if you want to go, I'm willing."

He took her hand and drew her down beside him, where he could look at her without twisting his neck. She was in a smooth gown of dark green. Her black hair was plaited in a single long braid, tied with red and gold ribbons, and a simple golden circlet ringed her brow. Princess was a beautiful woman, and the thought of having her seen by his old friends and colleagues was a tempting one; particularly tempting now that she could speak with a voice befitting her appearance, and was making such progress in her studies.

But Wizcon meant crowds. There would be welcome faces among them, guild members he knew by name and reputation but had never met, old companions too long unseen: all this was true. But crowds are crowds. Even nice crowds are still crowds, and Kedrigern found crowds unsettling.

If the crowding were not enough to discourage him, he had only to think of the horror of accommodations. At this late date it would be impossible to get a decent room, and the price of even a hovel would be exorbitant.

And then there was the traveling. Kedrigern disliked travel almost as much as he disliked crowds; but he consoled himself that his planned trip south with Princess would find no mob waiting at journey's end. *That* traveling, at least, would take him to repose.

With a sigh, he said, "No, my dear. We might have a bit of fun at Wizcon, but we'd only end up starting our vacation trip exhausted. I'd sooner stay at home and work on the counterspell against night visitations. I've promised it to old Bremborn before the solstice, and I want to get it out of the way."

"Whatever you like, Keddie. Are you ready for lunch?" Princess asked.

"I'm starving. This air does give one an appetite. Why don't we eat out here?"

She nodded in agreement with his suggestion, and he picked up a dainty silver bell and rang it lightly. As he waited for the house-troll to appear, he slipped his hand inside his tunic and touched his fingertips to the medallion that hung around his neck. His expression grew thoughtful.

Spot came bounding into view on huge flapping feet, ears and hands waving wildly in the speed of his passage. "Yah, yah!" the little creature cried, bouncing up and down eagerly.

Absently, as if his mind were busy elsewhere, Kedrigern said, "We will lunch out here, Spot. But stay a moment before you bring it."

"Is something wrong, awry, or amiss?" Princess asked.

"We're going to have a visitor. A member of the guild, I think, though I can't imagine why anyone from the guild would be visiting us."

"It must be important."

"Not to me. I withdrew from guild affairs long ago."

"Yah?" Spot inquired.

"Be patient, Spot. I'll tell you when," Kedrigern said. He drew out the medallion, and raising it to his eye he peered thorough the small hole at its center, the Aperture of True Vision. He looked all around, then upward, and fixed his gaze on a distant speck in the sky. "It's Tristaver!" he cried. "Spot, bring an extra tankard. And more cheese. And fill the large pitcher."

The troll went careening off, and Kedrigern explained to Princess, "Tris has always been good at shape-changing. He loves to have an excuse to fly."

"Can he really become a bird? It must be wonderful!"

"It's not all that difficult. I did it myself, a few times, when I was starting out. It's a lovely way to travel, if you don't get airsick. I wonder what brings him here. . . ."

A small falcon circled overhead. Kedrigern waved, and the bird answered with a sharp cry and shot off to disappear in the nearby woods.

"Tris will be joining us directly. He's shy about having people see him land. He's always been a bit clumsy, and landing is the hardest part," Kedrigern said.

"Why does he turn into a merlin? Wouldn't a peregrine be faster?"

"Just sentimental, I guess."

Spot arrived with a silver tray on which stood a brimming, frost-coated pitcher, three tankards, a generous platter of dark bread and soft pale cheese. As the little troll departed, a slender, elegant figure emerged from the trees, brushing vigorously at the leaves and dirt that clung to his garments. He waved to Kedrigern and Princess, and approached them with rapid strides. Kedrigern rose to greet him.

"Tris, how are you? It's been a long time!" he said heartily.

"Too long, Keddie!" the other wizard replied, throwing his arm around Kedrigern's shoulder. "Everyone's always asking about you. I must say, you look well. And is this Princess?"

"I'm happy to meet you, Master Tristaver," Princess said demurely, extending her hand.

"And such a lovely voice! I'm so pleased for you both. I had heard . . . Conhoon mentioned something . . . about a . . . a croaking problem," Tristaver said uncomfortably.

"That's all in the past. Well, come, sit down and join us for lunch, Tris. What brings you here?"

"Oh, a few of us were talking the other night, and your name came up, and I realized how long it's been since I saw you, so I decided to fly over first chance I had. Thank you," Tristaver said, taking the foam-capped tankard Kedrigern passed to him. "Actually, we were talking about that affair at Castle Grodzik. Everyone's impressed with the way you handled Grodz. He was a dangerous man."

"As a matter of fact, Tris, it was Princess's spell that did for Grodz. She's rather good."

"I learned it all from you, dear," Princess said, laying her hand on his.

"Well, we're all proud of you both. It's good to have this little visit, and a chance to chat."

"Purely a social call. I see," Kedrigern said, intently filling a tankard for Princess.

Tristaver smiled and smoothed his long snowy beard, but did not respond further. Instead, he toasted Princess, and then Kedrigern, and after refilling his tankard and breaking off a bit of bread he turned to the subject of the guild to which he and Kedrigern belonged. He spoke of old friends and old times, and Kedrigern joined in the reminiscences.

"Is Krillicane still active in guild affairs? She was one of the great ones," he said fondly.

"She retired shortly after you . . . withdrew from active participation," said Tristaver discreetly.

"Krillicane could do just about anything she put her mind to. Once, she actually made a street speak."

"Why would anyone make a street speak?" Princess asked.

"Urgent request from some infatuated prince, as I recall. Krillie took it as a challenge. It wasn't a street, actually. More like an alley: a little narrow passage running behind one of the prince's stables. It took awhile, but she made it talk."

"What did it say?" Tristaver asked.

"It said, 'We are not a mews.' She shut it up on the spot and never worked that spell again." Kedrigern sighed. "We had real wizards in those days, Tris. They'll never be forgotten."

"People still speak of you frequently, Kedrigern," Tristaver said. "I never chat with another guild member but your name comes up. People keep asking what's become of Kedrigern."

Kedrigern gave a little self-deprecating laugh. Waving off the remark with a gesture, he refilled his tankard. Princess, looking on in silence, could sense his pleasure at their visitor's words.

"I mean it sincerely. You really ought to be more active in guild affairs again. We need people like you," Tristaver said earnestly.

"I've done my share, Tris."

"No one can deny that. Still, it's been a few years. You must miss it sometimes. . . . The involvement . . . the sense of being in touch with events . . . the feeling of using your abilities to the full. . . . You're much too young to retire like this. You're not even close to two hundred."

"I don't think about the guild much these days, Tris," Kedrigern said cheerfully. "I still pay my dues, and I support its activities, but this is the life I prefer."

"You don't bear any grudge over that Quintrindus affair, do you? Everyone admits that you were absolutely right, and the rest of us—"

"No grudges, Tris. Let's just forget the whole thing."

"Of course, of course, Keddie. Anything you like. If it were up to me, I wouldn't say another word. But . . ."

Kedrigern sighed. "But the guild wants something, and it's your job to ask for it. I thought so."

"It's a very small favor. A matter of a few days' time, and no effort at all. Probably a bit of fun for you both. You see, Hithernils has vanished."

"I knew that was going to happen," Kedrigern said hotly. "He let everyone in creation know where he kept the guild's treasure. Some barbarian must have—"

"No, no, no, it was nothing like that," Tristaver broke in. "No barbarians. Hithernils is perfectly safe. He's at home now, in his study."

"You said he vanished."

"He did. He's invisible."

"How?"

"Someone on the Wizcon program committee asked Hithernils if he knew anyone in the guild who might be willing to offer a workshop on invisibility. Well, you know Hithernils."

Kedrigern nodded eagerly, and gave a low, involuntarily chuckle of anticipation. Tristaver was primly silent until his host urged him on.

"Hithernils doesn't know any more about invisibility than I do about chiromancy, but he loves an audience. So he gave them his own name, and then he went madly to work to learn something about invisibility spells. It seems he got one wrong."

Kedrigern stared at his visitor for a moment, then gave a whoop and doubled over, helpless with laughter. Princess and Tristaver looked on, exchanging awkward little smiles, as he struggled to regain his composure. The process took some time. At last, with one final giggle and a backhanded swipe at his tear-filled eyes, Kedrigern managed to ask, "And the guild wants me to work a counterspell and keep it all quiet, is that it?"

Tristaver leaned back and gazed off thoughtfully into the forest. "Well, actually, Keddie . . . no. It's the sense of the membership that Hithernils might benefit, in the long run, from this experience, and so we don't believe that it should end too soon."

"What do you want from me, then?"

"We wondered if you'd be willing to replace Hithernils at Wizcon. The program committee would love to have a panel on counterspells, and you're the obvious choice to lead it."

Kedrigern frowned thoughtfully and scratched his neck. "I hadn't planned on going to this one, Tris. Couldn't I just make Hithernils visible again, with a warning?"

"That might help Hithernils, but it wouldn't do much for the guild. The Wizcon people expect us to send a representative, and obviously we can't send Hithernils. He wouldn't dare show his face now."

"Why not? No one could see it."

"Well, of course, that's the whole problem right there. It simple wouldn't do. The mood at such conferences is very . . . very playful . . . and now that everyone knows of his unfortunate accident . . . No, Hithernils would never do. That's painfully obvious," Tristaver said.

"A lot more obvious than Hithernils," Kedrigern said, grinning broadly.

"Quite so. Will you do it, for the guild? For old times' sake?"

"Well . . . Princess and I were planning to head south. . . ."

"I don't see how you can refuse, Keddie. Your friends need you," said Princess solemnly.

"Don't you think we should talk it over?" he asked. He felt trapped.

"It would be a nice thing to do, and it would probably be fun besides. You could clear up a lot of misconceptions about counterspells. Everyone knows that you're the best there is when it comes to counterspells," she said.

"That's true," he admitted.

Tristaver added, "And, of course, you'd be honored guests of Wizcon. And you'd stay in the suite Hithernils reserved for himself."

"A whole suite?"

Stiffly, Tristaver said, "Anyone who represents the guild has to make a good showing. We can't have legendary wizards and beautiful princesses sleeping six to a bed in some fleabag."

"No, of course not."

"Besides, it's already paid for and the inn won't refund the money."

"All right, then, Tris—we'll go," Kedrigern said, rising and extending his hand while Princess looked on happily.

···<del>}</del> Two <del>}</del>···

welcome to wizcon

KEDRIGERN SAT ON the big lumpy bed, sulking. Princess seemed oblivious to his mood as she bustled about the room, humming a merry tune. She had deloused and defleaed the entire wing of the inn with a short-term spell, and was now engaged in more customary domestic undertakings. Here she arranged wildflowers in a chipped vase; there she shifted a threadbare doily. She plumped the cushions on the big benches by the fireplace, checked the water level in the fire buckets, tested the rushes on the floor for springiness. Her housekeeping done, she stood before the window, hands on her hips, and surveyed the room with a satisfied look.

"I don't want to give a party," said Kedrigern for perhaps the twentieth time since their arrival.

"Of course you do, Keddie," Princess said absently, looking into the other room.

"I don't."

"The guild has provided us with this nice big suite. We'd be terribly selfish not to give other people a chance to enjoy it."

"I won't enjoy it very much if it's jammed full of strangers."

"Just leave it to me. I'll invite a few people—the really interesting ones that I know you'll want to talk with—and we'll have a civilized evening."

With a scornful laugh, Kedrigern rose from the bed. "Do

11

you really think you can have a nice cozy party—a civilized evening—at a convention? You've never been to one of these, my dear. You don't know what the parties are like. Loud singing, everyone shouting back and forth . . . crowds . . . pushing . . . spells. Remember the spells.''

"What's wrong with spells? We both use them all the time. And this *is* a wizards' convention," said Princess complacently, smoothing the rumpled coverlet.

"There's nothing wrong with spells. But when people get into a party mood and then start showing off, there's bound to be trouble. At the conference in Gryphon Rock, for example, the stable boys at the inn were surly, and someone turned all the help into pigs. Believe me, there was a lot of explaining to be done when *that* got out. And a few years earlier, at Chateau Ravet, someone—''

"Just because there's been some rowdy behavior in the past, we needn't tolerate it here.''

"I'm talking about the present, my dear. Right now. There's a whole new element getting into the profession these days. Some of them wouldn't even make good alchemists.''

"Listen to yourself, Keddie. You're not even 170, and you're talking like an old fogy.''

"Then maybe I'm a young fogy," he said sullenly. "All I know is that I don't want to be in a room full of people like that.''

"We will set a respectable tone, and people will simply have to behave themselves.''

"Ordinarily, that might work. But this is Wizcon.''

Princess drew herself up. Her blue eyes flashed, and she said with a hauteur that would have snuffed the flame of an angry dragon, "This may be Wizcon, but *you* are a respected senior wizard, representing the most prestigious guild in the west, and *I* am a princess. There will be no rowdyism, boorishness, or indecorum.''

Kedrigern sensed that the final word on this particular topic had been spoken. He nodded, and said no more.

Princess was mollified. She smiled and said, "Good. It's getting late. Pull your boots on, so we can get to dinner. You have to prepare your remarks for tomorrow, and you'll want a decent night's sleep.''

As he tugged his boots on, Kedrigern muttered, "I'd better get my sleep tonight. Won't get a wink of it tomorrow night, not with a mob carousing through here until dawn. We'll head south looking like something dragged out of a necromancer's rubbish heap."

"Don't be moody. You might at least try to have a good time," said Princess patiently.

Kedrigern sighed. He knew that he was being selfish; even a bit childish. He knew that Princess had been longing to give a big party and that there was no opportunity for such things at home, and that this would make her very happy. He knew that it would be a good thing for the guild if everyone went home from Wizcon talking about what splendid hosts these wizards were. He even suspected that despite all his determination to the contrary, he might have a good time.

All the same, he hated noise and crowds.

About a dozen people were seated in the dining room. Kedrigern did not recognize a single one. They looked up as he and Princess entered, and their gazes lingered on Princess. She was resplendent in a close-fitting pale green gown, with a cloak of darker green thrown over her shoulders. Kedrigern, clean-shaven, in nondescript tunic and trousers of homespun stuff and a plain dark cloak, was given scarcely a glance. He found a corner table, small but relatively steady and less stained than the rest, and they seated themselves.

"Probably not a wizard in the place. I certainly don't see anyone who looks like a wizard," Kedrigern said morosely.

"You don't look like a wizard yourself," Princess pointed out.

"Well, of course not. It's just inviting trouble to go around looking like a wizard these days."

"Then why should other people do it?"

Kedrigern grunted, mumbled something, and took to staring at the tabletop. They dined well on grilled carp, mutton, and pheasant, plenty of fresh bread, fruit for dessert, and a good ale to wash it all down. The meal left Kedrigern in much better spirits. He and Princess were smiling at one another before they reached the dessert.

"You'll have a good time tomorrow night," Princess said, laying her hand on his in reassurance.

"I suppose so. It's been so long since I've been to a party that I've lost all taste for them," Kedrigern said listlessly.

Princess patted his hand. "All the more reason to have one of our own. You just leave it all up to me."

They left the dining room, which was a bit more crowded now as the late arrivals hurried to dine before the best food was gone. A low buzz of subdued conversation filled the air, louder as they stepped into the busy hall. Baggage was piled haphazard, and little groups stood about in lively dialogue. A number of people were standing near the stairway, and as he passed, Kedrigern heard, ". . . party in Crollo's room . . . tell the others . . . see you there," shouted contrapuntually by eager voices. Before he could comment triumphantly on this to Princess, a young man dashed up and stepped in front of them.

"I beg your pardon, are you Master Kedrigern? The wizard of Silent Thunder Mountain?" he asked.

"I am he," Kedrigern replied.

"Are you here representing the guild, Master Kedrigern? I'm on the committee. We were told there'd be a replacement for Master Hithernils . . . that he'd had some sort of accident."

"Yes, my wife and I are here for the guild."

"This is really exciting for us, Master Kedrigern! We've heard so much about you—your petrification of Buroc is a legend!"

A very pretty girl took Kedrigern's arm. "And the way you handled Fingard—that was the most courageous deed I've ever heard of!" she said.

"Fingard wasn't so terrible," Kedrigern said coolly.

"He was a fire-breathing dragon! And he was injured!" the girl said.

"You just have to show them who's master," Kedrigern said, smiling wisely.

"And Grodz—is it true you turned Grodz into a toad?" she asked eagerly.

"It was my wife who did that. Her first really major spell, actually, and it came off perfectly."

"No one else saw through Quintrindus's machinations. He fooled the whole guild—except you. Isn't that so, Master Kedrigern?" broke in a thin, intense young man at his other side.

"Well . . . Quintrindus was a clever man. He's deceived a great many people," Kedrigern said.

"But not you," the girl pointed out.

"No, not me," Kedrigern admitted with an easy shrug.

"Master Kedrigern, I know you have an early panel, but if you could spare a bit of time, we're having a little party tonight, and—" the first young man began.

Princess's firm voice broke in, and her grip closed on Kedrigern's free arm. "We're terribly sorry, but Master Kedrigern has a lot of work to do for his panel tomorrow, and he simply must have a good night's sleep," she said, sounding very much like the keeper of an absent-minded invalid. "If you'll excuse us, we'd best be getting to our rooms."

"Maybe tomorrow night . . . ?"

"We'll be hosting the guild's party tomorrow night. I hope you'll all be able to attend," Kedrigern blurted. "In our suite. Everyone will be there." His voice rose on the last syllable, as Princess's fingertips dug into his biceps.

As they entered the suite, Princess said in a frosty voice, "For a man who's lost all taste for parties, you've certainly turned into a jovial host."

"They seemed like such nice people," Kedrigern said guilelessly. "Not the kind of riffraff that trails around after alchemists. Nice decent young people. They had some sense. You could tell right away." He paused, and when no response came, he said, "Do you know, my dear, it might be a gracious gesture if we dropped in on their . . . party. . . ."

Princess looked at him icily, and said nothing. He scratched his chin, cleared his throat, and said, "I think I'll work on my opening remarks."

The panel went smoothly, all things considered. Only one panelist was totally incoherent, and he mumbled so low that not one in the audience could make out what he was saying. The others were well spoken, witty, and in good rapport with the sizeable crowd.

The only sour note of the morning's proceedings was the behavior of a short, pudgy, obstreperous man who kept interrupting the panelists with flatulent monologues thinly disguised as questions. After the man's fourth turgid display, Kedrigern ignored his wildly waving hand and peremptory cries for recognition, and the rest of the session was quite decorous.

Afterwards, one of his fellow panelists, a lean, swarthy sorcerer from the east named Abrazoul, complimented

Kedrigern on his handling of the noisy man, remarking that the fellow had the manners of an alchemist.

"He did, didn't he?" Kedrigern replied. "I wonder if there are any alchemsits here."

"A few, I'm sure. They want to see what they can steal from us," said Abrazoul.

A third panelist, Jaquinta, doyenne of the southern sorceresses, brushed back a lock of snowy hair and laughed contemptuously. "It would be like a monkey stealing an astrolabe: he can take it, but he'll never learn to use it properly."

"Well put, Jaquinta," said Abrazoul.

"Yes, very well said. By the way, I hope you'll both be able to come to the party in our suite this evening. It should get going just about moonrise, so if you—"

"I've received an invitation already," said Jaquinta.

"So have I. It was slipped under my door this morning," Abrazoul said.

"That explains what Princess has been doing all day," Kedrigern murmured.

Jaquinta smiled. "I do look forward to meeting her. From what I hear, she is a living testimony to the efficacy of your counterspells."

"And very beautiful besides," said Abrazoul.

Beaming, Kedrigern added, "She also has a definite gift for magic. She's learning at a great rate."

"I'm curious, Kedrigern: why didn't you have Princess speak at the panel this morning? She would have been a sensation. One doesn't often meet a princess who's been a toad."

"She's still a bit reluctant to talk about her past. After all, she spent a good many years sitting in a bog, snapping at flies, worrying about storks and snakes and cruel boys. . . . She wants to put all that behind her."

"I understand perfectly," Jaquinta said, squeezing Kedrigern's hand in a most maternal way.

Kedrigern passed a pleasant day exchanging news and gossip with old friends and meeting several people he had long been hoping to meet. A hurried note from Princess urged him to dine without her, as she was busy with last minute party preparations. He dined with Abrazoul, the three committee members he had met the previous evening, and two clever young conjurers.

Dinner was delightful, and they lingered long at table. It was close to moonrise when Kedrigern at last returned to his suite, in high spirits, whistling an elvish laughing-song. He found the rooms metamorphosed and Princess looking triumphant.

Flowers were everywhere, filling the suite with fragrance. Lanternglow and candlelight glinted off freshly polished wooden surfaces, and a fire sent highlights and shadows dancing in pursuit of one another. Near one wall stood a table on which were two kegs of ale, an assortment of stone jars containing local wines, and enough mugs and tankards for everyone at Wizcon.

"Well?" Princess asked expectantly.

Kedrigern took her hand and raised it to his lips. "My dear, you're a wonder. I must apologize for my peevish obstructionism. I should have known all along that you'd do everything to perfection."

"That's very sweet of you, Keddie."

"And you look absolutely marvelous, my dear! One would think that after working so hard all day . . ." He stepped back to admire her green and yellow robe, her glistening high-piled hair bound by the golden circlet. "Simply beautiful," he said reverently.

"Just a small spell here and there, Keddie. The staff did all the heavy work. They were very helpful. If it hadn't been for "

Three sharp knocks at the door announced the first arrivals. They were soon followed by others, and still others. Before the moon was above the treetops, the room was filled with people and the air was thick with talk and laughter.

There were wizards from all parts of the known world; there were magicians, witches and warlocks, conjurers and seers; there were followers of the subtle arts who had studied everything available about the subject and took advantage of this opportunity to meet the masters in person. Kedrigern dutifully made his way among the eddies of conversation. He came to rest with a trio of students from Rottingen, who were discussing the Iron Man that had made their city so famous.

"It's run by clockwork, isn't it?" he inquired.

"Correct, Master Kedrigern. When it's fully wound, it can do the work of six men in one day," said a dark-haired girl.

"That's very impressive. Does it do much work in Rottingen?"

"Unfortunately, it takes eight men two days to get it fully wound, so it's not yet practical," a young man said.

A second young man added, "But the inventor is working on another Iron Man. When it's done, they can wind each other."

Kedrigern paused for a moment's reflection, then nodded. "I see," he said, "Ingenious."

"The main problem is rust," the girl said. "After a day of rain, the Iron Man is bright orange. It still works, but it's bright orange."

"In Rottingen, we've given it a nickname," the second young man began. "We call it The Clockwork—"

"Oh, dear," Kedrigern broke in at the sight of a new arrival and her entourage. "I'm terribly sorry, but I must see someone right away," he said, working his way through the crowd.

The wood-witch stood just inside the doorway, looking around the room with a muzzy grin and slightly glazed eyes. Two of the inn staff were at her side, straining under their burden of a huge stone jar which they bore between them on a litter.

"Keddie, me love!" the newcomer shrieked at the sight of Kedrigern, and gave a wild cackle of glee that silenced the other party-goers in an instant. "You're throwing a party! Bloody miracle, that's what I calls it!"

"Hello, Bess. It's good to—" Kedrigern started to say, but was silenced by her strenuous bear hug and the wet kiss she loudly planted on his cheek.

"Now, where's Princess, so's old Bess can thank her proper for the invitation? I knows all this is her doing."

Princess glided to their side, aglow with the success of her party. "You must be Bess, the Wood-witch!" she exclaimed, giving the newcomer's ruddy cheek a quick peck. "Kedrigern's told me so much about you."

"Has he, now? Well, the worse it sounds, the truer it is, love," said Bess. She brushed back a loose, lank strand of hair and gave another unearthly laugh.

"We're so glad you could make it," Princess said gamely.

"It was good of you to invite old Bess, after all the trouble you had with that bloody crystal I sold to Keddie. I feels terrible about that, love."

"Now, don't you give it another thought. You're here to enjoy yourself," Princess said.

"Just to help things along, I brought a jar of me best. 'Old Fenny Snake,' I calls it." With surprising deftness, Bess plucked an empty mug from the hand of a conjurer and with a quick backhanded swipe, dipped a sample from the stone jar. "Here, now, you lads get that over to the table so's people can get their mugs into it," she ordered the two bearers. Turning to Princess, she extended the mug and said, "Have a sip, love. It'll do you good. Give you curly teeth and nice white hair, it will," and laughed once more.

Princess unsuspectingly raised the mug while Kedrigern, torn between politeness toward a guest and solicitude for his wife's well-being, looked on anxiously. At the first whiff of bouquet, Princess's head snapped back; her eyes crossed and began to water; she took two unsteady steps backward, gasping for air. Kedrigern snatched the mug from her shaking hands, lest it spill on her dress and eat through to the skin.

"Princess never drinks anything stronger than wine," he explained, putting a supporting arm around her waist.

"Sorry, love," said Bess, rubbing Princess's hands vigorously. "I keeps forgetting that it's an acquired taste."

Princess gasped, coughed, and tried to speak, but could manage no more than a strangulated squeak. Kedrigern helped her outside, where they walked for a time in the cool night air. Before long, her voice returned, and Kedrigern was surprised by her words.

"You once drank that stuff—for my sake," she said.

Kedrigern shuddered at the memory. "I did, my dear."

"And I was so unkind, ungrateful, and unappreciative the next day, when you felt so awful."

"As I recall, I botched things up a bit that day."

"I'm amazed that you could move and speak."

They walked once around the inn, and then Kedrigern said, "I think we ought to get back inside. We don't want to leave our guests on their own for too long."

"There's no hurry, Keddie. Everyone's behaving very well."

"They were before we had a jar of Old Fenny Snake on the premises. By now they may all be behaving like ogres."

Princess glanced at him apprehensively. Without another word, they hurried inside.

The atmosphere in the suite was subtly different. No one was actually sprawled prostrate on the floor, or swinging from the beams, but the mood was now one in which such behavior would not seem inappropriate. Kedrigern checked the stone jar and saw, to his horror, that it was nearly empty. He knew that the danger point was near; he hoped that it had not yet arrived.

As he stood by the jar, trying to decide what to do, an arm went around his shoulder and a numbing breath swept over him. It was the noisy little man of this morning, and he was well along to oblivion.

"Din' have a chance t' introduce myself 's morning," he said. "Name's Smarmax. Doc Smarmax, Al.D., Univers'y of Umleitung." Pausing to burp delicately, he murmured, "Great stuff in that stone jar. Won'ful bouquet."

Here was a beginning, Kedrigern thought. "I do hope we'll have a chance to chat when you're recovered," he said, taking Smarmax's arm and steering him to the door.

He eased out a reeling conjurer and a trio of young men who had just begun singing very indecent songs, and then his attention was caught by loud voices. They came from the center of the room.

"I know your type. You don't do any magic all year long, then you come here and try to pass yourself off as a big wizard. You're a phony!" one cried.

"Listen to boy conjurer," a second voice said scornfully in a heavy accent. "Check record, sonny boy—four spells and five counterspells last year I did, and am working now on seven-spell contract with local margrave."

"Wimp wizard!"

"Creep conjurer!"

"You couldn't spell your way out of a gunny sack!"

"Have never had to, creep. Am not dumb enough to getting into gunny sack in first places," the second speaker said. Suddenly there was a muffled cry, followed by triumphant laughter. Kedrigern pushed through the crowd in time to see a large gunny sack thrash about on the floor for an instant and then disappear. A stocky young man, swarthy and heavy-browed, his thick features scarlet with rage, jumped to his feet.

"All right, creep! You sneak-spell me, I show you what real wizard can do," he said, gesturing at the one who stood opposite him, laughing.

The laughing conjurer dodged. An elderly magician standing behind him, deep in conversation with a veiled seeress, sprouted a huge pair of antlers. The conjurer, meanwhile, made a complicated figure in the air, and the wizard roared in pain as a beehive materialized in his pants. The magician, becoming aware of his altered state, turned. The seeress stepped to his side. Their expressions were ominous.

Kedrigern worked a quick short-term immunity spell for himself, prepratory to stepping in and putting things in order. As he spoke the final phrase, Princess appeared, hands raised, at the center of the four figures. "That will be enough! I insist—" she declared.

Then she vanished.

"You bloody lot of nits! Look what you've gone and done to Princess!" Bess the Wood-witch shrieked in a bloodcurdling voice. The conjurer and the wizard disappeared. The antlered magician and his veiled companion turned on Bess menacingly, and Kedrigern quickly turned them to stone— temporarily.

The remaining guests departed in silent haste, without goodbyes. Kedrigern remained with Bess and two lifelike stone figures.

"What happened to Princess, Bess? Did you see?" he asked.

"One of them silly amateurs hit her with a spell when she stepped in between them. Maybe they both got her. Anyway, old Bess fixed them. Turned them into flies, that's what I did."

"Thanks, Bess."

"It's Bess should do the thanking, Keddie. Old Antlers and his lady friend were about to do me in."

"I think it was just a nervous reaction on their part. Understandable, certainly."

Bess nodded. "They had a drop or two of Old Fenny Snake. That makes some people jumpy."

Kedrigern thought that that was probably all to the good. When the magician and the seeress awoke from his spell the next day, they would remember nothing. Neither would the rest of the guests, in all likelihood. Old Fenny Snake had that effect on people.

"I botched it, didn't I, Keddie?"

"What?"

"Old Bess botched it. Brought along a jar of her best, and spoilt your lovely party," the wood-witch said. A tear trickled down her puffy red cheek.

"Don't cry, Bess. It wasn't your fault."

"Old Bess always does it," she wailed. "Never learns her lesson, not Bess. There's some as can handle Old Fenny Snake and some as can't, and I keeps encountering the second category everywhere I goes." She sniffed and wiped her eyes on a grimy sleeve.

"There, there, Bess," Kedrigern said, giving her a consoling hug. "We don't want to think about that now. What we have to do is find Princess."

"And it's about time, too," said a tiny voice.

"Princess! Where are you, my love?"

"Where I won't be stepped on by anyone's clumsy feet. Is it safe to come out?"

"There's only Bess and I, dear."

"And two statues," Bess added. "They won't hurt you, love."

From behind an overturned stool near the fireplace hopped an elegant little green toad with a tiny gold circlet on its head. Kedrigern covered his eyes, shook his head, and groaned, "Oh, dear me."

"Stop moaning and give me a hand," the wee voice said angrily.

Kedrigern stooped and extended his hand. Princess hopped to his palm, and he raised it to eye-level. She was a very attractive toad, as toads go.

"The important thing is not to get excited, my dear," he said. "We'll work this out. Everything will be all right."

"I'm not excited. I'm being very calm. Just get me back to human again as quick as you can."

"Of course I shall, my dear. Depend on it."

"Use the counterspell you used when we met. Just one more time. Hurry."

"Ah. *That* counterspell. Yes. Well, you see, my dear, that was a one-time counterspell. As a rule, that's all the situation requires."

"Are you saying you can't use it on me a second time?"

"I'm afraid not, my dear."

"Then get another one!" said Princess, sounding a bit more excited.

"Of course. I'll have to find the young man who enchanted you, and learn what spell he used. I'm sure I know a counter for it. Bess will help us all she can."

"I will! Oh, I will, love!" Bess said fervently.

"Well, where is he? What did you do to him?"

"Did you say you turned them into flies, Bess?" Kedrigern inquired.

"I did. It was the first thing came to me mind."

"Flies? *Flies?!*" Princess shrilled.

"That's right, my dear. So all we have to do—"

"Keddie, I ate them!"

"Ate them?" Kedrigern repeated numbly.

"All of a sudden I was a toad again, and here were two fat flies buzzing right in front of me, practically asking to be eaten. So I snapped them up. It was instinctive."

"This may complicate things a bit."

"Oh, Keddie!" Princess lamented in her tiny voice.

"Now, my dear, be brave. We've been through worse than this," Kedrigern said gently.

"He's right, love. Look on the bright side," Bess urged.

"There's isn't any bright side. I'm a toad again!"

"But you're speaking, my dear. Can you sing?"

In response to Kedrigern's inquiry, she ran through the scale. It came out sounding high and a bit tinny, but it was undeniably singing of a fair order.

"Well, now, you can speak and sing as well as ever. That's a good sign," Kedrigern said with forced heartiness.

"But I'm a toad, a paddock, a batrachian!"

"And I'm a wizard. Trust me, my dear."

"I hates to butt in, but I think you'd be wise to slip away quietly before sunrise," Bess said. "What with the disappearances and the statues and the rumors that are bound to spring up, that's the best way."

"I think Bess is right," Kedrigern said.

"Well, you'll have to pack. I can't pack."

"I'll pack, my dear."

"But why bother packing? What's the use? What need

have I of dresses and cloaks and slippers? All I need from now on is a lily pad and a few flies.''

"I shall pack every single item in your wardrobe, down to the last button. You'll be yourself again, Princess, I promise you.'' Kedrigern surveyed the room thoughtfully. "I imagine the best thing to do is move these statues out into the hall, and then tidy the place up a bit.''

"I'll do the tidying,'' Bess volunteered.

"I'll move the statues, and then start packing,'' said Kedrigern.

Princess gave a tiny disconsolate sigh. "I'll look for a nice dank spot where I'll be out of everyone's way.''

···❧ *Three* ❧···

as handsome does

THE DAYS WERE getting shorter, and so was Princess's patience. Two weeks had passed since her mishap, and Kedrigern had not yet found the counterspell. But one evening after dinner, he revealed his plans.

"The man to see is Fraigus o' the Murk. He wrote the standard text on transformation spells," he announced.

"Are you sure he'll help you?" Princess asked.

"He can't refuse, my dear. I was one of his best students. We were very close in those days, before he got so deeply involved in temporal magic. Fraigus was a legend in his own time, and now . . ."

"I never heard of him," Princess pointed out.

"Well, he wasn't a *universal* legend. More of a local legend. Those of us who knew him considered him one of the greats."

"That's not much of a legend."

Kedrigern shrugged. "It's better than nothing. Poor old Fraigus. Life has not been kind to him, from what I've heard. He's said to have gone quite to seed. I kept telling myself that I ought to pay a visit, try to cheer him up, but I put it off, and put it off. . . ."

"Oh, fine,' said Princess caustically. "You're going to turn my case over to some washed-up old—" In midsentence she snapped a careless fly out of the air in front of her, then

25

went on, "—wizard who can't even help himself. I must say, Keddie, I sometimes think you don't take this very seriously. It's not just inconvenient, it's extremely unpleasant."

The wizard looked down on his tiny green wife, seated on the table before him in a golden bowl of damp moss, and felt an upwelling of pity. He had never personally experienced the sensation of being turned into a toad, but he was willing to believe that it was not a pleasing one. Particularly for a beautiful princess like Princess.

"My dear, I do understand, and I deeply sympathize. But you must admit, your case is most unusual. It's not every day that a woman who's been turned into a toad and then turned back into a woman is turned into a toad a second time. It may be unique in the annals of sorcery," he said.

"Maybe I'll be a legend in my own time. Like Fraigus."

"Don't let it make you bitter."

"It's just that nothing is being done, Keddie. You're a wizard, and a leading authority on counterspells. So why am I still a a toad?"

"My dear, I know my field much too well to take these things lightly. Magic is a very tricky business. Why, we still don't know exactly who placed the spell on you, much less the details of the spell itself. If I just made a wild guess, you might end up as . . . well, as something much worse than a toad."

"There *is* nothing worse. Especially with winter coming. Winter is a very bad time to be a toad, Keddie," she said in a sad, tiny voice that tugged at his heart.

"Winter is still weeks away. I'll be off to see Fraigus in the morning, and back before the first hard frost. Spot can look after things until I return."

"Are you sure Spot understands? If he gets confused, I might end my days in a ragout."

"No need for concern. I've made it clear to Spot that you are not an ordinary toad. And in case he should forget, I've placed a Sphere of Protection around you. You'll be perfectly safe."

She sighed an almost inaudible sigh. "All this waiting," she said disconsolately. "I really don't see why I can't try one of my own spells on myself. You told me I was coming along at an amazing rate."

"Banish the thought!" Kedrigern said with alarm. "Even

the greatest wizards don't unspell themselves. 'She who unspells herself has a fool for a wizard' may be an old saying, but it's true.''

"All right, Keddie. I'll wait. But please hurry.''

"I will. I'll leave at dawn, and be back at the earliest possible moment, I promise you.''

The hovel wherein dwelt Kedrigern's old friend and teacher, Fraigus o' the Murk, lay west of the Dismal Bog. A fine high road, smooth and straight, skirted the bog and passed near Fraigus's dwelling. But at the first fork, Kedrigern turned aside and took the low road that passed through the heart of the bog.

This was the short cut, but that was not Kedrigern's reason for choosing it. He would never have admitted to the charge, but Kedrigern was a sentimental man. When he realized that he was so near the place where he had met his lovely Princess and won her heart, he could not resist the chance to revisit the happy scene.

At a little knoll that rose between the road and the edge of the bog, he reined in his shaggy black steed. Setting the horse to graze, the wizard hunkered down by the knoll and gazed on it fondly. On this very spot, he had freed Princess from a cruel enchantment. Looking more closely, he could make out faint traces of his work. Here were the impressions of the stones that had formed his pentacle, and a smudge of the powder he had used to mark the necessary runic figure. He smiled wistfully at the recollection.

In a little while he rose, went to his horse, and took his scrip and water bag. Settling down comfortably by the knoll, he began to chew thoughtfully on a thickly-buttered slab of golden bread, and sip cold water. The thought of Princess had made him homesick, and he longed to be back in his cozy house on Silent Thunder Mountain.

But love and loyalty won out over homesickness. Of all his wizardly acquaintances, only Fraigus was likely to know the proper solution to this complicated re-enchantment. He owed it to Princess to make this journey. And Fraigus himself was in need of a friend.

If rumor was true—and it sometimes is—Fraigus was in a bad way and steadily worsening. It is a sad thing to see a man go downhill. When the man is a great wizard, it is even sadder, and also unnerving. Kedrigern had indeed thought once or twice of visiting poor old Fraigus and attempting to bring him around. When he began to hear rumors of spells cast in anger, and capricious enchantments, he knew he must make his visit soon. Princess's present difficulty had provided the final incentive.

As Kedrigern sat thinking of his absent wife and hearth, and recalling Fraigus at the peak of his power, he heard a small voice nearby. At once he was alert.

"Alas," said the voice. "Alack and welladay."

"Is someone addressing me?" Kedrigern said aloud.

"Woe is me," the voice went on, trailing off in a tiny sigh.

Kedrigern had an overwhelming sensation of *déjà vu*. It was under such circumstances as these that he met Princess. But surely there could not be two enchanted maidens sharing this bog. It was too great a coincidence.

"Oh, that I was ever born to suffer such a fate," said the voice.

"If you'll stop lamenting for a moment and explain your problem, I may be able to help," Kedrigern said. "No promises, mind you, but I'm willing to listen."

A toad leaped out of the bog, landing squarely in the middle of the knoll. "Release me from this foul enchantment! Make me a prince once more!" it cried.

"Are you really a prince?"

"Of course I'm a prince. Don't I look like a prince?" the toad retorted angrily.

"No. You look like a toad."

The little creature was silent for a time, and then it said petulantly, "I suppose I do. I'm not accustomed to this sort of thing, you know."

"That's understandable."

"Well, are you going to do something? You'll be well rewarded, I assure you. My father is the King of Kallopane. He is a generous man."

Kedrigern had heard that sort of thing before, and did not pay it heed. He was not doing this for profit, but out of pure sentiment. There were a few facts he had to know before he could begin, and he dropped to one knee before the toad, who seemed pleased with the gesture.

"You must tell me the circumstances of the enchantment.

It's particularly important that I know whether it was a spur of the moment act, or was planned ahead of time," he said.

"It was definitely extempore. My oldest brother's child was being christened, and we were very careful to invite all the local fairies, witches, and wizards. We know what happens when they're left off the guest list. Everyone was having a very pleasant time, and then my father, the king, thought he'd have a bit of fun with one of the bog-fairies."

Stunned, Kedrigern said, "Don't tell me your father teased a bog-fairy!"

"My father, the king, has a famous sense of humor," said the toad huffily.

"Bog-fairies, as a rule, do not. But go on with your story."

"I don't remember much. My father, the king, made a witty observation about how farsighted he and my mother, the queen, were to have had all sons, and never have to worry about having a daughter turned into a toad. I laughed along with the rest, and suddenly everything seemed to flicker for a moment. And there I was, little and green and clammy."

Kedrigern rose and nodded confidently. "That's an on-the-spot spell, all right. There seems to be a lot of it going around lately."

"Can you help me?"

"I think so. Just stay right there. Don't move, and don't say another word."

Kedrigern quickly prepared the ground, then circled the knoll in the prescribed manner. That done, he began to recite the counterspell. At the last word, he brought his hands together. A great peal of thunder rolled over the bog, and an instant of darkness enveloped them.

When the light returned, a handsome prince stood poised on the knoll, his golden hair gleaming in the sun. Considering the circumstances, he was remarkably self-possessed. He was dressed in pale green tights, a green silk doublet gorgeously embroidered in gold, a dark green cloak lined in white, and close-fitting white boots. He turned languidly to Kedrigern and said, "Fetch me a mirror, there's a good fellow."

Kedrigern, frowning, said, "It's customary to express one's gratitude when one is freed from an enchantment."

"My father, the king, will see to that. A mirror, fellow,

and quickly. It's been ages since I've been able to admire myself.''

"There is no mirror within six days' riding. If you want to look at yourself, look in the bog.''

The prince, flicking unseen dust particles from his arms and shoulders, said, "Very well. Lay down your cloak. I would not soil my knees.''

"I would not soil my cloak, either,'' said the wizard.

The prince's deep-set dark eyes flashed angrily under long lashes. The cleft in his chin deepened, and his elegant nostrils flared. "You are saucy, fellow. Know that I am not only the handsomest prince in all the world, but also the quickest to anger. When I express a wish, it is obeyed.''

"Sure, Prince,'' Kedrigern said. He picked up his water bottle and whistled for his horse. The shaggy black steed came to his side and the wizard mounted.

"What is the meaning of this?'' the prince demanded, arching a magnificent eyebrow.

"I'm leaving, Prince. Your kingdom is back the way I came, then off to the east, I think. If you start walking, you can be there in a few weeks. Just don't tease any bog-fairies on the way.''

"A prince does not walk!''

"Then run. Or hop. I don't care. I'm sorry I ever bothered to help you.''

"Surly knave! Dismount at once, and give me that horse!'' the prince commanded.

Kedrigern held back the phrase that he was tempted to shout. The prince was probably as impenetrable by insults as he was by reason or simple gratitude. Perhaps a good long hike would teach him manners, though the wizard had his doubts about that.

"Have a pleasant journey, Prince,'' he said with a parting wave.

"The horse, you churlish miscreant!''

Kedrigern reined the horse to the westward path. He had proceeded about a half-dozen paces when a painful light burst into fragments inside his head; turf and treetops whirled around him, and he pitched over and fell heavily to the ground.

He awoke at dusk, with an agonizing throb in his head. The prince was gone. The horse was gone. Food, and pack, and water bottle were gone.

He sat up cautiously, and felt the back of his head. He winced as his fingertips brushed a blood-encrusted lump behind his left ear. The handsome prince had a good eye and a strong throwing arm.

Kedrigern stood, swaying a little, gulping at the nausea that surged through him with the motion. He murmured a quick spell against headache, and at once felt better.

Fraigus's hovel was a good many days' walk to the west. The bog water was drinkable, provided one did not examine it too closely. Berries, nuts, and mushrooms would allay his hunger. The long walk would clear his head. Kedrigern had no desire to squander magic on a traveling spell, or enchanted refection. He wanted to have every bit of his power ready for his next meeting with the handsome prince.

He took a deep breath and started walking.

Declining and despairing he may have been; bloodshot of eye and rubicund of nose he certainly was; but Fraigus o' the Murk was a goodly host. When Kedrigern arrived at his hovel one day at sundown, footsore and weary, sick to death of foraging, Fraigus welcomed him like a long-lost brother. Within minutes Kedrigern was seated before a fire, his boots off, feet up on a cushioned stool, with a tall tankard of cold ale in his hand.

Fraigus, in an armchair facing him, beamed and raised his tankard. "Good it is to see you, lad, after all these years. It's long and hard you've traveled to see your old teacher. Drink deep, now, and refresh yourself."

The ale was delicious. Kedrigern wiped his lips and said, "It's long since we sat and talked together, Fraigus. A lot has happened in all the years."

"Aye, lad, a lot. I hear that you've gone and got yourself married to a bonnie princess, and you live in a wee cottage on a mountaintop."

"Yes. Princess and I are very happy together," Kedrigern said. He judged it best to keep his problem to himself for a time, until the proper moment presented itself.

"And do you keep up your temporal magic, Keddie? You had a real knack for filching goods out of the future."

"I don't do it anymore. It was easy to bring the things back, but I could never figure out what they were for. The house was getting cluttered with junk."

"Ah, now you talk like a married man, Keddie," said the old wizard. He drank deeply, and both were silent for a time, gazing into the fire.

After a while, Kedrigern asked, "Are you keeping up with your own magic, Fraigus? I haven't heard anything about you for some time."

"I've done nae magic at all these thirty years, lad," said Fraigus. "Aside from the small necessities."

"The last thing I recall hearing," Kedrigern said, frowning with the effort to remember, "was that you had changed the whole aim of your magic. You were still reaching into the future, but you weren't bringing objects back anymore."

"Aye, that's right, lad. I got weary of handling bits and pieces. I wanted to see how they all fit together. I wanted a good look at what the future held."

Fraigus raised his tankard. Finding it empty, he hurled it across the room, where it landed with a thump on a disgusting pile of trash and rags. To Kedrigern's amazement, the pile gave a cry, a sort of bleating, mewling, syrupy gurgle, and moved.

"Stir yourself, you filthie staumrel knurlin!" Fraigus cried. "Fetch more ale or I'll whang your hurdies!"

The pile rose on hideous misshapen stumps and scuttled out of the room with a lurching, crablike motion. It snuffled and whined as it went.

"What's that?" Kedrigern asked in a subdued voice.

"It's my new servant. They're always trouble at first. This one's learning, but I'm footsore from kicking the donsie thing," said Fraigus.

"What happened to the house-troll you used to have?"

Fraigus glanced at him uncomfortably and said, "He's nae use to me now, Keddie."

Kedrigern did not press his host. He emptied his own tankard just as the servant made its erratic, sidelong way back into the room with two fresh tankards of ale. Fraigus rewarded the creature with a wallop, and snarled, "You'll be quicker than that if you know what's good for you, you cankrie wee coof!"

They drank in silence for a time, Kedrigern sipping while his host gulped his ale down noisily, and at last Kedrigern asked, "Did you ever manage to get a glimpse of the future, Fraigus?"

The old wizard sighed, drank deeply, and said, "Aye, lad, I did. Thirty years ago, it was."

"And . . . ?"

"I've been drunk most of the time since then, Keddie. I thought it would help. But it does nae good at all. I still remember what's to come."

Kedrigern shuddered and emptied his tankard. The ghastly little servant was quicker this time, and was spared a blow from its master, though Fraigus abused it with more unintelligible terms from his native highlands.

They ate, and drank considerable amounts of ale, and Kedrigern awoke the next afternoon on the floor of the main room, before a dying fire. He sat up, made a wry face at the taste of his tongue, and started at the sight of the servant near at hand. The thing seemed, by its attitude, to be looking at him intently, but it was difficult to be sure. Its features, grotesque in themselves, were so scrambled about that its expressions were indecipherable.

"Go away. Please," Kedrigern said hoarsely.

The creature lurched, quivered, and hobbled off, groaning wetly. Kedrigern looked after it, fascinated. It was the most hideous object he had ever seen. He could not make up his mind whether it was animal, vegetable, mineral, or manifestation. Whatever it was, it was the quintessence of ugliness.

It was not a very good servant, either. Kedrigern wondered what had become of Pudmox, the troll who had served Fraigus so faithfully for close to two centuries. The old wizard had been evasive when asked about him, and Kedrigern, though he was puzzled, did not press the matter. He had other concerns.

He did his best to exert a good influence on his old teacher without acting like an insufferable prig. And whether it was as a result of Kedrigern's efforts, or embarrassment, or a surfeit of ale, or the knowledge that his wisdom and long experience was still respected, Fraigus o' the Murk began to behave more like his former self.

In a few days, Kedrigern noticed a definite physical improvement in his host. Fraigus's eyeballs no longer appeared like egg yolks draped with fine red lace; his nose bore less resemblance to a carbuncle. His voice softened. He drank less and less ale, and talked more and more, and Kedrigern rejoiced that his presence had had such a healing effect on the unhappy old wizard.

Over dinner on the tenth day of his stay Kedrigern broached the subject of Princess's retransformation. Fraigus listened without speaking, and when Kedrigern was finished, shook his head in a solemn manner.

" 'Tis a serious business, lad," he said darkly.

"Very serious. That's why I've come to you. If anyone in the world knows what to do, it's you, Fraigus."

"I must ponder it for a time. It's long since I've dealt with such matters."

"Of course, Fraigus. I wouldn't try to rush you."

"You've handled your part well, you and the bonnie lady both. You were sensible enough to try nae home remedies."

"I know enough about remedial magic to use it cautiously. I'd never try a counterspell without at least some knowledge of the spell and who cast it."

"You do know something of counterspells, then, do you, Keddie?"

"I have a small practice," said Kedrigern modestly.

"Aye. Aye," Fraigus said thoughtfully. He was silent for a time, nodding, and then he rose. "I must consult my books. Make yourself comfortable, Keddie, and rest assured I'll do my best to make your wife a bonnie lady once again."

Kedrigern saw no more of his host until the second morning following, when Fraigus settled at the breakfast table weary and worn, but triumphant. Kedrigern looked to him eagerly, and the elder wizard nodded.

"I've found what you must do, Keddie," he said. "It's a chancy business, and you'll have to do some long traveling in nasty weather through places you'd nae choose to be. But if you follow it through, you'll find someone who can help bring your Princess back to what she was, and nae have her a wee toad."

Kedrigern gulped loudly and reached across the table to clasp Fraigus's gnarled hand. "I don't know how to thank you, old master. If there's anything . . . anything at all . . . any way I can show my gratitude . . ."

"There is a wee small favor you might do me," Fraigus said, staring down at the tabletop.

"Name it."

"Well, you mentioned a knowledge of counterspells," said Fraigus, avoiding Kedrigern's eyes.

"That's my speciality."

"Aye. Well, you remember Pudmox, my old house-troll. . . . A gawsie auldfarrant swankie it was, Pudmox," said the wizard, shaking his head wistfully. Kedrigern, uncertain whether the troll was being praised or damned, waited for further information. "I put a spell on it, Keddie," Fraigus blurted, looking at him with guilt-haunted eyes. "My fine, loyal old troll, who's served me faithfully for near two centuries, and I've annihilated it. The poor creature dropped a keg of my best ale, and in my boozie rage I turned it into a handful of dust!" He buried his face in his hands and began to weep piteously.

Kedrigern laid his hands on the old wizard's shoulders. "Let me have a look, Fraigus. I think I can do something for Pudmox."

"Och, that's nae all, Keddie. After I turned it into dust . . . I sneezed! I blew the poor old troll all over my workshop!"

"Oh, dear," Kedrigern murmured. "That may complicate things. But I'll do what I can. Let's go to your workshop and have a look."

With an occasional sniffle, Fraigus led the way to a room at the rear of the hovel. It contained all the customary apparatus of a wizard's workshop, but was much neglected. Dust lay thickly on every surface.

"It was here I destroyed the poor faithful creature," said Fraigus gloomily.

Kedrigern looked the room over, shaking his head. "Have you dusted the place since then?" he asked.

"Dusted? I've nae dusted since I came here, lad."

"Then we'll dust. Let's get all the dust in this room into a heap, right in the center of the floor."

Proceeding with great care and caution, they did exactly that. With the assistance of the hideous little servant—which was just the thing for getting at confined spaces and the undersides of things—they soon had a mound of dust in the middle of the floor, and the rest of the room spotless.

"Nice workshop you have here," Kedrigern observed.

"It is, lad. I've forgotten how nice."

"You could do some good things in a workshop like this."

Fraigus shook his head decisively. "Nae mair spells for

me, Keddie. I've abused my talents, and I don't deserve to practice.''

"You could start working on remedial magic. There's a real need for it these days.''

"If you can bring Pudmox back, Keddie, I'll have faith in your remedial magic.''

"Fair enough. I'll need a few ingredients for the counterspell. How are your supplies?''

"I'm fully stocked, lad, and it's all at your disposal.''

"All right, then. Sit over there, Fraigus, and don't say a word.''

"What about this thing?'' Fraigus asked, nudging the little servant with his foot.

"It can stay, as long as it behaves.''

The thing gave a bubbly sigh and scuttled under a bench. Kedrigern set about preparing the counterspell, a brief task, and then took up his position before the mound of dust. It was all over in a matter of moments: a brilliant burst of light, a slight tremor, and there was Pudmox, as squat, knobby, warty, and ugly as ever, blinking its tiny eyes, its gap-toothed mouth wide in astonishment.

"Pudmox, you're back!'' cried Fraigus, bounding to his feet. "Och, you've put on weight!''

"It couldn't be helped. There was no way of telling which was Pudmox and which was only dust, so I used it all,'' Kedrigern said apologetically.

"Say nae mair, Keddie. It'll be stronger than ever with a bit more bulk to it.''

Pudmox prepared a superb dinner that evening in celebration of its return. Kedrigern ate sumptuously, drank moderately, and was ready to depart early the next morning. He felt very good. The trip had been an unqualified success. The only sour note of the entire journey was his encounter at the Dismal Bog, and he was so pleased with Fraigus's rehabilitation and the promise of help for Princess that he was almost willing to forgive the vain and ungrateful prince. The small likelihood of their ever meeting again made it still easier to be maganimous.

As they said their final farewells at the door of the hovel, Fraigus grinned broadly and knowingly and said, " 'Tis a long walk you have ahead of you, Keddie.''

"I'll be all right, Fraigus. I'm used to walking.''

"Och, now, I can't send you home to your bonnie lady all footsore and frazzled. You must go home in proper style."

"Really, Fraigus, I don't mind—" Kedrigern started to say. He fell silent at a familiar clopping sound coming from around the corner of the hovel. He turned in time to see Pudmox, a happy smile on its barrellike face, leading a shaggy black steed to his side. It was Kedrigern's own stolen horse. The scrip was filled with cheese and bread, and the water bottle was full.

"A fine creature, isn't he, Keddie?" said Fraigus proudly. "He came into my possession just before you arrived, and I forgot all about him in my pleasure at seeing you. Now he's my parting gift, to show my gratitude for your loyal assistance to me in my hour of need."

The horse had stepped to Kedrigern's side, and was rubbing his master's shoulder fondly. Kedrigern turned to stroke the steed's muzzle and murmur a greeting.

"Look how he's taken to you, Keddie!" Fraigus crowed. "Glad I am to see it."

"How did you happen to get him?" Kedrigern asked casually.

"He just . . . came by one day," Fraigus said.

"No rider? All alone? A fine horse like that?"

"Och, now, Keddie, here I am, holding you up with my prattle and you anxious to be on your way home," said Fraigus, bustling about with a great display of concern. "Make a back, Pudmox, so my good friend can mount up and be off to his bonnie Princess. There's a good troll."

Kedrigern knew that he would learn nothing more from Fraigus. He turned to mount, and stepped in something squishy. With a cry of disgust, he drew back. The hideous little servant wambled aside with a croupy moan, narrowly escaping a kick from Fraigus.

"Crowling wee blastie! Always hanging about and getting stepped on," Fraigus said angrily. The creature hopped back and forth, making eager glucy noises. "I think it likes you," said Fraigus. "Do you want the glaikit thing? I've nae use for it since you brought my Pudmox back."

The little monstrosity throbbed with excitement at Fraigus's words. Kedrigern was beginning to put things together, and he had suspicions. He accepted the offer. Pudmox picked the creature up, stuffed it into a sack, and fastened it to the saddle, and Kedrigern was on his way.

He did not remove the thing from its sack, despite its whining and burbling, until he was back in the Dismal Bog, at the very spot where he had met the prince. Here he dismounted, took down the throbbing sack, and dumped its contents on the knoll. Stepping back, he folded his arms and addressed the misshapen heap.

"I have a few questions, and it would be well for you to answer truthfully," he said in a stern voice.

The creature seemed to understand. It quivered a little, but did not make a sound.

"You needn't try to speak. If the answer is *yes,* move one of your . . . well, move something twice. Once for *no.* Do you understand?"

A misshapen clawlike limb moved twice.

"I suspect that you're the erstwhile handsome prince—and former toad—who bashed me on the head and stole my horse. Is that correct?"

The thing shrank in upon itself. Feebly and reluctantly, it waved a stump, twice.

"Aha. And you followed the wrong road, to the hovel of Fraigus, where you demanded food, shelter, and obsequious service . . . and when Fraigus was reluctant to obey your commands, you insulted and threatened him. Correct?"

An indescribable lump on the thing's back moved twice.

"So Fraigus turned you into that. Of course. I should have known at once. Fraigus never did like handsome princes." Kedrigern looked down, shaking his head. The thing on the knoll jiggled excitedly. "And now I suppose you want me to disenchant you."

The thing stopped jiggling. It moved a flabby protuberance, something like a limp eggplant, twice, and then it froze in expectation.

"You don't deserve a bit of sympathy, you know. You deserve to be exactly what you are . . . whatever that is," Kedrigern said. But he knew in his heart that nothing on earth deserved to be that ugly, and he hoped that the experience might have taught the handsome prince a valuable lesson. As for himself, he had no desire for revenge. Fraigus had outdone anything he might have contemplated. With a resigned sigh, he said, "All right, I'll see if I can do something. But mind you, now—oh stop bouncing—mind you, I can't be sure what's going to come of it. You've been enchanted, and disenchanted, and re-enchanted. That complicates your situation. I'll try to make you a handsome prince again, but I can't guarantee what you'll turn into, only that you won't be what you are. Is that acceptable?''

The thing waved an appendage twice, decisively and enthusiastically, and then was still. Kedrigern prepared the knoll, using an all-purpose rune this time, and stepped well back to intone a generalized detransformational spell. He clapped his hands. Treetops and waters quivered under a blast of sound, and a darkness passed over all. The horrid thing was gone. Kedrigern looked down on the knoll.

"At least you're a handsome toad," he said. "That's something."

The toad glared up at him with baleful eye. It puffed up, then with a single graceful bound it soared from the knoll to land with a loud plop and disappear in the dark water.

Kedrigern shook his head ruefully and walked to where his horse waited. He patted the big steed's neck and said, "That's princes for you, old friend. Arrogant and ungrateful to the end. Not even a *brereep* for my troubles."

He rode home under a lowering sky. Winter was closing in. Snow began to fall as he reached the foot of Silent Thunder Mountain, and he barely made it to his cottage before the full force of the blizzard struck. There would be no traveling for a time; and until he could travel, Princess would remain a toad.

All the same, it was good to be home.

···⚐ *Four* ⚐···

a name to conjure with

A LATE WINTER storm assailed the cottage, hurling hail and
sleet and rain against the windows, ruffling the thatch, making woeful moan in the upper reaches of the chimney. Its
efforts were wasted. Withindoors warmth and coziness
prevailed.

Kedrigern sat by the fire in slippered comfort, thinking
kindly thoughts about Vosconu the Openhanded, whose vine-
yards produced wine fit for kings and emperors and most
pleasing to the palate of a tired, thirsty wizard. A brimming
goblet of Vosconu's finest stood near at hand. The fire crack-
led. Shadows swayed and swooped gracefully about the room.
Kedrigern reached out languidly for the goblet.

"Go ahead, drink yourself into a stupor. Don't think about
me," said a tiny voice.

Kedrigern drew his hand back quickly. "My dear, I think
of you incessantly," he said.

"Fine way you have of showing it. You stay locked up in
your study all day long, and you don't say two words to me
at dinner, and as soon as dinner is over you can't wait to
guzzle wine."

"One small goblet of wine is hardly 'guzzling,' " Kedrigern
said, sounding injured.

"If you really cared for me at all, you'd be working day
and night to despell me," said the wee voice righteously.

Kedrigern turned to the table, where Princess sat daintily on a clump of damp moss in her golden bowl, her lustrous eyes glinting in the firelight. It was difficult to interpret her expression, but Kedrigern caught the suggestion of impatience in her voice.

"I'm moving as quickly as I can under the circumstances," he assured her. "The next step requires traveling, and I must have some information before I can set out."

"I appreciate, condone, and approve of your being careful, concerned, and solicitous. I just want you to be a bit quicker, speedier, and more expeditious."

"I'm glad you're keeping up your vocabulary exercises, my dear. It's good to keep your mind occupied at a time like this." Princess sighed softly, but said no more, and Kedrigern went on, "Caution must be our watchword. You have a complicated history. The more one is spelled and unspelled and respelled and despelled, the more sensitive one becomes to side effects. I told you what befell that obnoxious prince I despelled on my way to visit Fraigus. We don't want such things happening to you. That would be terrible."

"A terrible thing has already happened to me, Keddie. I'm a toad," said Princess coldly.

"Only temporarily."

"So you keep telling me. Winter is nearly over, you've gone to see Fraigus, and I'm still a toad. Meanwhile, you're working away at spells for strangers while I sit in my bowl of moss and wait for flies to pass."

"Panglunder is not a complete stranger, my dear. And there's no one else who can help him. Believe me, I'm not happy with his case, but I can't turn him away."

Princess gave an impatient little sniff of the sort to which a sensible man attempts no reply. Kedrigern gazed into the fire and reflected on the problem Panglunder had saddled him with. Outwardly, the wizard was the picture of repose, but he was actually quite annoyed and angry at having been called in on this affair when he had such pressing concerns of his own.

Kedrigern was an easygoing man, even for a wizard. He disliked few things, and hated scarcely any at all. Chief among his antipathies were travel, urgent deadlines, and night work. Panglunder had brought down all three upon him at once.

Panglunder the Unyielding, Lord Paramount of the Dark Wood, dwelt in a gloomy castle some nine days' unpleasant travel from the comfortable cottage on Silent Thunder Mountain. Kedrigern was not particularly fond of Panglunder, but he owed him a favor and the Lord Paramount had sent to demand immediate payment of a kind that required the wizard's personal attention. Kedrigern had been working hard, with very little sleep and no noticeable results, since the messenger's arrival three days past, and was nearing the end of his patience.

He rubbed his weary, burning eyes and sighed. Why did Panglunder have to be both impetuous and unyielding? If he'd only used his head, none of this would have happened. When a man has reached an understanding with an enchantress, that man should not suddenly get himself betrothed to a princess—not even if she's a beautiful, nubile princess with a dowry exceeding the wildest fantasies of avarice, and he's a powerful lord accustomed to having his will in all things. Sorceresses are not the kind of people to take rivalry in good humor.

Despite his mood, Kedrigern smiled. There was a lighter side to this, though Panglunder might not find much in it to amuse him. Memanesha had a sly sense of humor unusual in a sorceress. Imprisoning the beautiful Princess Lalloree behind a barrier of fire was a distinctive touch. The lovers could exchange sighs, ardent words, and passionate glances, but nothing else. If they came within arm's length of one another, they would be singed. A genuine masterstroke, Kedrigern thought, just a bit enviously.

He had a countermeasure in mind, but it was going to be a delicate and touchy business. A Celtic water spirit could pass through the fiery barrier and remove Princess Lalloree unharmed. But afancs were hideous things, and easily upset. Lalloree would have to be warned not to start screaming at the sight of her rescuer. Afancs did not take kindly to threats, either. Panglunder would have to hold his temper, even if they treated Lalloree less than gently. And there was Memanesha to consider, too. Kedrigern had no wish to antagonize a colleague. Memanesha would just have to accept the fact that business is business; the customer calls the tune; sometimes you cast a spell, sometimes you lift one. The more he recalled about Mcmanesha, the less likely it seemed that she would accept his counterspell with good grace.

He groaned in frustration. Exhausted though he was, he could not relax. Too much on his mind. Yet it was reckless to work on spells—particularly unfamiliar spells—when one was not at one's peak. This whole affair was becoming a source of great bother.

"Are you all right, Keddie?" Princess asked.

"Yes. Just thinking."

"What about?"

"Spells. Enchantments. Beautiful princesses."

"I was a beautiful princess . . . once," said Princess with a sigh.

"And shall be again. When I met you, you were a toad, but before that, and then when I despelled you. . . ." Kedrigern fell silent, gazing thoughtfully into the flames, frowning slightly.

"Keddie? Don't doze off."

"Something just occurred to me. Odd that I never thought of it before."

"What is it?"

"You did start out as a beautiful princess, didn't you? I mean, there's no possibility that you were turned into a beautiful princess somewhere along the line, but were originally—"

"I was born a beautiful princess!" Princess cried indignantly. "How dare you insinuate otherwise! Of all the nerve!"

"My dear, I insinuate nothing. I must ask these questions in my professional capacity. Despelling an enchantee without full knowledge of her background can have awkward consequences. I remember the time I—"

"No digressions, please. Stick to the problem."

"I shall, my dear. Well, then. You were a beautiful princess until your twenty-first birthday, when a—"

"Eighteenth. My eighteenth birthday," Princess corrected him sharply.

"Ah, yes, your eighteenth birthday. On which sad occasion the curse of Bertha the Bog-fairy turned you into a toad, which you remained until I released you from the spell."

"Partially."

"It was a very complicated spell. And in a short time I had you back to yourself."

"Yes," Princess admitted. "But I spent altogether too much time looking like a beautiful princess and croaking like a toad."

"As I have pointed out, it was a complicated spell. Bog-fairies are as methodical as they are malicious. In any event, you were thoroughly despelled at last," Kedrigern said brightly.

"All too briefly."

That observation brought on a profound silence, in which Kedrigern took up his goblet and sipped noiselessly. At length Princess sighed and said, "Oh, if only we hadn't gone to Wizcon."

"No point in crying over a spilt potion, my dear. I'll have you back on two feet soon," Kedrigern said, setting down the goblet on the opposite side of his chair. "At least we can still hold a conversation."

Princess looked up at him from the bowl of damp moss in which she sat. She was a pretty little creature, as toads go. She did not move, and her expression did not alter in any way that Kedrigern could discern, but a large tear ran from each glittering eye.

"I was doing so nicely. . . . Building my vocabulary . . . learning magic . . . ," she said in a small sad voice.

"Your progress was most impressive."

"I was better off with the body of a beautiful princess, even when I could only croak like a toad. At least I could read. Now I can't even turn a page."

"Spot might be of some help there."

"Not really. Spot tends to get excited. It tears out the pages and starts eating them."

"I'd forgotten. Trolls will be trolls."

"What does it matter? What good is a rich vocabulary to a toad?"

"You can still speak, my dear."

"Who wants to listen to a toad?"

"I do. And I should think your magic would be even more useful to . . . to one in your present condition."

Princess sighed, but said no more. Kedrigern, his fund of encouraging observations depleted, sat silent. Outside, the storm raged on, its ferocity unabated. The logs settled with a gentle crunch and a spray of sparks, accentuating the snug domesticity of the scene.

"I'd be better off back in the bog, even on a night like

this," Princess muttered. "At least in the bog I had plenty of company, even if I was a toad."

"You were a very nice little toad," Kedrigern pointed out.

"Don't be patronizing. This is bad enough without your being patronizing."

"Merely trying to elevate your spirits."

"The difference between a very nice toad and a beautiful princess is considerable, Keddie. Handsome princes don't set out on perilous quests, nor do valiant knights slay dragons and inflict grievous bodily harm on one another to win smiles from a very nice toad. Even her own *husband* doesn't do anything for a woman when she's a toad."

"My dear, I'm gathering information. It takes time."

"It certainly does," said Princess sullenly.

"Fraigus could only tell me *where* to look. He couldn't give me names. And to wander aimlessly, especially in this weather . . ."

"You hate to travel in *any* weather."

"True," he conceded, "but I find it particularly repellent in weather like this. It's not a fit night out for man nor beast."

Even as Kedrigern spoke these words, there came a loud pounding at the door. Kedrigern and Princess both looked up sharply.

"Who can that be?" Princess asked.

"Probably an ogre, asking the way. Ogres get restless in this kind of weather, and they have no sense of direction."

"I don't want ogres in the house, Keddie," said Princess as Kedrigern rose from his chair and straightened his robe.

"I won't let it in, my dear. I'll just give it directions and send it on its way."

As Kedrigern reached the door, his house-troll scooted into the room and began bouncing up and down, eagerly crying, "Yah, yah!"

"It's all right, Spot. I'll take it," Kedrigern said.

"Yah?"

"You might put another log on the fire. Lay it on gently, please. Don't hurl it across the room."

Working a quick short-term all-purpose protective spell, Kedrigern reached for the latch. The pounding came again, not the sound of knuckles but of wood on wood. Blasted pushy ogres, he thought; but he realized at once that the door was not shaking as it would under the blows of an ogre's cudgel. Someone was rapping with something lighter; a stick, most likely. With a shout of welcome, Kedrigern flung the door wide. He was bespattered by a wet blast, and barely escaped a hard blow on the forehead.

"Bess! Come in, Bess," he said to the wet and windblown figure who stood on his threshold, broomstick in hand, poised for a resounding thump on the door.

"Ah, bless you, Keddie, it's a bad night to be up. I was able to keep above the storm most of the way, but landing was awful. I'm afraid I ruined your blackberry bushes," Bess said as she entered.

"What on earth brings you out in such weather? Here, let me take your broom."

"No need, Keddie," said Bess. Standing the broom at her side, she said, "Wait for me in the corner. Behave yourself, now."

The broom gave a little shake, turned, and obediently waddled to the corner of the hall, where it leaned against the wall. A puddle began to spread on the flagstones around its base.

"You don't mind, do you, Keddie? I hates to leave me broom out on such a night. It gets soggy and hard to manage."

"No trouble at all, Bess. Come inside. Princess will be glad to see you. She loves to have company."

"Will she, now, or are you just being polite? I could understand her being angry with me and blaming me for her troubles."

"She doesn't blame you, Bess. Come on."

"Well, it's good news I bring. I've been asking around all this time, Keddie, and I finally learned something useful. That's why I flew right over," Bess said as they made their way to the fireside. "Have you ever heard of an old wizard named Arlebar?"

"The name is not familiar. What's his field?"

"Oh, he does a little of this and a little of that. He's been retired for the last eighty years. Lately he's been doing a bit of private instruction—in transformation spells," Bess said with a knowing smile.

"I see. And where can I find Arlebar?"

"You'll have a long trip to do that, Keddie."

"Does Arlebar by any chance dwell over the Barren Moun-

tains, past the Dismal Bog, through the Dark Wood, across
the River of Misery and the Desolation of the Loser Kings,
and a harsh and perilous journey beyond the Inn on the Outer
Edge into the heart of the Dragonback range?''

Bess stopped in her tracks, astonished. ''The very place!
But you told me you didn't know the man!''

''I don't. I didn't know his name until you mentioned it, or
the fact that he's a wizard. I wasn't even sure he'd be human.
But I knew that somewhere out there I'd find help for Princess.''

''You've been doing some fancy magic, have you?''

''Well, actually, someone told me. I went to visit my old
teacher, Fraigus.''

''Fraigus o' the Murk?''

''Himself. Come along, Bess, you're soaking the carpet.''

''Fraigus o' the Murk,'' Bess repeated, shaking her head
slowly in wonder. ''I thought the poor old soul was dead and
buried these thirty years.''

''He's kept to himself,'' Kedrigern said as they entered the
room. ''Princess, it's Bess the Wood-witch, come to bring
good news.''

''Welcome, Bess. Make yourself at home,'' Princess said
sweetly.

''Ah, that's good of you, love, after all the trouble old
Bess has caused.''

''Now, don't talk that way, Bess, dear. Keddie, pull up a
chair for Bess.''

''Sit right here by the fire and dry off, Bess,'' the wizard
said.

''If you don't mind, love, I'll stand over here and dry
meself off with a little spell. I gets nervous when I'm too
close to a fire.''

''Of course, Bess.'' Kedrigern carried the chair to the far
side of the table, where Bess was already enveloped in a
cloud of frowsty steam. She settled into the soft cushions with
a long sigh, extended her feet before her, and looked from
Princess to Kedrigern and back again to Princess, smiling
maternally.

The fresh log was slow to catch fire, and the light in the
room was subdued. Bess was transfigured. Her cheeks, which
time, wind, and weather had worn to the color and texture of
an oxhide jerkin, were softened by the gentle light. Her warts
and the whiskers that made her resemble an aging tomcat

scarcely showed, and the tracery of rufous veins that covered her noise was invisible. Even her nose appeared less bulbous. She looked like a kindly old peasant woman deep in thoughts of home and family.

Without warning, Bess threw her head back and gave a hair-raising cackle of laughter. Kedrigern straightened in his chair, and a loud splash came from the golden bowl.

"So you knew about Arlebar all along. You're a deep one, Keddie, that you are," she said.

"I don't know much, Bess. Not really."

"Don't you, now? Sounds to me as if you could find his house in the dark."

"Hardly that. Even if I can make it to the Inn on the Outer Edge, Arlebar's home is still a harsh and perilous journey away. Just how long a journey, I can't say."

"You'll find him, Keddie. You have to. Arlebar's the man who can help Princess."

"What makes you so sure?"

"Old Bess has been busy talking to people and asking questions of them as knows things. That pair of young rowdies as caused the trouble at Wizcon each spent some time studying transformation spells with Arlebar," said Bess, winking wisely and laying a finger to the side of her nose.

"Then Arlebar will know what spell is on me, and Keddie can remove it without any danger of side effects!" Princess said happily.

"Well done, Bess," Kedrigern said. "I'll finish up here tomorrow, and be on my way by . . ." He paused, then said, "Bess, do you know anything about summoning up water spirits?"

"It's a part of me education that's totally lacking. Sorry, love."

"Just thought I'd ask. Panglunder of the Dark Wood needs a water spirit fast, and since I have to pass through the Dark Wood on my way to the River of Misery . . . Oh, well, I'll work on it along the way."

"When do we leave?" Princess asked excitedly.

"I leave tomorrow. Alone. I wouldn't think of bringing you, my dear. It's much too dangerous."

"You can protect us with your magic."

"I'm not made of magic. I could burn up all my power

protecting us along the way, and have none left when I find Arlebar.''

"You won't burn up any more protecting the two of us than you will protecting yourself,'' she pointed out.

"That's just it, my dear: traveling alone, I can take risks I wouldn't dream of taking if you were with me. Meanwhile, you'll be completely safe here. I won't be worrying about you. I can concentrate on the task at hand.''

"And what will I concentrate on as I sit here in a bowl of damp moss?'' Princess demanded. "Don't you think I worry? What if you get yourself killed?''

"At least one of us will still be alive.''

"One of us will still be a *toad*!'' Princess cried in a shrill angry voice. "Keddie, either I go with you, or I go back to the bog.''

"My dear, be reasonable.''

"She's being reasonable,'' Bess said. "She wants to go with you, and not spend the next few months sitting in a bowl, waiting.''

Princess said nothing, but an indignant little splash came from her bowl. Kedrigern rose and paced the length of the room. Flinging out his arms, he said, "But it will be dangerous! Doesn't anyone understand that? *Very* dangerous!''

"She don't care, Keddie,'' said Bess.

"Let her speak for herself,'' Kedrigern snapped.

"I don't care if it's dangerous. I want to go,'' said a brave little voice from the bowl.

"There you are,'' said Bess, smiling benignly.

Kedrigern sank into his chair and sat staring up into the darkness with a martyred expression. "Oh, dear,'' he said softly. "Oh, dear me.''

"Now that everything's settled, I'll be on my way. You'll be wanting to get an early start, I expect.''

"Yes,'' Kedrigern said dully.

"No need to go up in this weather, Bess. Spend the night here and we can all leave together in the morning,'' Princess said.

"That's kind of you, love, but I've got something on the fire and I don't dare leave it unwatched for long,'' said Bess, rising from her chair and rubbing the small of her back.

"You could leave first thing in the morning.''

"The dear knows what I'll find if I'm not home within the

hour. It's terrible flying weather, but there's no help for it, love.''

"I'll get your broom,'' Kedrigern offered.

He went into the hall where Bess had parked her broom. There was a puddle in the corner, but no broom to be seen. Kedrigern noticed a wet track leading into the kitchen. He followed it to the broom closet. The door was ajar, and he heard soft rustling within, followed by a giggle.

"All right, out of there, all of you,'' he commanded, flinging the door wide.

There was a subdued scuffling sound, and Bess's broom came forth, followed by a slender mop, somewhat tousled. An aged, much-worn besom swept out at a tilt behind them, looking very disapproving.

"A fine way to behave,'' Kedrigern said scathingly. "You have a perfectly nice dry corner all to yourself, and you had to trail water all over my floors—'' At this, the little mop tried surreptitiously to wipe up the track of puddles. Kedrigern put a stop to this with a wrathful look. "And lead my household astray. Not that they put up much resistance,'' he continued, and the mop shrank back to the stolid companionship of the old besom. "Well, come along. Bess is waiting. Back in the closet, you two.''

The broom waddled across the kitchen and into the hall, swaggering a little. At the sight of Bess, standing with arms folded and a stern expression on her formidable face, the broom slowed and edged its way to the wall, out of her immediate reach.

"Up to your old tricks, are you?'' she demanded.

The broom shrank into the corner, sagging and trying to look small. Bess glowered at it. Kedrigern, at her side, added his own cold look of censure.

"In the broom closet, was he?'' Bess asked.

"Yes.''

Turning to the broom, Bess chided, "Couldn't behave yourself in a decent wizard's house for ten minutes, could you? It's ashamed you should be. Go on, get outside and wait for me. And don't get yourself all wet.''

Kedrigern unlatched the door, and the broom skulked through the narrow opening. When the door was shut, Bess said ruefully, "I'd get rid of him in a minute, only that he's the smoothest ride I've ever had. And fast, too. There's no other broom I'd trust on a night like this. But he's a terrible one for fooling with the young mops, he is."

"He did no harm, Bess. Just a bit of flirting."

"No harm here, maybe, but I can't keep another broom, or a mop, in the house for the goings on of him. I've got me reputation to think of."

"I can see how it might be awkward."

Bess sighed and nodded. Brightening, she said, "It has its compensations, Keddie. He'll get me home double quick now, to get back on me good side, and give the house a nice sweeping tonight, while I'm asleep. It's just that I has to keep an eye on him."

"I understand perfectly."

"So you'll be leaving tomorrow, you and Princess?"

"We will, Bess. I really wish I could persuade her to stay here. Perhaps if you spoke—"

"I will not," Bess said flatly. "Her little heart is set on going, and I'd not thwart her."

"But the *danger!*"

"Ah, Keddie, you're a grand wizard but you know nothing about women. She has no wish to be safe while you face perils of all sorts for her sake. No woman does."

"She doesn't?"

"No. And remember, Keddie, Princess isn't your ordinary princess. She knows a bit of magic herself. You might be glad she's along."

"I hadn't thought of that," Kedrigern admitted.

"Men never do. And while I think of it, here's something else you might be glad to have along," Bess said, groping about under her frazzled shawl and extracting a securely stoppered flask. "Old Fenny Snake. It's a fresh batch."

"I really don't think I should," Kedrigern said, raising his hands, shaking his head, and backing away.

"It's cold and wet and raw where you'll be going, and a couple of swallows of Old Fenny Snake will put the heart in you. And there's nothing like it for lighting a fire," said Bess, pressing the flask on him. "Just don't let it get on your skin."

"I'll be careful. Thanks, Bess."

The wood-witch made a smooth takeoff, then circled and set out for home at a great clip, assisted by a lusty tailwind. Inside the house, Kedrigern shook himself dry, latched and

barred the door, and returned to the welcome warmth of the
fireside. Princess was sleeping soundly on her bed of damp
moss, and the house was still.

He looked longingly at the goblet of Vosconu's excellent
wine, scarcely touched. But the spell for Panglunder needed
more work, and spell research called for a clear head. And
after that, there was packing to be done. Princess could not
help, and Spot would only mash everything into a small wad.

And tomorrow, the journey.

···❧ *Five* ❧···

when lovers prove unkind

UNDER A BRIGHT sun and clear blue skies, the crossing of the Barren Mountains was easy; indeed, to Kedrigern's great annoyance, it was almost pleasant. The trails were dry and free of snow, the wind was mild, the air bracing. Kedrigern did not have occasion to utter a single cross word or voice a solitary complaint on this leg of the journey.

The lowlands were quite a different thing. The forest air was heavy and dank and smelled of the death of winter. In sheltered hollows lay speckled patches of rotting snow, exhaling cold mist. Water dripped from the black trees, and the patter of the drops was a background to the splash and sucking withdrawal of their great horse's hooves as he plodded down the muddy trail.

"Isn't this exhilarating?" Princess asked from her perch on Kedrigern's shoulder.

He answered with an indeterminate grunt.

"It's wonderful to travel. We don't travel enough, Keddie. If we're not careful, we'll become dull."

He did not respond to that observation.

"Just smell that air!" Princess said brightly.

In a sudden outburst of frustration Kedrigern cried, "This is the worst place I've ever been, and this is the worst time of the year to travel! We could be at home, by a nice fire, wearing dry clothes, and look where we are!"

Coolly, Princess replied, "*You* might be sitting by the fire in nice dry clothes. *I* would be hunkered down on a clump of damp moss, trying not to think of flies. I do wish you'd show some consideration for me, Keddie."

"My dear, I'm only making this filthy trip for your sake. But it's still the worst time in the year to travel."

"You think every season is an awful time to travel."

"I do, because they are. But the end of winter is the worst. All that dampness. And the mud," said the wizard with loathing.

"And what's wrong with dampness and mud? Some of us happen to think they're very nice."

"They're not for everyone, my dear."

"Well, they're for me until I'm despelled, and it appears that that's a long time off. Why can't we go right to Arlebar? Why must we stop off at Panglunder's?"

"It's on our way. We needn't stay long. I only have to release Lalloree from the flames and we can leave the next day. It'll be a relief to sleep indoors again."

"For *you,* maybe."

"I'll see that you have a nice bowl of moss."

"Thank you very much," said Princess.

They proceeded in silence for a distance, coming at last to the edge of the Dismal Bog. The air was chill and misty. Barren limbless trunks loomed eerily among the wisps of whiteness.

"Keddie, let's stop here for a while. I'd like to splash around and have a good soak," Princess said.

"Certainly, my dear. Capital idea. I'll take a snack and walk about a bit while you're splashing."

Kedrigern dismounted carefully, so as not to dislodge Princess from his shoulder, and stooped to facilitate her descent. She hopped headlong into the bog, splashing like a child in a tub and making merry little sounds of sheer batrachian bliss.

Kedrigern seated himself on a relatively dry stump, took a piece of bread from his scrip, and nibbled on it as he looked on affectionately. Princess was a tidy, graceful little toad, quite different from the gross and sullen creatures squatting motionless along the edge of the bog. A common lot, they were. Breeding shows, he reflected, even in a toad.

His collation finished, Kedrigern rose, stretched, and began to pace slowly along the edge of the bog. Toads of all sizes plopped into the water as he passed, making little squonking noises of alarm and displeasure. Kedrigern smiled on them, placing his feet carefully to avoid injury to the unwary and the preoccupied.

He came to a familiar knoll and paused for a moment. A large toad was seated squarely on it, glaring at him.

"Good day to you, toad," said the wizard amicably. When he received no response but an uninterrupted cold stare, he went on, "You've chosen a historic place to rest, though I'm sure you don't know a thing about it. On that very knoll I freed a beautiful princess from a spell that had turned her into a toad. And only last fall, I did the same for a handsome prince."

The toad did not move or make a sound. It fixed a glittering eye on Kedrigern, and sat.

"Poor prince," said the wizard with a sympathetic sigh. "I had to turn him back into a toad not long after. At that, I think the poor fellow came out ahead. If you had seen what Fraigus had made of him, you'd—"

At the name of Fraigus, the toad let out an enraged "Brereep!" and began to hop furiously up and down on the knoll. Kedrigern gave a start at the outburst, and then recognition came upon him.

"Prince! Poor fellow, I didn't mean to rub it in. Oh, dear," Kedrigern said as the toad, with one last irate "Brereep," leapt from his station and described a long graceful arc not bogward but into the long grass by the roadside, where the great black steed browsed serenely. Kedrigern looked after the toad for some time, but could find no trace of his progress. Shaking his head sadly, he returned in a somber mood to where he had left Princess.

She hopped from the bog to meet him, and her high spirits lifted his own. She suspected nothing, and he made no reference to his encounter with the unhappy prince.

"How absolutely delightful! How refreshing!" she gushed. "I must say, Keddie, the life of a toad does have its moments. Just being able to splash about, and frisk and frolic and plop—it's wonderful!"

"Surely a princess can frisk and frolic. Even plop, if she's so inclined."

"Oh, my, no. Not at all. A princess can't just hop into the water and enjoy herself. A princess doesn't swim, she *bathes*. It's an elaborate ceremony. I used to have attendants everywhere to make sure no one could peek, and there'd be women to help me undress, and others to lather me up and rinse me down and towel me dry, and some to scent me afterwards, and brush my hair, and attire me in fine raiment."

"It sounds very luxurious," Kedrigern observed.

"Well, yes, I suppose it was. But it was always so *crowded*. It's nice to have privacy."

"You had privacy at our cottage," he could not resist pointing out.

"That was in a bathtub, Keddie. It just isn't the same thing as a bog."

"Tell me, my dear, what else to you remember about the old days in your father's kingdom?" he asked.

"Well, I remember bathing. And I remember my eighteenth birthday. I won't forget *that* in a hurry. And I remember the jugglers Daddy used to bring in for the holidays."

"Do you know, my dear, you've always been reticent about your family. I don't believe you ever told me your father's name."

Princess was profoundly silent for a time and at last, in a subdued voice, said, "To be perfectly honest, Keddie, I still don't remember."

"How about your mother's name?"

"I can't remember that, either. I don't even remember what they look like."

"Regal?" he suggested.

"Certainly. She was . . . very beautiful, and he . . . he had a black beard. I remember that much. A scratchy black beard. But if they came and sat down beside you now, I wouldn't recognize them."

"They probably wouldn't recognize you, either."

"Keddie, have I lost my memory forever? Is that part of the spell?" Princess cried in alarm.

"No, my dear. A transformation spell doesn't incur memory loss, as a rule. That would undercut the entire point of it."

"Maybe I was misspelled somehow. Or maybe this comes of all the other magic that's been used on me. It's all gotten mixed up together, and gone bad."

"Don't get upset. We can work on your memory once you're back in your proper shape," said Kedrigern.

Princess was not ready to be comforted. "Bad enough to be a toad, but a toad without memories . . . ," she moaned.

"You haven't forgotten our life together. You recognized Bess the other night."

"That's true."

"And you must remember Tristaver. And Grodz. And Conhoon, and Buroc, and Rhys ap Gwallter. You can't have forgotten Rhys ap Gwallter."

"I remember them all. I can remember the day you came to the bog, and how sad and lonely you looked when I first saw you. I didn't know who you were, but I thought you were a very pleasant looking man."

"Well, there you are," Kedrigern said cheerfully.

"Not what one would call stylish, or dapper, mind you," she continued. "As I recall, you were wearing the very same outfit you're wearing now. But you had an honest, pleasant face."

"Your memory seems perfectly intact, my dear."

"It doesn't go back very far. Before you, it's all bog."

"We'll work on that when we have you despelled," Kedrigern assured her. "Are you ready to go now?"

"Are we leaving the bog?"

"We'll be traveling along the edge for a few days. You'll be able to get more good swims."

She hopped to his outstretched hand, thence to his shoulder, and when she was comfortably settled, he remounted. The road rose a bit at this point, and was consequently a bit drier and firmer. The horse kept up a steady canter. Neither Kedrigern nor Princess spoke for a time, and then a thought occured to the wizard.

"Have you any idea how long you were in the bog, my dear?" he asked.

"Oh, it must have been . . . well, it was quite some time. Perhaps as much as a year. Maybe a few years."

"Could it have been longer?"

She pondered for a moment, then said, "I suppose it could. One day is pretty much like another in a bog. Why do you ask?"

"Just curious, my dear."

As they continued to skirt the bog, Kedrigern was daily reminded of Princess's observation on the uniformity of quotidian life in such a setting. After a few days, he had the feeling that he had been here half a lifetime, waiting for something interesting to happen. Whatever it might offer in the way of aquatic recreation, a bog was not a place that attracted or pleased him.

They left the Dismal Bog at last, and entered the Dark Wood, a gloomy place, but less dank than the bog's environs and very quiet. They slept soundly at night, secure behind a warning spell that extended about a furlong in every direction. There were patches of tender new grass for their horse, and an abundance of clear cold springs for their water supply and Princess's frisking. Kedrigern found the rich soil a good source of rare and useful simples. The road was firm, and travel was easy and comfortable. There were no alarms; not the slightest hint of a threat. And yet, for all the undeniable advantages the woods offered the traveler, Kedrigern and Princess found themselves uneasy in this place.

They saw a few birds, but heard no song. Now and again a squirrel blurred around a tree trunk, but there was no other sign of animal life, and not a trace of man. The silence that had been lulling at first grew oppressive and at last foreboding. Kedrigern tried reciting verses to raise their spirits, but the sound of a solitary voice in that immense stillness was funereal in its effect, and he did not get past the first stanza of "The Jolly Juggler." After that, they both kept silent for a long time.

"Keddie, how much farther is Panglunder's castle?" Princess asked as they rested of an afternoon.

"It's not far now. We should be there by tomorrow at this time."

"Thank heaven for that. This is a depressing place. I can almost feel the sadness in the air," said Princess with a tiny shiver.

"It *is* rather cheerless here," Kedrigern agreed. "This place was much livelier a few years ago. It was worth your life to travel through Dark Wood in those days. There were thieves, brigands, robbers, wild men, outlaws, barbarians . . . a family of trolls . . . an ogre . . . all of them very nasty."

"At least there was something going on."

"Indeed there was. Murder, robbery, rape, mutilation, torture, pillage, orgies, massacres . . . never a dull day in Dark Wood. Panglunder stopped all that, though."

"He seems to have stopped everything."

"Panglunder is a very thorough man."

They passed a time in reflective silence, then Princess said, "It seems like more than just the absence of noise and crowds. It's as though the place itself is saturated in gloom and depression and unhappiness."

"Odd you should say that. There's a legend about Dark Wood. There's a legend about *everything* in these parts."

"What's the legend?"

"The usual thing. Handsome king and beautiful queen and wicked spell on their only child and desperation and grief and finally everything falling to pieces and nothing but wind over crumbling ruins and misery all around. You know."

"You might try to be a little sympathetic," Princess said with mild vexation.

"My dear, one hears the same story everywhere. Pass by a collapsed cowshed, and there's sure to be a peasant near at hand to blame it all on a wicked spell. Sometimes it's simply a question of poor construction and shoddy workmanship, but you'd never think so to hear the legends. Everything that goes bad is the fault of a wizard or a sorcerer with a wicked spell."

"Why do *you* think Dark Wood is such a miserable place?"

Kedrigern weighed her question. He rose and brushed his cloak, frowning thoughtfully all the while, and knelt to take up Princess. They remounted, and rode for a time, and still he was silent.

"Well?" she demanded.

"Probably a wicked spell," he said.

She gave him a withering glance, but he kept his eyes innocently fixed on the roadside.

They camped on higher ground that night, and next day the road ascended steadily, at a shallow angle. That afternoon, from the top of a rise, they saw Panglunder's castle on a hilltop to the north.

It was a grim, businesslike pile of dark stone, square and blocky, with a watchtower at each corner and a keep rising in the center. As a stronghold it was formidable; as a residence, even for a single night, it was uninviting, at least in Princess's opinion.

"It looks like a place where you'd send people to be impaled," she said.

"It wasn't designed as a pleasure dome, my dear."

"That's obvious. I can imagine what Panglunder must be like."

"He's a decent sort. A bit unpolished, perhaps, but a good fellow."

"I can picture him now. Red face, barrel chest, hairy nostrils, no neck. Full of strange oaths. Swilling ale by the potful and singing war songs, then collapsing into sodden sentimentality about dear friends far away. Disgusting."

"Is that what they did at your father's castle?"

"That was uncalled for, Keddie," she said frostily.

"You gave such a graphic description, my dear, I was certain it had been drawn from the life."

Princess gave a very superior sniff and was silent for a time. When they were back on the forest trail once again, and Panglunder's castle was lost to view, she said, "Actually, I was describing a neighbor of ours, a great brute of a fellow. Whenever Daddy got angry at me, he'd threaten to marry me off to him."

"Your memory seems to be coming along nicely, my dear."

"Not all that nicely. I can't recall his name."

"I shouldn't think you'd want to."

"That really isn't the point."

"No, I suppose not. But you needn't expect to meet such a brute in Panglunder. I think you'll be pleasantly surprised."

"I'll be pleasantly surprised if he has a neck," said Princess.

When they came to the clearing in which it stood, Mon Chagrin, the castle of Panglunder, looked even more forbidding, looming granitically over them at the crest of a long upward slope. Kedrigern reined in his big black horse at the edge of the wood. For a time he studied the castle with his unaided eyes, and then he drew out the medallion of his fellowship and peered through the tiny hole at its center, the Aperture of True Vision. He replaced the medallion in his tunic and continued to gaze on the castle.

"Something's wrong. I know it," said Princess.

"No, nothing's wrong. Odd, but not wrong."

"What's odd?"

"It looks . . . well, it looks *nice*. There are pots of flowers by the gate. The tower hoardings have been painted. There's a very pretty ground cover at the base of the towers; it brings out the natural color of the stone. About the only thing missing is a welcome sign."

"Maybe it's under new ownership."

"Couldn't be. Not this quickly. It wasn't three weeks ago that I had the message from Panglunder, and a seige takes . . . now, what in the world . . . ?" said Kedrigern, fumbling in his tunic for the medallion and raising it to his eye.

"What's happening?"

"Two of Panglunder's men are putting out a welcome sign. I must say, Panglunder has gotten very gracious since I was here last. I'm impressed."

"Obviously a woman's influence," Princess said airily.

They started up the long broad road that led to the castle. Scarcely had they emerged from the wood when a figure on horseback burst from the castle gate and rode toward them at a great clip, waving exuberantly as he came nearer.

Kedrigern returned the wave. "It's Panglunder. He's coming out to meet us himself," he explained.

"I'm just going to jump into your hood."

"No need for that, my dear. Panglunder will be glad to see you."

"Keddie, I'm not looking my best."

"He'll understand. I'll tell him—"

"Keddie, I'm a *toad*! I don't want to meet anyone while I'm a toad!" she cried, and hopped gracefully into his hood.

"As you wish, my dear."

"And don't tell anyone I'm with you," said Princess, her tiny voice muffled.

Panglunder pulled up at his side in a great billow of dust, and Kedrigern wished that Princess had stayed for a glimpse of him, for he was quite different from the neckless brute she had anticipated. For one known—justifiably—as the Unyielding; for a man who had earned the title of Lord Paramount of the Dark Wood and held it against a score of challenges; Panglunder was an unprepossessing figure. He was short, and slight of frame. His hands were small, and the fingers that were not smashed out of shape or missing altogether were long and delicate. His eyes were blue and watery, and he blinked a lot, as if continually surprised by what met his gaze. His hair, a nondescript brownish thatch, was unruly on the sides and thinning on top. He had a long, narrow, high-bridged nose and a rather weak chin. All in all, Panglunder did not look much like a successful warlord, but it was unlikely that anyone had ever pointed out the fact to him.

His welcome was boisterous and hearty. "Oh, I say, it's good to see you, Kedrigern, old fellow!" he cried in a voice that filled the clearing and echoed off the castle walls. "What a delightful surprise! Whatever brings you to Dark Wood, old chap?" Before Kedrigern could respond to his surprising greeting, Panglunder added in a hoarse undertone, "Not a word about being sent for, whatever you do. You just happen to be passing by, that's all," and then roared, "You must stop for dinner. Stay the night, honored master! Stay the summer! It's a pleasure to see you."

Through the dust of Panglunder's arrival, Kedrigern could see a palfrey approaching. He could just make out the rider, a woman of dignified mien. She looked familiar, but the dust made it hard to be certain.

"Memanesha?" he asked.

"Yes. She mustn't know," was the whispered reply, followed by a booming "Best surprise I've had all year! What are you doing up this way, master?"

"I just happened to be passing," Kedrigern replied loudly. "I'm on my way across the river to see a man about a spell. How is everything with you, Panglunder?"

"Wonderful. Absolutely marvelous. Never better."

"I'm glad to hear it."

"Oh, yes, things are going well. Isn't that so, my Memanesha?" Panglunder said, addressing the woman who had just joined them.

"Quite well, Pannie dear," said Memanesha. She fixed her dark eyes on the wizard. "I expect they will continue to go well, as long as no one interferes in our affairs."

"No fear of that," said Panglunder heartily.

"I do hope so. You're looking quite well, Kedrigern. Are you still specializing in counterspells?" she asked with a sweet smile.

"I work a small counterspell from time to time, Lady Memanesha. Now and then. Here and there. You know how it goes."

"Here?" she repeated, with emphasis. "Now?"

"Oh, no, nothing here or now. I'm traveling on a purely personal matter. I have to find an old wizard who dwells somewhere beyond the Inn on the Outer Edge."

"I see. Just passing through," said Memanesha.

"Just passing through, I assure you, my lady."

"Then we must make you as comfortable as we can during your all too brief stay, and send you on your way refreshed. Come along, Pannie," said the sorceress.

She turned her palfrey toward the gate. Panglunder rode to her side, tipping a quick wink of relief and gratitude to the wizard, who fell in behind the pair and followed them to Mon Chagrin in silence.

After a warm bath and a refreshing nap, in garments vigorously brushed and boots brightly polished, Kedrigern partook of a leisurely dinner superbly prepared and accompanied by wines approaching Vosconu's in quality. He sat long at table with his host and hostess, and found them an attractive couple. The centuries had been kind to Memanesha. Her skin was unlined, her figure svelte, her hair a lustrous crown of amber flecked with gold. The only evidence of a long and eventful life lay in her smoldering dark eyes. The man who looked unguarded into those eyes might lose himself forever. Even Kedrigern, forewarned and protected, felt vague stirrings within him at each lingering glance, and did his best to keep his eyes busy elsewhere. Panglunder, for that reason, received closer scrutiny than might otherwise have been given him.

He looked no more formidable than he had on greeting his guest; indeed, in a loose fur-trimmed robe that was much too big for him, he looked almost like a child *en dishabille,* not someone who would be characterized in earnest as "The Unyielding." But unyielding he most certainly was. What Panglunder said he would do, and set out to do, he did.

It must be this force of character, Kedrigern thought, that made Panglunder so attractive to a woman like Memanesha, who in her time had been the consort of kings. Panglunder had attracted other women, too—the as yet unmentioned

Princess Lalloree, for one. It had to be his character that attracted them, Kedrigern judged. It wasn't his good looks, or witty conversation.

During a lull in the table talk his thoughts turned to Lalloree. Her name still had not come up, and he found the silence ominous. Perhaps Memanesha's enchanted fire had flared up, and the unfortunate girl was now a heap of ashes. That was unpleasant to contemplate, particularly in view of the cheery mood that prevailed in the castle. Panglunder was unyielding, but not heartless.

It might be that Memanesha had simply effaced all memory of the young princess from Panglunder's mind. But if that were so, why had the Lord Paramount hastened forth to enjoin Kedrigern to silence? It was all very puzzling.

"Pannie and I have been wondering about your journey, Kedrigern. Did you say you were going to seek a wizard?" Memanesha asked, breaking abruptly into his musings.

"That's correct. I have to get some information about a spell I mean to counter."

"You did say that this wizard dwelt somewhere beyond the Inn on the Outer Edge, didn't you?"

"I did. I'm not exactly sure where, but I'll make inquiries at the inn."

"I say, Kedrigern, what sort of place is this inn?" Panglunder asked.

The wizard and the sorceress exchanged a guarded glance of professional concern. Memanesha nodded, deferring to Kedrigern, and he said cautiously, "It's a very . . . interesting place. Not like your ordinary inn."

"Do you mean it's clean?" Panglunder said, and laughed loudly at this sally of wit.

"It's very clean," Memanesha assured him.

"That's an odd name, Inn on the Outer Edge. Outer Edge of what? The edge of the world is hundreds of leagues from here. I know. Met a man once who'd seen it. Looked over and got dizzy. Nearly fell off. What's this inn on the edge of, anyway?"

"It's sort of on the edge of . . . things," Kedrigern said uneasily.

"What things? Rocks? A river?"

"No, nothing like that."

"Woods, then? A forest? Is it at the edge of the sea?"

"It's at the edge of reality," Kedrigern said. When Panglunder merely blinked, a bit more rapidly than was his custom, the wizard explained, "It's a sort of crossing point for what is, and what might have been but wasn't, and what wasn't but should have been."

"And for what must never be," Mcmanesha added.

"Yes. And what will be."

"It sounds like a very strange place," said the Lord Paramount.

"It is, sometimes. And sometimes it's just a nice clean inn amid the Desolation of the Loser Kings on the way to the Dragonback Mountains. But under certain conditions, unusual things happen. I stayed there once when I was a student. That was awhile back. Oh, my, yes, quite awhile back," Kedrigern said, looking off into a shadowy corner in a mellow, reminiscent mood. "Another student and I decided we'd go and see for ourselves if all the stories we'd heard were true. Poor old Derrigash. I haven't seen him for ages."

When Kedrigern had been silent for a time, Panglunder cried, "What happened to him?"

"Derrigash? He washed out, poor fellow. He was never comfortable around spells. Used to get nervous and stammer in the middle of them, and summon up things that were not at all what he intended. Couldn't have that, of course. I think he finally went into alchemy."

"I mean at the inn. What happened at the inn?"

"Oh, the inn. Not much, actually. A man down the hall claimed that Arthur's last weird battle in the west had been fought in his room during the night, and one of the servants turned to glass while we were having breakfast, but that was all. Everyone said it was a quiet time."

"Turned to glass? Real glass?"

"Yes. Unfortunately, another servant bumped into him and knocked him over, right on the flagstone floor." Kedrigern shook his head sadly at the memory of this mischance, and fell into a melancholy silence.

"Who is the wizard you seek?" Memanesha asked after a polite interval.

"All I know is his name. It's Arlebar."

"I see. And is it important that you find him?"

"Very."

Memanesha favored him with a smile that would have brought a statue to its knees whimpering with desire, and turned a subdued version of that smile on Panglunder. "Pannie, I think we've found a solution to our little difficulty," she said.

"You mean . . . that unhappy child?"

"Exactly what I mean, Pannie." She returned her attention to the wizard. "You see, dear Kedrigern, I know Arlebar. Our acquaintance was brief, but . . . close," she said, demurely lowering her eyes. "I'm sure he has tender memories of me still, and would outdo himself for one who came to him bearing my letter of introduction."

"My lady Memanesha, I don't know how to thank you for such kindness," said Kedrigern.

"I can easily tell you. We have with us at Mon Chagrin a young lady—a child, an infant, really—who must be returned to her family. They dwell on the plain south of the Dragonback Mountains. It is likely that your quest will bring you near her parents' kingdom, and you will be able to return her to her family and claim a suitable reward," said the sorceress.

"Is Arlebar's home near this kingdom?"

"Unfortunately, I know Arlebar's exact whereabouts no better than you do. It's been some time since we were . . . in conversation, and he is something of a wanderer. But he's sure to be in the general area."

"You'd be doing us a great service," said Panglunder.

"We would be deeply grateful," Memanesha purred.

"I'll help you all I can. Horses. An armed guard to the bridge," Panglunder eagerly offered.

"I will weave a protective spell to bring you safely across the Desolation," Memanesha added.

"That's very good of you," said Kedrigern warily. "I'd love to help. I really would. But—"

"I'm prepared to be generous, Kedrigern. And her father absolutely dotes on the girl. He'll give you her weight in gold. Maybe even diamonds."

"A not inconsiderable amount. She's a buxom little baggage," Memanesha pointed out.

"As I said, I'd love to help. It's rather out of my way, though. It could make for a long journey."

"It need not be an unpleasant one," said Memanesha, smiling and glancing sidewise at the wizard. "There are those who consider the child comely, in a callow sort of way, and on a long journey—"

"Now, just one minute!" cried a tiny, irate voice from Kedrigern's pocket. An instant later, Princess hopped to the table. "That's quite enough of *that* talk!"

"What's the meaning of this? You're a toad!" said Memanesha with loathing.

"Politeness prevents me from saying what *you* are, madam, but it happens that I am a princess, presently enchanted, and the wife of Kedrigern."

"Oh, I say . . . Congratulations to you both," Panglunder said numbly. He shrank back in his chair, blinking quite a lot.

Memanesha looked down on Princess for a time, then glanced at Kedrigern, who nodded in affirmation of Princess's words. The sorceress flashed a radiant smile, and in a voice of transcendent sweetness said, "My dear, forgive me! I didn't know. How thoughtless of our Kedrigern not to share the wonderful news with us. But surely now you see what I was thinking. A man like our Kedrigern really must have a wife, and there is no better wife for a wizard than a beautiful princess."

"That's true enough," Princess conceded distantly.

"Of course it is, dear. And yet they're always throwing themselves away on handsome princes, expecting to live happily ever after. Well, we all know what happens when you marry a handsome prince. Hopeless."

"So I've heard," said Princess.

"It's absolutely true, dear. I confess it, I was matchmaking. But now it turns out that Kedrigern has already married a princess, and that makes everything perfect."

"It does?" said Kedrigern, looking around in perplexity.

"It removes the last possible objection. Now it will be quite respectable. Princess Lalloree will return home properly chaperoned, in the company of a decent married couple."

The mention, at last, of the girl's name answered one pressing question: Lalloree was alive, and fit to travel. There remained only the question of her willingness.

"Would it be possible for us to speak to the young lady?" Kedrigern asked.

"Not at present, I'm afraid," Memanesha replied. "She's in an enchanted sleep behind a curtain of magic fire. For her own protection."

"But she's well."

"Oh, perfectly. It's very restful, actually."

"And she's willing to return to her family."

"Quite willing. One might even say eager. The only thing delaying her is the problem of finding a suitable escort. We can't just send the silly little thing off by herself. And Pannie and I are far too busy with matters here in Dark Wood to spare the time for a long journey. That's why I put her in the enchanted sleep, you see—it makes the waiting easier."

"How did Lalloree come to be here, anyway?" Kedrigern asked.

Panglunder paled and looked suddenly ill. Memanesha, with a quick sidelong glance at him, gave the wizard one of her most incapacitating smiles and laughed lightly and merrily. "Dear Kedrigern, it's such a mix-up! I'll have to tell you the whole story someday, but I'm sure you're tired after all the traveling you've done, and you'll want to get an early start tomorrow," she said, rising gracefully from her chair. "Pannie will show you to your room. Is everything quite all right?"

"Oh, yes. Fine," Kedrigern said, rising.

"And you, Princess—is there anything you require? A basin of mud, perhaps? Some flies?" the sorceress asked.

Princess's tiny voice was icy. "Nothing, thank you, madam."

"How wonderful it must be to have such simple needs," Memanesha said sweetly as she turned to make her departure.

When the door closed behind her, Panglunder leaned across the table, clasped Kedrigern's hands in his, and said hoarsely, "Kedrigern, get that princess out of here, please. I can't stand this much longer!"

"What's going on, anyway?"

"It's all a misunderstanding. The marriage would have been a purely political arrangement, but try to tell that to a sorceress. Now I don't know what to do. I can't take her back to old Brindom myself, and I can't just keep her on here indefinitely."

"Why not? She's in a trance," Princess pointed out.

"There's no telling what Memanesha's liable to do. She

might wither Lalloree up into a crone. Or turn her into a . . . into something loathsome.''

"Into a toad! You were going to say 'into a toad'!" Princess cried in a rage.

"No! I was going to say 'into a monster.' I *like* toads. We have lots of toads around Mon Chagrin.''

"Well, I haven't seen any.''

"They keep to themselves.''

"You're asking a lot, Panglunder," Kedrigern said. "We're going on a long and perilous quest, and having a lovesick, homesick princess on our hands is not going to make things easier for us.''

"Lalloree's not the least bit lovesick, I assure you, old fellow. And she's quite a good traveler. Knows hundreds of songs. Riddles. Word games. She'll be loads of fun. The journey will be over before you know it.''

"And what does this whimsical Lalloree look like?" Princess asked.

"Oh . . . attractive, I suppose, in a kind of juvenile way.''

"'Buxom' was the word your lady friend used when she suggested sweet dalliance en route. Hardly a word one applies to tots.''

"My dear," said Kedrigern in a wounded voice, "surely you don't for a moment think that I could . . . Princess, you wrong me grievously.''

"When a woman suddenly finds herself little and green, Keddie, she is not anxious to have her husband thrust into the company of a buxom young princess. I accuse no one. I wish to wrong no one. I merely—''

"You could keep her in a trance!'' Panglunder broke in with great enthusiasm. "That's it! Just pack up so she gets a little air, and she won't be any trouble at all. I'll give you a cart.''

"I am a wizard, not a delivery man," said Kedrigern with great dignity.

"Then do something magical and get her out of here! I'll take good care of you, I swear. Two of my best horses for each of you, an armed escort to the bridge, and a bag of gold. Memanesha will guard you with a spell until you reach the inn.''

Kedrigern scratched his chin thoughtfully. He raised Princess to his shoulder, so they could confer privately, and said, "I'm inclined to do it. The child won't be any trouble, really, and Memanesha's spell will enable me to save my magic until it's needed. Besides, I do owe Panglunder a favor."

"You don't owe his lady friend anything. I don't trust her, Keddie."

"Neither do I, but I trust Panglunder. He'll take good care of our horse, and a bag of gold may come in handy."

"Well . . . if you think so," said Princess dubiously.

"I do. And you mustn't give a thought to Lalloree, my dear. No other woman, however buxom or merry, could interest me for a moment."

···✠ Six ✠···

the desolation of the loser kings

"Ninety-nine knights went a-riding;
    They spied a lady fair,
With dainty foot and cherry lip
    And lovely golden hair.
The seventy-third brave knight did speak,
    He spoke out bold and free:
Oh, merry, merry maiden,
    Wouldst deign to marry me?
*With a hey! And a ho! and a lully-lully-loo,
    And a fa-la-la-la-la all the day!*"

"AND MOST OF the night, too," said Princess acidly. "She hasn't shut up since we left Mon Chagrin."

"Youthful exuberance my dear. We must remember, she's been in a trance for weeks," Kedrigern replied.

"Now I understand why," Princess muttered.

"Ninety-nine knights went a-riding;
    They spied a lady fair,
With dainty foot and cherry lip
    And lovely golden hair.
The seventy-fourth brave knight did speak,
    He spoke out bold and free:
Oh, merry, merry maiden,
    Wouldst deign to marry me?"

71

Lalloree turned to the men-at-arms escorting them, and said, pouting, "You're not singing along. You're supposed to join in the chorus, but you're not singing."

"Out of breath, my lady," said the nearest. "We sung along with the first sixty choruses."

"Aye, and we was singing all yesterday and night," added the man at her other side.

"Oh, you're no fun, any of you. Everyone in my father's kingdom sings all the time," said Lalloree with a toss of her head.

Kedrigern heard the words with revulsion. He pictured merry peasants, bright-eyed and apple-cheeked, going about their toil with a lully-lully-loo and a fa-la-la-la-la while good King Brindom beamed and twinkled and beat time with his scepter and the courtiers clapped their hands and tapped their toes in perfect time. It was an appalling prospect. He began to sympathize with Panglunder and even, though very slightly, with Memanesha.

"Well, if nobody will sing along, I'll sing for myself," said Lalloree defiantly, and began to hey, and ho, and lully-lully-loo with renewed vigor. The men-at-arms exchanged agonized glances and began to edge slowly away from her horse.

Princess endured for a time, and finally said, "Keddie, have some compassion for the men. Put her back into an enchanted sleep."

"That would not be practical."

"Well, this is impossible. I'm going into your hood and try to get some peace and quiet.'"

As Lalloree was about to repeat the inquiry made by the seventy-seventh brave knight, Kedrigern relented. He called out to her, "May I have a word with you, my lady?" and pulled his horse up beside hers.

"Of course you can, Uncle Keddie. Then we'll sing together."

Ignoring the muffled laughter from inside his hood, the wizard said, "We'll be making camp in a little while, and for safety's sake, we must travel in silence from this point on."

"Do you mean I mustn't sing anymore?"

"I'm afraid not. It might attract a lawless element."

"But we have men to protect us."

"Only six men, Lalloree. They can't fight off an armed

band. We must be silent." Turning to the men-at-arms, he
asked, "Isn't that so?"

A chorus of varied but heartfelt affirmatives arose from the
weary soldiers. Kedrigern looked at the crestfallen Lalloree
and shrugged.

"You could shield us with your magic," she said.

"I must save my magic. We'll need it later. No singing,
Lalloree."

"But it's so *boring* when I can't sing," she complained.

"You might observe the birds and wildflowers."

"That's dull."

"Do intricate mental calculations."

"Ugh."

"Practice conjugations and declensions."

"That's all so *boring*, Uncle Keddie! I like to *sing*, and to
hear stories of bold knights and handsome princes and how
they struggle and wander all over the world and suffer untold
agony and die horrible *deaths* just to win one kind glance
from a beautiful princess."

"Why don't you make up your own story as we go? Just
do it quietly. In your head."

"That's too *hard*," she whined.

"Sorry, Lalloree, but that's how it has to be."

"I'll sing very softly. I'll just sing to myself, and nobody
will hear it but us."

"No," said Kedrigern firmly.

They rode on for a time, and Lalloree, sullen and silent,
did not look at the wizard riding by her side. At length she
said, "I won't sing if you tell me something."

"What is it?"

"That little frog that rides on your shoulder sometimes—is
it really your wife?"

"It is."

"And was she really a beautiful princess?"

"She was, and will be again."

"Why is she a little frog?"

From Kedrigern's hood came a tiny voice, trumpet-clear.
"Because I sang when I should have been quiet."

Lalloree's eyes widened. Kedrigern nodded solemnly. They
rode on in blessed silence.

Panglunder's men-at-arms left them at the entrance to the

great arched bridge over the River of Misery. After crossing, the three travelers rested at the far bank. Princess had a good soak while Kedrigern napped and Lalloree paced up and down the path, enumerating the ways in which everything around them was boring.

Her complaint was not wholly unjustified. The Desolation of the Loser Kings was a great semicircle of flat dreariness, from the mists of its northern reaches to the foothills of the Dragonback range far to the south. The Dark Wood was a carnival of diversion in comparison.

Lalloree's murmurs and deep sighs went unheeded. Princess splashed happily in the shallows at the river's edge, while Kedrigern dozed in the shade of a stunted tree on the bank. Suddenly Princess let out a startled cry and came hopping headlong toward their camp. Kedrigern sat bolt upright and looked wildly about, momentarily befuddled.

"Keddie, it's enchantment! He's enchanted! He spoke to me!" Princess cried in great agitation.

"Who? Where? Who spoke?"

"The toad! The big toad! *Him!*" Princess shouted as a large green toad looking somewhat the worse for wear bounded into view and squatted down about five paces from them.

"He spoke to you?" Kedrigern asked.

"He did. He asked me to help him."

"If that's all, why did you panic?"

"I was surprised. One doesn't expect a toad to strike up a conversation," Princess said with dignity. "*My* situation is rather unusual."

Before Kedrigern could respond, the visiting toad took a cautious hop toward him and in a mellow, resonant voice said, "Kedrigern, great wizard, master of all the gentle arts, aid me, I implore you." The voice was familiar.

"We've met somewhere," Kedrigern said.

"Indeed we have, gentle master. You once took pity on me and freed me from a cruel enchantment. But I, alas, was ungrateful—"

"The handsome prince of Kallopane!" Kedrigern exclaimed.

"A handsome prince? Where?" said Lalloree, suddenly interested in the proceedings.

"Right here," said Kedrigern, pointing.

Lalloree hurried to his side, looked in the indicated direction, and turned on him with a moue of elegant distaste. "That's a *toad*."

"He used to be a handsome prince."

After a reflective pause, Lalloree stooped and asked the toad, "Is that true?"

"Indeed it is, fair damsel. And by the power and compassion of the great wizard Kedrigern, I hope I may be so again," the toad replied in a rich baritone.

Lalloree turned to Kedrigern, her blue eyes bright with excitement, her features animated. Clapping her hands together, she cried, "Oh, Uncle Keddie, do it, please! Change him back! Oh, please, *please* change him back!"

"Not the remotest chance, my child," said the wizard.

"Is this the handsome prince you met on your way to see Fraigus o' the Murk?" Princess asked.

"The very same."

"Please, Uncle Keddie! Oh, *please*!"

"No! The last time I changed him back into a handsome prince, he tried to knock my brains out."

"Oh, kind wizard, merciful mage, be as forgiving as you are wise. I was confused and upset. I had long been a toad. One forgets the finer points of civilized behavior when one is among toads," said the erstwhile handsome prince.

"That's true, Keddie," Princess softly said. "It's terribly difficult to keep up the graces. I've slipped a bit myself."

"*You* didn't hit me on the head with a rock. You didn't steal my horse, and my food, and my water. You didn't insult a wizard," Kedrigern reminded her.

"I may have had a better upbringing."

"No doubt, my dear. Whatever the—"

"Please, Uncle Keddie! Please, please, *please*! I won't sing. I won't even hum. I'll make up a story in my head, like you said, all about a kind, generous, wonderful wizard who finds an enchanted toad and turns him into a handsome prince who—"

"*Back* into a handsome prince," the toad at her feet corrected her.

"Oh, yes, yes, *back* into a handsome prince, and he meets a beautiful princess and is smitten by her grace and her lovely voice and vows to return her to her father's kingdom and beg for her hand in marriage, and he does bold deeds and faces great danger but in the end everything works out and everyone is happy,'' said Lalloree, pausing to gasp for breath.

"Lalloree, my child, let me make a few things clear,'' said the wizard. "Sit. Be comfortable. Listen.'' When Lalloree was seated demurely beneath the tree, the princely toad at her side, Kedrigern said, "First of all, you must learn that a responsible wizard does not simply disenchant people upon request. Some spells have nasty aftereffects, and hasty disenchantments can lead to very unpleasant surprises. The prince is already well aware of that fact.''

"I am indeed, gentle and most wise mage. You warned me fairly, and I am most grateful for it,'' said the newly arrived toad.

"Secondly, you must never think that this sort of thing is easily done. It is not. If I could disenchant an enchanted toad with a few words and a wave of the hand, my wife would now be a beautiful princess,'' Kedrigern went on. "Thirdly, I mean to use no magic at all on this portion of the trip except in emergencies of the most dire nature, because I may need all I've got once we reach the Inn on the Outer Edge and pass beyond. And fourthly, my wife takes precedence over all others. When there's a despelling or a disenchantment done, it will be done first to Princess.''

"But couldn't you please just make him a handsome prince, Uncle Keddie, couldn't you, please? He could protect us against ogres and miscreants, and do great feats of arms and—''

"Lalloree, my sweet child, the last thing I want on this journey is bold deeds and feats of arms. They're noisy, and they take up altogether too much time. And someone always gets hurt.''

Lalloree's pretty face fell. She bowed her head, and her long golden tresses curtained her features. Her shoulders shook. Kedrigern reached over to her, lifted her chin, and looked into big blue eyes that glittered with tears.

"Now, now, Lalloree . . . oh dear, oh dear . . . oh dear me,'' he said at the sight of her tear-stained cheeks.

"Please, Uncle Keddie. Just this one bit of magic,'' she said softly, her sweetly dimpled chin a-tremble.

"It's impossible at the moment, Lalloree. However . . .''

"Yes? What?'' she exclaimed, brightening as quickly as the sky after a summer shower.

"Well, maybe when our quest is over, and Princess is herself again, and you're safe at home, I might possibly be able to do something for this unfortunate prince. Mind you, I promise nothing. It's all very—"

"Oh, you *will* do it, Uncle Keddie, I know you will! Tell me, is he really handsome?"

"As I recall, he's quite well proportioned, clean-featured . . . piercing eyes, square jaw, golden hair . . . all the usual."

"My deepest and most heartfelt thanks to you, kind mage," said the toad.

"I haven't done anything yet."

"You have given me hope, and for that I am eternally and sincerely grateful, goodly wizard. You have also described me very accurately."

"He can ride with me, Uncle Keddie, right on my shoulder, the way Princess rides on yours. I can make him a little cloak out of my green hankie, and make a pad for him out of a leaf, and at night he can sleep on my—"

"At night he will sleep in my saddlebag. I am your chaperone, Lalloree, and your sleeping arrangements are my responsibilty," said Kedrigern firmly.

"It shall be as you say, gentle master," said the toad, adding with a sigh, "I have grown accustomed to sleeping in a saddlebag. One might do worse."

Kedrigern looked at him thoughtfully. "*That's* how you came to be here. When I saw you at the Dismal Bog, you . . . the saddlebag . . ."

"It was the impulse of a moment, my benevolent benefactor. When I spied you at the bog, I wished to beg your forgiveness and implore your aid, but at the crucial moment my courage—and my voice—failed me. In desperation, I leapt into your saddlebag."

"A bold and decisive move. Well done."

"Thank you, good Kedrigern."

"What's your name? If we're going to be traveling together, we ought to know your name."

"I was known everywhere as the handsome prince of Kallopane. No name was ever necessary."

" 'Handsome' will do, I think. Well, Handsome, this is Lalloree, daughter of King Brindom. You've met my wife, Princess."

"Charmed, ladies," said Handsome, bowing as gracefully as his configuration permitted.

"Isn't he *wonderful*, Uncle Keddie?" Lalloree gushed, clapping her hands.

"His manners have certainly improved since our first meeting," Kedrigern conceded, pulling himself to his feet and stretching. To his little company, he said, "And now, I think we'd best be moving on. It's not yet midday, and we have a long way to go."

In the Desolation of the Loser Kings, all ways seemed long and all days dreary. As the travelers headed eastward, and the river vanished from sight, a languishing came over them, and they progressed in moody silence. Late in the afternoon, when a broken wall loomed on the horizon ahead, Kedrigern reined his horse to a halt. Princess left her shelter in his hood to perch on his shoulder, and Lalloree drew up beside them.

"It's so desolate out there. Terribly depressing," Princess said.

"This place has a sad history, my dear." Kedrigern looked out over the bleak flatness, shaking his head ruefully. The few trees in sight were gaunt and leafless, more like twisted gallows than trees. Skeletal ruins stood near the broken wall directly before them. There were no other signs of past, and none at all of present life. "A very sad history," the wizard repeated.

"History is so *boring*," Lalloree declared.

"I know nothing of the subject, but if you say so, I accept it as proven, gracious lady," said Handsome.

"This bit of history is most instructive, particularly to those of royal blood," Kedrigern said sternly. He nudged his horse into motion, and as they rode toward the ruin, he related the story of their surroundings. "The first of the true Loser Kings was Karl the Listless. He reigned for sixteen years and achieved almost nothing. His son, What's-his-name the Apathetic, ruled even longer and accomplished far less. He's the only king I ever heard of whose subjects kept forgetting his name. When they finally realized that he was dead, a collateral line assumed the throne. They were no improvement. Hrunk the Unnecessary was followed by Hrunk the Incapable and his son Hrunk the Bewildered. When that line died out, there was no king for eleven years. Hardly

anyone noticed. At last the crown was forced on a distant
cousin, Edward the Terrified, but by then there was no kingdom left, only the desolation you now see. The peasants who
hadn't slipped away had given up and died of sheer misery.''

"For a man who doesn't care for politics, you know a lot
about it,'' Princess observed.

"Politics had nothing to do with it. You'd hardly think so
now, my dear, but this was once lovely countryside . . .
fertile, picturesque, full of happy peasants, working and
playing. . . .''

"Did they sing?'' Lalloree asked eagerly.

"Not that I'm aware of. They preferred dancing. Hardly a
week passed without some kind of merry festival.'' Kedrigern
sighed deeply and made a vague encompassing gesture. "And
look at it now.''

"What befell them, mighty master of those who know?
Tell us, that we might be forewarned. We will be most
grateful,'' said Handsome.

"It was a war of magics. Karl the Listless took no interest
in affairs of state, but he liked magic. He filled his court with
sorcerers, wizards, magicians, witches, warlocks, all of them
jockeying for his attention and his favor. Now, you take that
kind of rivalry, and add the usual court intrigue, and it's only
a question of time before the nasty spells and wicked enchantments are flying around like hail. By the time the rivals had
exhausted all their magic, there was nothing left to fight over.
The land was blighted. Spells of every kind had been placed
on it, and demons from every corner of the earth had been
summoned to it. Even now, there are deadly pockets of
enchantment here and there. You still hear of careless travelers disappearing, or turning into something unpleasant. It's a
bad business,'' Kedrigern said sighing once again.

They rode on for a time, all of them thoughtful, no one
speaking, their eyes on the long shadows that went before
them. Abruptly, Kedrigern blurted, "Sometimes I think I
should just give it all up—break my staff, drown my books,
clean out my study— and take up something constructive, like
woodworking, or pottery.''

"That's a fine way to talk,'' said Princess impatiently. "If
you abjure magic, what's to become of me? I've been enchanted and disenchanted so many times there's no telling

what I might turn into. And what about poor Handsome? What about yourself?''

"What do you mean?''

"You're over a hundred and sixty, Keddie.''

"My dear, for a wizard that's practically boyhood.''

"What if you stop being a wizard? Won't it all catch up with you?''

After a profound pause, Kedrigern said in a subdued voice. "I hadn't thought of that.''

"Think of it.''

"I'd still like to be in a field that doesn't have such a terrible potential for doing harm to people.''

"If I can think of one, Keddie, I'll let you know," Princess said. "Meanwhile, why don't you just try to be a good wizard?''

Kedrigern spoke no more about abandoning his magic, and the others were silent out of uneasiness at the gathering dark and the cheerless surroundings. They camped for the night in the shelter of the broken wall. Kedrigern laid a small quieting spell on the immediate area, to discourage the curiosity of any insects, field mice, and other small creatures that might be about. He used no further magic. For protection against larger creatures and residual spells, he trusted to Memanesha's promised protection. To conserve magic, he built a fire and erected Lalloree's tent with his own hands. The tent was a shaky and somewhat asymmetrical structure, but it served as adequate shelter from the night chill.

The little band of travelers ate a quiet, thoughtful meal as the moonless night closed over them. When Lalloree had entered her tent and tied the flap shut, Kedrigern placed Handsome in a saddlebag and secured it. Fixing a bedroll for himself near a cozy puddle where Princess could rest in comfort, he banked the fire and turned in.

He was awakened twice during the night by disquieting sounds, but they were far off and did not come closer. Toward dawn the ground trembled, as if under heavy footsteps, but the vibration diminished steadily. Whatever had been passing was moving away. Just as Kedrigern was getting back to sleep, a light drizzle began. He tried to ignore it, but at last gave up in disgust and dragged himself from the bedroll.

It turned out that no one had slept well. There had been

more night noises and peculiar phenomena than Kedrigern had been aware of—slow breathing sounds, menacing laughter, the flapping of wings, words and phrases muttered just below the threshold of intelligibility, wet plops and sharp crunches and other sounds less easily described—and they started on their way sleepy and dull-spirited. Kedrigern's repeated reassurances that they were under Memanesha's protection, and that sounds had never hurt anyone, did nothing to lighten anyone's gloom. They were all wondering how many such nights they would have to pass before arriving at the inn.

In midmorning they halted by a gnarled and stunted oak tree. It stood in incongruous solitude, the only tree to be seen in all directions over the empty plain.

"This place feels funny, Uncle Keddie," said Lalloree uneasily as soon as her feet touched the ground.

"She's right, Keddie," Princess said.

"It's the only shady spot we're likely to find. Let's try to enjoy it," said the wizard as he took down the saddlebags.

"But it's *funny*. The air is all tingly."

"Perhaps it's going to rain, Lallaoree. There was a bit of a sprinkle this morning, you recall."

Lalloree and Princess said nothing more, but did not appear reassured. As Kedrigern busied himself kindling a very small fire from the available bits of wood, Handsome hopped to his side and said in a low, confidential voice, "Am I in error, or is there something odd about this place, great wizard?"

"There's something odd about every bit of the Desolation," Kedrigern replied impatiently. "It's probably just the weather. Maybe a vestige of old magic. Don't worry about it. We have Memanesha's spell to protect us until we reach the inn."

A thread of smoke arose, and Kedrigern prepared to nurse it gently into flame. As he bent forward, a terrified shriek rent the air and he very nearly pitched into the little pyramid of kindling. He scrambled to his feet to see a giant gray-green hand and forearm emerging from the ground before Lalloree. Another hand burst from the earth as he watched, and then a third.

Lalloree stood frozen with fear, screaming uncontrollably as the hands groped in the air around her, coming ever closer. Kedrigern frantically uncorked his water bottle and ran to the

writhing hands, splashing each with water and uttering a
phrase of power as he did so.

Forearms stilled. Fingers twitched, then froze in position.
As the travelers looked on in awe, the arms swelled into
trunks, the fingers stretched into branches, and in the space of
a few moments the single oak had become a grove of four, all
equally stunted and twisted.

"It's all right now, Lalloree. Just a residual spell. You
must have set it off somehow," he said in a soft, consoling
voice.

"It was *awful*!"

"Well, no harm done," he said, patting Lalloree's trembling
hand. "But I wonder why—oh dear!"

The ground had heaved violently under his feet. As he
sprang back, dragging Lalloree with him, a jet of sooty black
smoke shot forth, spreading and billowing, thickening as it
rose, forming into a giant figure in distorted human form. Its
legs were stumpy and bowed, its arms huge, ending in hooked
talons of red horn. Its chest was massive, and on top of the
chest was not a head but a low hump slit by a many-toothed
slobbering mouth. The head was studded with small red eyes
set in no discernible pattern.

Kedrigern worked an emergency protective spell for himself and his companions, then stepped in front of Lalloree,
raised his arms, and made a sign that forced the apparition to
regard him.

"How dare you menace travelers protected by a spell!" he
cried. "Begone, or suffer a wizard's wrath!"

The dark shape hunched forward a little, studying him, and
then turned several of its hot red eyes on Lalloree. Kedrigern
stood his ground confidently, arms folded. The thing placed
its hands flat on the ground, lowered its head, and stared at
him.

Kedrigern picked the largest eye and glared angrily into it.
"I won't tell you again," he said.

"You come not protected. Little spell now. No spell when
I appear," said the crouching thing. Its voice was deep and
slow, its breath sulphurous and hot as a furnace blast.

"That's impossible. Memanesha promised that she'd—"
Kedrigern stopped abruptly at the realization that he and his
companions had been properly had. Memanesha had deceived
them, and they had suspected nothing.

"No spell. No protected," said the sooty, slobbering, red-eyed monstrosity looming hungrily before them.

This was a serious turn of events. Kedrigern's protective spell was a quick light-duty affair meant only to supplement Memanesha's more comprehensive magic. But there was nothing to supplement, and all by itself, Kedrigern's spell could barely hold a small fiend at bay, let alone a towering cacodemon. There was no time to work a proper full-strength protective magic. Flight was impossible. Bribery was absurd. Kedrigern bit his lip and concentrated. He felt a soft hand on his arm and turned to see Lalloree smiling expectantly.

"Are you going to make him disappear now, Uncle Keddie?" she asked. She spoke as calmly as if she were anticipating a clever card trick.

"Not right this minute, my child. Trust me," he said. Returning his attention to the thing, he said, "I suppose you mean to eat us."

The cacodemon responded with a burst of hot, loud, foul-smelling laughter, and leered at them.

"I see," said Kedrigern. "Well, there's one thing I will not permit. You must not eat my medallion. It would only make you sick, anyway."

"Medallion?" the thing roared, laboring over the syllables.

"Yes. It's the source of all my power and wisdom, but it wouldn't do you any good at all. It's no use even thinking about it." Reaching into his tunic, Kedrigern drew forth the medallion of his guild, displaying it with an elaborate gesture. Stooping, he scratched a shallow hole in the earth at his feet and laid the medallion in it, loosely covering it again. He straightened, brushing his hands, and said, "There. You must not touch it, you understand. Above all, never think of swallowing it."

The thing looked at him with most of its eyes. "No swallow medallion. Swallow you," it said.

"Just a minute, now. Don't you *want* to swallow my medallion?"

"You say, make sick."

"Must you believe everything I say?"

"Wizard always full of tricks," the cacodemon rumbled suspiciously.

"Is everything all right, Uncle Keddie? It's still here," Lalloree whispered.

"Of course everything is all right. The thing is stupid, that's all. Don't worry," Kedrigern said, doing his best to sound supremely confident while inwardly calculating how long his spell would hold. Then inspiration burst upon him. "Sing, Lalloree! Sing the song about the ninety-nine knights! Go ahead, good and loud!"

Lalloree sang. Her voice was sweet and clear, and very enthusiastic:

> "Ninety-nine knights went a-riding;
>   They spied a lady fair,
>   With dainty foot and cherry lip
>   And lovely golden hair.
>   The very first brave knight did speak . . ."

The apparition turned all its glowing red eyes on her and stood as if hypnotized. Once Kedrigern was certain of its preoccupation, he dug into various pouches and pockets and set about a complicated but sure-fire antidemon spell, while Lalloree sang blithely on.

He was a fast worker. Before Lalloree had come to the forty-first brave knight's endearments, the spell was ready. Wiping his hands on his cloak, the wizard gestured for her to cease. As soon as she stopped singing, the thing turned on him, rumbling in a nasty way.

Kedrigern tried to be fair, even to demons. He raised a hand for attention. "I must warn you, thing, that we are now protected by a spell that will make it very unpleasant for anyone who tries to devour us. You had your chance, but you missed it. I suggest you go back underground for another millenium or two, and learn to concentrate. There's nothing for you here," he said.

The cacodemon reared up and flailed its long, taloned arms in a terrifying display of rage. Kedrigern, who knew the ways of these creatures, did not budge. His expression grew severe.

"Devour! Devour everybody!" the thing roared.

"Don't be so obtuse. We didn't come here to be devoured."

The thing settled on its haunches, sniffed the air, and said, "Big spell now. Protected plenty."

"That's exactly what I just told you."

"No devour today," it said sadly.

"I should hope not. Well, go on. Be off with you!" said the wizard with a wave of his hand.

The thing swelled into a formless sooty cloud speckled with darting red lights, like popping sparks on a hearthstone. With a roar that diminished to a whoosh and then to a whistle it flowed rapidly back into the earth, dwindling and fading and finally vanishing.

"That was wonderful, Uncle Keddie!" Lalloree cried, clapping her hands delightedly.

"It certainly was," said the wizard, patting at his forehead with his cloak. "I only hope that thing doesn't have friends and relatives all along the way to the inn. I'll be out of magic before we're halfway there."

"Is it really gone?" said a tiny voice from a puddle a few paces away.

"Of course it is, my dear. Are you all right?"

"Yes. I jumped in here when that thing appeared. So did Handsome, I think," said Princess. "Oh, Keddie, if anything had happened to you . . ."

Another small voice from the puddle added, "Dear master, do be careful—for all our sakes."

"I'm afraid I have some bad news," Kedrigern said to his companions. "We've been tricked. Memanesha didn't put a protective spell on us. She did nothing at all—which means that we have a long and dangerous journey ahead."

"You'll protect us with your magic, won't you, Uncle Keddie?"

Kedrigern seated himself with his back to a tree and stretched out his arms wearily. "My dear child, if every day requires as much magic as I've just used, I'll be completely out of power by the time we reach the inn," he said. "And that's if we're very lucky. I might run out a lot sooner."

"But you're a wizard! You're a *great* wizard!"

"That's true, but even the greatest wizard doesn't draw his magic from a bottomless well. It's more like drawing from a cistern. One must allow time for refilling."

Princess and Handsome hopped from the puddle. They and Lalloree exchanged looks of serious concern. All three drew closer to the wizard.

"We could gallop all the way to the inn. That would save time," Princess suggested.

"An excellent suggestion, my dear. Just give me a few minutes to rest up, and I'll—"

"Uncle Keddie, the horses—they're gone!"

Kedrigern looked to where the horses had been tethered and let out a groan. They had broken free and run off, taking most of the supplies with them. All that remained was the scrip of food that hung at the wizard's belt, and a pair of water bottles.

"Are you going to bring them back by magic means?" Lalloree asked.

"Not if I can help it. I hate working magic on horses. They're too high-strung," the wizard replied, climbing to his feet.

He reached into his tunic and drew out the medallion of the guild. Raising it to his eye, he peered through the Aperture of True Vision, slowly turning to scan the surrounding wasteland in all directions. Scowling, he replaced the medallion inside his tunic and rubbed his eye with the heel of his hand.

"Not a trace of them," he muttered. "They've probably been devoured by something."

"Oh, Uncle Keddie, this is turning out to be a real *adventure*!" said Lalloree, clapping her hands and smiling brightly.

"There's no need to be ebullient," Kedrigern said sourly.

"I'll dress up like a boy! Don't you think that's a good idea? I'll smudge my face, and tuck my golden tresses under a rude cap, and no one will suspect—"

"You will do no such thing," Kedrigern broke in impatiently. "That sort of trick only works on the stage, and only if one starts with a girl who looks like a boy. You do not. You would fool no one, Lalloree."

"But how will I guard my virtue?"

"At present it's not in danger. The things you're liable to meet out here are interested in you as an article of diet, not as an object of illicit dalliance. Still, you raise a good point. Once we reach the inn, there's no telling . . ."

He fell silent, rubbing his chin slowly and thoughtfully, and after a time he broke into a melancholy smile and shook his head. The others watched, and finally Princess asked, "What are you thinking about?"

"Imberwick, my dear. A wizard I used to know," he replied absently.

"I've never heard you mention him."

"There's not much to say about Imberwick. He specialized narrowly, and became absolutely expert at one thing: he could turn a beautiful young maiden into a fat ugly old man."

"Not much call for that sort of thing, is there?"

"As a rule, there isn't, but during the War of the Six Princes, Imberwick had more work than he could handle. It was a time when beautiful young maidens were not safe and ugly fat old men were. Of course, once the war was over . . . The spell was irreversible, you see, and I don't think Imberwick always took the time to explain that to anxious parents."

Kedrigern sank into a reverie, from which Lalloree roused him with a timid question. "Uncle Keddie . . . you're not going to turn me into a fat ugly old man, are you?"

"Of course not, child. I'll think of something else once we get to the inn. Our main problem right now—"

"Is *that*!" Princess shrieked, and made a great leap for her puddle. Handsome followed instantly.

"What? Where? Not another demon!"

"There, Uncle Keddie!" Lalloree said, pointing up into the clouded sky.

Kedrigern beheld a distant speck that circled and cavorted in a manner that could only be playful. He foresaw no threat. But in the very instant of his scrutiny, all frolicking ceased. Swift and straight as the flight of an arrow, the flying object came directly at the wizard and his companions.

···⚶ *Seven* ⚶···

the inn on the outer edge

"RUN, KEDDIE! HIDE!" Princess cried, her tiny voice strained with fear.

When the wizard did not move, she bounded back to his side, hopping up and down in extreme agitation, and at last described a headlong arc into his hood.

While Princess thrashed anxiously about, Kedrigern groped for his medallion. He drew it out and sighted through the Aperture of True Vision. The activity in his hood made it difficult to hold the medallion steady, but once he had a clear view the wizard let out a burst of happy laughter and began to wave his arms.

"Keddie, what are you doing? Stand still or they'll see us!" cried Princess.

"It's all right, my dear. I know one of them."

"*One* of them? How many are there? And what are they?"

"Dragons. Only two."

"*Dragons*! Oh, what an *adventure*!" Lalloree squealed. "If only there were a handsome prince to slay them!"

"Fortunately, the only handsome prince currently available is hiding in yonder puddle. One of these dragons happens to be an old acquaintance of mine. I removed an arrow from his claw."

"There are two of them," Princess pointed out.

"And one is female. I think old Fingard has settled down,"

said Kedrigern, waving furiously, chuckling expectantly as the two dragons sped toward them.

"Keddie, dragons eat princesses!"

"Uncle Keddie, don't let them eat us!" Lalloree cried as the negative possibilities of this glorious adventure dawned upon her.

"Ladies, your fears are groundless. Dragons have no special fondness for princesses."

"But I *read* it, Uncle Keddie! Whenever people wanted to attract a dragon, they'd chain a maiden to a rock, and a dragon would come for her!"

"Lalloree, my child, they used to chain the maiden to a rock to attract a crowd. It was the crowd that caught the dragon's attention. Please stop your worrying."

"Keddie, I'm terrified! I've never seen a dragon."

"Just stay in my hood and keep very still. You'll be as safe as a spell."

"What about me, Uncle Keddie?" Lalloree asked, her manner much subdued. "Is there anything I should do? Should I sing?"

"By no means. Stay next to me. Be demure."

"What about Handsome?" she whispered, though the dragons were still well beyond earshot.

"He's safe in his puddle."

There was no more movement in Kedrigern's hood. He stood patiently, waving to the approaching pair with one arm. Lalloree clung desperately to the other, pale, her blue eyes wide with fear and awe. The approach of dragons was an impressive sight.

Fingard and his mate circled once, lazily, then came to earth, touching down simultaneously with a picturesque upward sweep of wing that smoothed into a graceful folding motion. So light and expert was their landing that scarcely a puff of dust was raised.

"Well met, Fingard," Kedrigern greeted the larger dragon. "You're looking quite splendid. How's the foreclaw?"

The dragon boomed:

> "Wizard worked wonders,
>   Healed hurt done by hunters,
>   So foreclaw feels fine again,
>   Better than before."

"I'm glad to hear it, Fingard. Will you introduce me to your charming companion?"

Fingard puffed himself up, gave a flirt of his wings that sent dust swirling about the little group, and said proudly:

> "Wizard, meet wife,
> Lovely, lissom Ti Lung,
> Dearest and daintiest of dragons.
> Wife, meet wizard,
> Worker of wonders,
> Kedrigern the clever, the kindly,
> Magnanimous man mighty in magic."

Bowing deeply, Kedrigern said, "I am honored to meet the beautiful Ti Lung."

Ti Lung was slender and sinuous, a lithe figure clad in iridescent scales of the palest gold that glittered as she moved. Her willowy grace was a charming contrast to her husband's imposing bulk, her brightness all the brighter beside Fingard's tarnished-brass hue. She ducked her head, and looked up at Kedrigern shyly out of eyes like emerald lozenges.

"The master of all wizards is too generous to this unworthy person," she said in a voice like crystal bells in the gentlest breeze of the spring. "Truly all honor is mine, to be noticed by him whose name is heard with dread and veneration wherever the sun shines and the rain falls."

A tiny snort of impatience came from Kedrigern's hood. He cleared his throat loudly to cover the sound and said, "Ti Lung is as gracious as she is lovely. May I present Princess Lalloree? I'm escorting her back to her father's kingdom, far to the south."

Lalloree curtseyed rather stiffly and in a hushed unsteady voice said, "I'm very pleased to meet you."

The two dragons bowed their heads politely, and Kedrigern went on: "I must congratulate you on your good fortune, Fingard, and wish you ten thousand years of happiness together. You make a most attractive couple."

> "Wife works with water:
> Running rills, rapid rivers,
> Lochs, lagoons, and limpid lakes;
> Can force forth fierce floods

Or dry up with dreadful drought.
Fingard favors fire,
Breathes burning brimstone,
Spews sulphurous smoke.
Together, make terrific twosome."

"I'm sure you do. No fire and flood near settled areas,
though, I hope. You did promise me, Fingard."

"Fingard faithful to friend;
Gratefully gave
His word to wizard,
Bond of behavior."

"Very good, Fingard. That shows admirable self-control.
I'm very proud of you."

The dragons exchanged a meaningful look. Fingard gave a
steamy sigh and added in an undertone:

"Sometimes slip slightly,
But wife is watchful—
Floods flames forthwith,
Quickly quenching."

"They do say that opposites attract," Lalloree said, smiling nervously.

"All the more reason to rejoice in your marriage, Fingard.
And my profound thanks to the vigilant Ti Lung, on behalf of
flammable creatures everywhere," said Kedrigern, bowing
once again to the golden dragon. With these courtesies at-
tended to, he asked Fingard, "What brings you to the Desolation of the Loser Kings? Honeymooning? Visiting the family?"

"Taking Ti Lung
On sightseeing sojourn—
Magnificent mountains,
Colossal cataracts,
Rushing river,
South's splendid spectacles."

"South? You're going south? Past the Inn on the Outer
Edge?" Kedrigern asked excitedly.

Ti Lung softly replied, "Honored master, this unworthy one has long yearned to acquaint herself with the fabled magnificance of your land, and is already awed to numbness by the beauty of this desolation in which we stand. Noble husband has promised even greater spectacles one day's flight to the south, and this lowly person palpitates with anticipation of wonders that await her undeserving eyes."

"You won't be disappointed, Ti Lung, I assure you. There's some mighty impressive scenery to the south. You'll love the Dragonback Mountains, I'm sure. I wonder if . . . oh, no, I mustn't impose on you," said Kedrigern, raising his hands in a gesture of renunciation.

> "Whatever wizard wishes
> It pleases this pair to perform—
> Ask favor freely, friend of Fingard."

"Well, you see, we're heading south ourselves, to the Inn on the Outer Edge, and we've run into some difficulty," Kedrigern began. He proceeded to summarize their adventures, assisted by vigorous nodding and eager exclamations of an affirmative nature by Lalloree, and concluded, "In short, Fingard, we could use a lift, and since you're passing the inn, if you wouldn't mind . . . I realize it's an imposition, and if we weren't in such straits I wouldn't dream of asking . . ."

The dragon replied grandly:

> "Passengers no problem.
> Fingard feels flattered,
> Happy he can help."

"Passengers," Lalloree repeated weakly, turning to the wizard with stark terror in her eyes. Kedrigern felt a sudden stirring in his hood. He knew that he must act with dispatch, before the first shock wore off and Princess and Lalloree flatly refused to budge from this spot.

"We'll just get our things together and be ready to leave in a moment," he said. Tugging Lalloree aside, he instructed her in an undertone, "Get Handsome out of the puddle and stick him in your hood. Tell him not to stay a word, and don't you let slip that he's a handsome prince. Dragons don't like handsome princes. Go on, look to it." Reaching back to give his hood a comforting pat, he said softly, "Relax, my dear. We'll be at the inn before dinner time."

"Keddie, I'll die of fright," came a tiny whisper.

"There's nothing to fear. Just stay in my hood and keep your eyes closed."

"Princesses don't fly!"

"Dragons do, and very well."

"What if we fall off?"

"We won't."

"What if we *do*?"

"Fingard will catch us before we hit the ground. I've seen him fly, my dear. He's one of the best."

Princess said no more, but Kedrigern could feel her trembling inside his hood. Lalloree returned from the puddle, drying her hands on her cloak, and with a quick nod assured the wizard that all was well with Handsome. There was nothing more to pack, and no reason to delay. Kedrigern handed a water bottle to Lalloree, took the other one for himself, and announced their readiness to depart.

Ti Lung made a comfortable cradle of her foreclaws, and Lalloree nestled snugly inside, looking slightly less fearful than she had been. Kedrigern was reminded of a child in a swing. He opted for a better view, and seated himself on Fingard's back, near the dragon's head, in the depression between the two great humps of shoulder muscle.

With a sound like the snap of a pennant in a sharp gust, Fingard unfolded his wings. One mighty, whooshing beat, and then another, and up they rose from a ring of dust into the gray sky, Kedrigern holding his breath and clinging tightly to one of the hornlike protuberances that jutted from Fingard's skull.

The dead land fell away beneath them. The horizons opened. Off to the right, Kedrigern saw the River of Misery, widening as it flowed south; beyond it was the deep massed green of Dark Wood, and beyond that the cold gray of the Barren Mountains. Far ahead, on this side of the river, loomed the lower, longer range known as the Dragonback Mountains. Lalloree's home lay on the other side of those jagged peaks, and one day soon he would take her there. But Princess came first, and Lalloree would just have to wait until he had found Arlebar.

The panorama was so vast, the ride itself so exhilarating,

that Kedrigern forgot all else in the sheer delight of the journey. He had done some flying in his younger days, but it had all been very businesslike and methodical: short-range, low-level, point-to-point heats as a merlin or kestrel, strictly to demonstrate his shape-changing skills. Now he was free to enjoy the experience of being airborne for its own sake, and he loved it. Once this quest was over, he promised himself, he and Princess would take a long trip. Ordinarily, he loathed travel, but it was quite different by air. They would go as something big and sturdy. Albatrosses, say. It would not require an excessive amount of magic, and it was really a marvelous way to see the countryside.

The thought of Princess's metamorphosis jolted Kedrigern out of his innocent woolgathering. He was getting ahead of himself. There were problems to be solved before any trips could be taken, and the problems were of a nature that might preclude any future shape-changing on the part of his wife. Having been turned from a beautiful princess into a toad, then back into a beautiful princess, and now back to a toad, she might understandably be reluctant to attempt any further transformations. And he himself, for all his skill and knowledge, could take warning from her variegated history. Perhaps it was best to let well enough alone. If men were meant to fly, they would have been given dragons.

There had been no sound or motion from his hood for some time. Turning his head, he said, "Are you all right back there, my dear?"

"Are we landing?" said a wee, frightened voice.

"Not quite yet. Soon."

"Ask me when we've landed."

Kedrigern perceived that his enthusiasm for flying was not shared. Of course, traveling in a hood is not the height of comfort, and deprives one of the chief joy of flight, namely the grand vista of the world at one's feet. Realizing this, he asked, "My dear, have you looked out?"

"No!"

"You'd feel different if you did, I'm sure."

"I'd feel nauseous."

"It's really quite striking. Marvelous view."

"I don't want to look down and see a lot of emptiness. I want to be on solid ground. Preferably damp ground. Can't you make Fingard hurry?"

"He's flying as fast as he can. It won't be much longer."

And indeed it was not, for even as Kedrigern spoke, he saw the smoke rising from the chimneys of the Inn on the Outer Edge. Fingard and Ti Lung made a smooth descent to a level stretch of ground across the road from the main entrance. With a thoughtfulness seldom encountered in dragons, and which Kedrigern credited to the gentling influence of Ti Lung, they circled so as to avoid an overflight of the stables, thus sparing the domestic livestock some anxious moments.

"Thank you, Fingard. It was a delightful trip," Kedrigern said as soon as his feet touched the ground.

> "Fingard good friend—
> Happy to help
> Wizard in want,
> Serve stranded sorcerer,
> Please pretty princess."

Lalloree sprang lightly to the ground, and at once turned to plant a kiss on her mount's cool golden cheek, saying, "Thank you, Ti Lung. That was *wonderful*!" She turned to Fingard, as if to bestow on him a similar token of appreciation, but hesitated at the sight of his spiny, prickly, bristling hide and finally settled for a friendly pat on the smooth leading edge of his wing.

Uneasy at the display of gratitude, the dragon said awkwardly:

> "Time to travel on,
> Swiftly speed southward
> Seeking scenic splendors."

"This unworthy one is overwhelmed by joy to have been of use to such paragons of wisdom and beauty," Ti Lung added. "And now is time to remove our humble selves and seek the wonders of your magnificent land."

Without further ado they lifted off, described a great lazy half-circle, and with a farewell dipping of wings, headed for the mountains to the south. Kedrigern and Lalloree returned the salute and stood watching until the dragons had vanished, then the wizard turned and took a good look at the Inn on the Outer Edge.

It was a sizeable establishment, with a large main building

and several outbuildings, all in decent repair. For all the tales that were told of it, the inn looked surprisingly ordinary and very quiet. While the ordinariness was reassuring to Kedrigern, the quiet was not. He reasoned that anyplace where a pair of dragons could land, discharge passengers, and take off again without so much as one curious glance from a slavey or stable boy was bound to be accustomed to the unusual. It behooved him to be prudent, he thought, until he knew the situation better.

Lalloree jarred his reflections with a question. "Uncle Keddie, why do they talk that way?"

"What way? Who, the dragons?"

"Yes. They talk funny, don't they?"

"Not for dragons. Ti Lung is a bit more courteous in her speech than most people you meet, I suppose, but I wouldn't say she talks funny."

"Fingard does."

"That's just his alliteration. He's from the north."

"Does everyone talk that way in the north?"

"Only dragons and poets."

"Are we down? Is it safe to come out?" asked a small voice from Kedrigern's hood.

"Yes, my dear, we're safe and sound. There's the inn," he replied. "Did you doze off?"

"I fainted," Princess said indignantly.

"I regret any discomfort you've suffered, my dear. At least it's all over, and we're safely here. I'll see about getting us a meal and someplace to sleep. We'll need horses, too. And supplies."

"I'd like some damp moss," Princess said.

In a muffled voice from the recesses of Lalloree's hood, Handsome added, "So would I."

"I'll do my best to make comfortable arrangements for all of us," Kedrigern said. "I think our best course is to tell the truth, but not too much of it."

"I prefer that you say nothing about me. I don't want to meet new people looking like this," Princess said.

"I feel the same way," said Handsome.

"All right. Just stay in the hoods and don't speak, that's all. I'm going to tell the innkeeper who I am, and say that I've been asked to escort a young lady back to her family after a tragic betrothal. You'll have to look tragic, Lalloree."

"I'll try, Uncle Keddie," she said brightly.

"Start now. I'll say that I want to meet with my renowned colleague Arlebar while I'm in the neighborhood. Someone here is sure to know the way to his home. Remember, now: silence and a tragic demeanor, and all will be well."

The innkeeper was not obliging. Harry was his name, and he was a bald, bearded, serious-mannered fellow with a nose like a soft roseate gourd. He listened with respectful attention to the wizard's account of his travels, adding a nod or a sympathetic grunt at the proper intervals. When Kedrigern was finished, Harry thoughtfully rubbed the bulbous tip of his nose between thumb and forefinger for a time before observing, "Busy journey you've had, Master Kedrigern."

"It was rather taxing," the wizard allowed.

"Oh, aye, taxing. You'll be wanting clean comfortable beds and some good food after such a journey."

"We've been thinking of nothing else."

"Oh, aye. I wish I could help you."

"Surely, Harry, in an establishment this size . . ."

"Ah, well, you see, Master Kedrigern, it's the height of the questing season. We've got little bands and troops and fellowships from all over creation, not to mention those as comes from the Other Places. And there's the rooms that up and disappear on us every now and then. It's no easy thing running a place like this, I tell you."

"I don't require a suite, Harry. As long as the young lady has safe and comfortable lodging, I can put up with the most austere accommodations."

"Well, I'll see what I can do, Master Kedrigern. If it was anyone but a great wizard like yourself, I'd tell him it's a pile of clean straw in the stable or nothing," the innkeeper said. "But I don't think it's good business to treat wizards like that."

"You're right, Harry. It isn't," Kedrigern said, smiling pleasantly.

"While I look around, you and the young lady might want to go and have a good tuck in. Rabbit stew today, hot and spicy. All natural ingredients, too, no magic added. Plenty of fresh bread. Best ale east of the river."

"An excellent suggestion, Harry. We will dine, and await your news."

Kedrigern and Lalloree entered the spacious dining room of
the inn by a small side door, their arrival noticed by only a
few of those within. The wizard guided Lalloree to a table in
a shadowy corner, and seated her where she was shielded
from the general view. He placed his own chair so as to be
able to inspect the room unobtrusively.

The occupants of the dining room were odd and varied.
Most of them were ordinary human beings—archers, woods-
men, thieves, swordsmen, and a few cloaked figures whom
Kedrigern recognized as fellow practitioners, though none of
any standing. Here and there, surrounded by a faint glow or a
vague shimmering in the air, were others not so ordinary.

Kedrigern's examination of his fellow diners was interrupted by a tiny whisper from his hood. "You didn't ask
about Arlebar," Princess said.

"All in good time, my dear," he responded softly.

"Well, he's our only reason for coming here, isn't he? I
mean, why come all this way and not even mention his
name?"

"In dealing with wizards, it's usually best to—Lalloree,
don't stare!" Kedrigern said sharply.

Lalloree's head snapped around to face him, her eyes still
wide in stunned amazement. "Uncle Keddie . . . those . . .
those *creatures*," she said dazedly.

At a table along the side of the room near the hearth, a man
enveloped in blue flame was conversing earnestly with a
yellowed skeleton clad in rotting silks. A muscular giant with
rough brown skin and glossy green hair and beard sat between
them, listening intently. On his shoulder was perched a trans-
lucent lady about a hand's-breadth tall, with iridescent wings.
Little dots of light swarmed and swirled in the air above her
head.

"Oh, they're just some questing fellowship. As Harry
said, it's the peak of the questing season right now."

"But they're *strange*."

"You may see stranger things before we leave. This place
borders on the impossible, and there's a lot of crossing back
and forth."

"Uncle Keddie, I'm *scared*."

"Fear not, fair maid," came a bold little voice from her
hood. "Though I am but a toad, my strength and devotion are
at your service."

"Not so loud, Handsome," Kedrigern admonished him.

"I merely wished the lady to know that she is not without a willing champion."

"Chivalrous of you, Handsome, but it's not necessary. There's no danger as long as Lalloree doesn't stare, doesn't point, doesn't cry out in astonishment, and doesn't talk to anyone."

"What'll I *do*, Uncle Keddie?" she moaned. "It'll be so *boring*!"

"Once you get a room, stay in it. Keep the door locked. If you get too bored, sing to yourself."

The barmaid placed a steaming bowl of thick rabbit stew before them, and left a loaf of bread and a jug of ale. They fell to at once. The stew was delicious, the bread crisp and no more than a day old, the ale excellent, and their appetites ravenous. To dine well at an inn was a rare feat in Kedrigern's experience; to dine in any public place was entirely new to Lalloree; consequently, they ate in appreciative silence, their attention focused on the bowl before them.

As Kedrigern mopped up the last of his stew, Princess asked *sotto voce*, "What about us? What are Handsome and I supposed to eat?"

"I'll save some bread and make little pellets."

"That's hardly a feast."

"I can't order a dish of flies. If you're patient, I'm certain that once we have a room, you'll have all the flies you could ask for."

"Harry said there were no rooms."

"Never fear. He'll find something for us," Kedrigern whispered over his shoulder. Glancing out over the dimly lit room, he saw a familiar figure approaching their table and said, "Here he comes now. Not another word until we're settled."

Harry stood before the table for a moment, massaging his nose. Kedrigern invited him to join them, but the host declined the offer, saying, "Ah, thank you, Master Kedrigern, but I have too much work waiting. I'm having trouble finding a room for you."

"That's not good, Harry."

"But I think I may have found something suitable for the young lady," the innkeeper quickly added.

"Much better."

"It's a wagon what I've had on hand since last fall. Perfect accommodations for a lady, it is, too. It belonged to that nice little princess what got herself carried off by the afreet. You must know all about it, being a wizard and all."

"I haven't heard a word, Harry. News travels slowly in Dark Wood. An afreet, you say? They don't generally operate in these parts, do they?"

Harry pulled up a chair, seated himself, and leaning forward over the table said in a low confidential voice, "It's the first afreet anyone in this place ever saw, Master Kedrigern. Must have been brought in here during the Wizards' Wars and never used, and then just forgotten. The poor little princess was sitting over there, by the window, when she must have set off the spell. All of a sudden, there was this big afreet leering at her—fair filled the room, he did—and then they both vanished."

"Amazing. Has anyone tried to bring her back?"

"There was one young lad tried his hand at it, but he didn't have much luck. As a matter of fact, we lost him, too."

"Oh dear."

"After that, I discouraged further attempts. Especially by the wild young lot you've got working magic these days. Anyway, Master Kedrigern, the nice little wagon she was traveling in, *that* didn't vanish. Her servants all ran off in a panic and took the horses, but I've got the wagon out back in a shed. I keeps it nice and clean, just in case she gets back somehow, but I don't much expect to see her again."

"It's unlikely you will. Afreets are a possessive lot."

"Well, then, maybe the young lady would consider staying in it. It's very comfortable, and snug as a mitten."

Kedrigern turned to Lalloree. "Shall we inspect this wagon, my lady?"

"If you wish, Uncle Keddie," she said demurely.

"Another good feature about this wagon," Harry informed them as they made their way from the room, "It's got a nice wide driver's seat, all cushioned, with a canopy overhead. Even has a curtain, against the rain. If you don't mind sleeping outside, you could keep right close to the young lady and make sure she's absolutely safe during the night."

"We'll see, Harry," said the wizard cautiously.

The host paused at the bar to light a lantern. Taking the lead, he started across the spacious innyard. As they passed thc stables, Kedrigern noticed a particularly fine warhorse. He asked Harry to stop so he might have a closer look.

"A splendid animal, Master Kedrigern," the innkeeper said warmly, raising the lantern higher. "Belongs to Conrad Coeur du Fer de la Tour Brisée, he does. This whole string of horses is all his."

"Do you think Sir Conrad might be willing to sell us a pair?"

"Oh, no, Master Kedrigern. He's on a great guest, Sir Conrad is. He came here some days ago, him and his squire and cook, and a minstrel, and a brute of a swordsman. He still needs three more people to fill out his band, and he's been holding interviews every day. Once he gets them all together, he'll need every one of these horses."

"Too bad. We need horses ourselves."

"If you was to go on quest with Sir Conrad, he'd give you the horses."

"I'm already committed to a quest, Harry, and it's very important to me. Perhaps there are other horses about."

"Oh, aye, plenty of horses. But none for sale."

"In that case, we may be with you for a while. Let's see that wagon."

The wagon of the unfortunate princess turned out to be a charming conveyance, expertly designed to be twice as roomy inside as it appeared to be from outside. It had been kept spotlessly tidy. The cushions were plump, the linen was clean, and there were fresh flowers in a crystal vase on the neat little dressing table. Lalloree was delighted, and declared for it at once. Leaving her to poke about inside, Kedrigern and Harry withdrew to examine the driver's seat. It was indeed spacious, comfortable, and sheltered from the weather.

"It has its points, Harry," the wizard said. "Still, I was hoping for a room."

"It's not as if I was charging for it, Master Kedrigern. There'd be no charge, not to a wizard like yourself."

"Ah. But what if the princess returns? Worse yet, what if the afreet comes back for the wagon? It's risky."

"Oh, but you could put a spell on it to protect the pair of you. That'd be nothing to you, Master Kedrigern."

"I suppose I could do something like that."

"You'd be doing my establishment a great honor, Master Kedrigern. I'll throw in meals, if you take the wagon."

"Ale, too?"

"All you want."

"Done," said the wizard, extending his hand.

Even as the two men clasped to seal the agreement, cries of delighted surprise were coming from within as Lalloree acquainted herself with the contents of drawers, chests, and cupboards. When Harry had left, Kedrigern climbed inside. He found Lalloree flushed with excitement, gorgeous robes piled about, and Handsome seated in a shallow bowl on the tiny wash stand, looking on foldly.

"Oh, Uncle Keddie, look at all these wonderful gowns! And there's a whole drawer of lovely slippers, and a cupboard full of cloaks! What a grand place you found! It's a thousand times nicer than that dreary old Mon Chagrin! Thank you, Uncle Keddie," Lalloree babbled as she dashed about, picking up a gown, tossing the first aside for a second, holding up first one, then another, matching slippers to gowns to robes to cloaks and generally behaving like a child on a particularly successful birthday. Princess hopped to Kedrigern's shoulder, watched for a time, and gave a small, sad sigh.

"Alas! Will I ever be a beautiful princess again?" she said.

"Before you know it, my dear. I'll start asking about Arlebar in the morning. Why don't you have a good splash, and then we'll all turn in."

"Not that I doubt your power, oh mighty mage," said Handsome, "but what if the afreet really does decide to come back for the wagon?"

"If the afreet, or anything else, comes near this wagon, he, she, it, or they will regret it. Trust me, Handsome, and get a good night's sleep. You and I will sleep on the driver's bench, and let the ladies enjoy the privacy of the wagon. Hop to it, my boy."

····⊰ *Eight* ⊱····

swordsman, giant, squire, knight, minstrel, wastrel, sorcerer, sprite

LALLOREE WAS CONTENT to spend the next day reveling in the contents of the wagon, every item of which seemed to fit as if made to her measure. Kedrigern brought her a generous breakfast, picked two large clumps of sopping wet moss for Princess and Handsome, and left the trio in the wagon under the protection of a spell. He had work to do.

The inn was surprisingly busy. It seemed even more crowded than it had the day before, though Kedrigern had heard no new arrivals in the night. As he looked around, he saw that the newcomers were not of the kind whose arrival was heralded by hoofbeats or creaking wheels. They were all from Other Places.

The ghosts were the least troublesome of the lot. They did cause something of a chill when they passed, or when he passed through them, but they took up no room at all, being quite insubstantial. The pixies, elves, and leprechauns were decent little folk, but their diminutive size made it necessary for him to watch his step, and the fairies darting about in the air had him blinking and ducking his head until he realized that they were being playful, and that there was no danger of a collision. He ceased flinching at their near misses, and they soon left him alone.

The green-haired giant and his gossamer companion were seated by themselves in a corner. The skeleton and the burning man were nowhere in sight. The other tables were occupied by ordinary humans. Kedrigern made his way through the crowded room to the bar, where Harry was filling a large piggin with ale. When it was filled to brimming, he placed it on the window ledge beside two others, and started filling a fourth. A huge hand appeared at the window and took two of the piggins.

"Good morning, Master Kedrigern," said the innkeeper without pausing in his labors. "I trust you slept well."

"A most relaxing night, Harry. I see you're busy this morning."

"Oh, I am indeed. Those giants do have a thirst," Harry said, placing the fourth piggin on the window ledge just in time for a pair of enormous hands to snatch up both. "Drowning their sorrows, so to speak."

"One seldom thinks of giants as being sentimental," Kedrigern observed.

"This lot have had a hard blow," said Harry, taking up another piggin. "Lost someone very close to them, they have."

"Sorry to hear it."

"Oh, base ingratitude!" a deep voice outside the window rumbled, and a different but equally reverberant basso profundo added, "Thoughtless, thankless, heartless minx!"

"It's that Snow White," the innkeeper said indignantly. "She up and walked out on them, after all they've done for her. Took her in when she was running for her life, they did, and hid her from that wicked stepmother of hers, and all they asked in return was a little help in keeping the place tidy. A bit of cleaning and dusting and washing, some cooking and mending, a spot of gardening—little enough to ask of a healthy girl. But she claimed that keeping house for seven giants was taking up all her time and wearing her to a frazzle. Said she hadn't a free moment to keep a lookout for a handsome prince, and if one should happen to come by he wouldn't look at her twice, she being so worn out and bedraggled with all the work."

Kedrigern shook his head and made a little clucking sound of disapproval. "That's your biggest problem with princesses. They all expect a handsome prince to come along and marry them, and live happily ever after."

"Aye, that's true enough, Master Kedrigern."

"There are some pretty sorry specimens of handsome prince

out there, too. I heard of one king's son who kissed a beautiful princess and sent her and her entire household into a deep sleep. Someone finally had to send for an old witch to come and prick everyone's finger with a spindle in order to get them moving again. By then, the king's son was a laughingstock in all the neighboring kingdoms. Poor fellow wandered off and became a hermit. Handsome princes are not what they used to be, Harry.''

"Indeed they are not. Nor are the princesses, either. This Snow White, now—what did she do but go off and find herself a position with seven dwarfs.''

Kedrigern raised an eyebrow and nodded thoughtfully. "I imagine that cuts her workload considerably.''

"Well, there's no denying that it's easier to keep house for seven dwarfs than for seven giants, Master Kedrigern, but all the same, it's a shocking display of ingratitude,'' Harry said, placing another piggin on the window ledge. "But that's how it is these days. People are all out for themselves.''

"I'm afraid so, Harry.''

"And cruel, too. You wouldn't believe the cruelty that's about. It's a terrible world.''

"It is indeed. All the more reason for us to perform whatever little kindnesses come to hand. Which reminds me, Harry, do you know the way to Arlebar's house?''

"Arlebar?'' the innkeeper repeated with an expression of bewilderment.

"Arlebar the venerable wizard. He lives somewhere to the south, and since I'm headed that way, I'd like to pay a call and wish him well.''

"That's decent of you, Master Kedrigern. Let me think, now. Arlebar . . . is it Arlebar what does the transmutation of base metals?''

"I'm almost certain he doesn't. That sort of thing is strictly for the alchemists. Arlebar is a respected elder wizard. Very elder.''

"Does he conjure up demons?''

"Not to my knowledge. Last I heard, he was retired, giving lessons now and then. Transformation spells, mostly.''

Harry rubbed the rounded tip of his nose thoughtfully. "Arlebar . . . Arlebar the elder wizard. Transformation spells,'' he repeated, frowning in the effort of concentration.

Kedrigern was aware of someone beside him. He turned

and found himself eye to eye with a heavy-browed scowling man in a dusty traveling cloak. The man took a step back and with his hands on his hips, looked from wizard to innkeeper, then fixed his steady gaze on the wizard. As the cloak opened, Kedrigern glimpsed a richly embroidered tunic and the handle of a dagger.

"I heard the name of Arlebar," said the stranger, as if he were making an accusation.

"You did, my lord, you did indeed," said Harry cautiously.

Slipping his hand into his tunic and resting his fingertips on his medallion, just as a precaution, Kedrigern said, "I've been making inquiries about Arlebar. Is he a friend of yours?"

"Never saw him in my life. Mean to, though, and soon. Who are you?"

The man was confoundedly pushy, Kedrigern thought. A sharp reply seemed warranted, but he checked his tongue. The man had done nothing threatening; he was merely rude. And if he knew anything at all about Arlebar, it would be foolish to offend him.

"I am Kedrigern of Silent Thunder Mountain," he announced.

The reaction was astonishing. The scowl disappeared from the stranger's face, giving way in an instant to a look of delight. "Kedrigern . . . Master Kedrigern . . . the great sorcerer of Dark Wood!" said the man.

"Wizard, actually," Kedrigern said, smiling.

"But that's the same thing as a sorcerer, isn't it?"

"It's fairly close."

"Master Kedrigern, forgive my brusque manner. I'm under something of a strain these days. Can you spare me a few moments?"

"Of course," said the wizard.

He followed the stranger to a corner of the room where they could speak without being overheard. As they seated themselves, a muscular swordsman with bulging shoulders and a shaven head took up a stance between them and the rest of the patrons.

"Rospax will see that no one disturbs us," the man explained.

"I don't doubt it," said Kedrigern, glancing at the huge blade that hung in a plain scabbard at the swordsman's back. It was almost as tall as he was.

"I am Conrad Coeur du Fer de la Tour Brisée, and I am on a quest. I seek the Magic Fly," said the man.

Kedrigern scratched his chin. "I don't believe I ever heard . . . Magic fly, you say?"

"Correct, Master. Actually it is no fly, but a distant cousin under an enchantment. She is a very beautiful lady of noble birth. I must find her and free her."

"I see."

"The wizard Arlebar, I have heard, knows the spell to disenchant her."

"An interesting coincidence, Conrad. I'm looking for Arlebar myself."

"Then you will join my quest!" Conrad said, reaching across the table and clasping Kedrigern's forearm in a manly grip.

"I'd be glad to ride along, but I don't see any real need for my services if Arlebar knows—"

Conrad, with vigorous manual gestures and much head-shaking, silenced the wizard and said intently, "There is a need, Master. I must have you as part of the quest. It's all in the spell. I can't change it."

"Perhaps if you could explain . . ."

"Under the terms of the spell, my cousin Lazica must be sought by a picked band of eight questers, constituted as follows: swordsman, giant, squire, knight, minstrel, wastrel, sorcerer, sprite," said Conrad, counting off each title on a finger. "Of course, I am a knight, and have a squire. My cook, fortunately, is a wastrel. I know Rospax from a number of campaigns we fought together, so he is my swordsman. On the very day we left, a minstrel turned up at my gates, seeking a place in my service." Conrad paused, then said, "He's not much of a minstrel, but I was pressed for time."

"Your quest was off to an auspicious start."

"I ran into trouble immediately. It's a lot easier to find minstrels and swordsmen than it is to find giants, sorcerers, and sprites. I wandered for weeks, searching, and was beginning to grow desperate. Then I met an old friend who told me of the Inn on the Outer Edge. He said I'd be likely to find anything I needed here."

"And have you?"

"Only yesterday, I signed up a giant and a sprite, and now I've found my sorcerer."

"Wizard, actually," Kedrigern corrected him.

"Close enough. And since you, too, seek Arlebar, we'll be doing each other a favor."

"Do you know where to find Arlebar?"

"I have clear directions to his house."

"He's said to move around a lot."

"But he always returns home."

Kedrigern nodded. He wanted time to weigh the proposition. Conrad, seeing his hesitation, leaned forward and said, "Though a wastrel, my cook is a master of the culinary arts. You'll eat like a prince. And I have the best horses in six kingdoms."

"I've seen them. Marvelous animals."

"You'll have your pick—my own steed excepted, of course."

It was a fair offer. Conrad had a point about their both being after the same goal. He also had directions and horses. And supplies and a good cook. Still, it never hurt to bargain.

"I must make a few things clear, Conrad," the wizard said. "Once I've learned what I seek from Arlebar, it may be necessary for me to leave the company to pursue my own quest."

"No problem there. A certain amount of attrition is normal. What's important is to start out with the full complement as called for in the spell."

"Good. There is also the question of Princess Lalloree. I've promised to conduct her safely to her father's kingdom once my quest is done."

With a dismissive wave of his hand, Conrad said, "What you do when the quest is over is no concern of mine."

"Yes, but she's with me now, here at the inn, and I must bring her along."

"A princess? On *my* quest?"

"It's been done."

"Not by Conrad Coeur du Fer de la Tour Brisée, it hasn't."

"She's a very small princess. Hardly more than a child. Beautiful singing voice. Loads of fun," Kedrigern said.

Conrad appeared to soften. "Sings, does she?" he asked.

"Incessantly. And sweetly."

"I love to hear a woman sing," Conrad said softly.

"Then Lalloree will make you very happy. It's good to have a princess along on a quest, Conrad. Keeps people on their best behavior. Gets them to wash a bit more often. Beneficial all around."

"All right, Master Kedrigern. She can come."

"Can you provide a horse and a tent for her?"

"Horse, yes. Tent, no."

"She must have her privacy, Conrad."

"I don't *have* a tent."

They pondered the problem in silence for a time, Kedrigern growing steadily more annoyed at the complications that had intruded into a perfectly straightforward quest. He should never have agreed to take Lalloree home. Conrad should have thought of tents. What kind of man goes on a long quest without tents? What else had Conrad overlooked?

"The baggage wagon! I could rearrange the baggage wagon so Princess Lalloree can stay in it. Would that do?" Conrad asked.

"I think it might. Yes, it would, Conrad."

"Good, then it's settled. There's nothing else, is there?"

"There's only the pet toads."

"Pet *toads*?"

"She's very attached to them."

"What kind of princess keeps pet toads? What is this Lalloree like, anyway? She sounds odd to me," Conrad said uneasily.

"She's a charming little creature. Fond of animals, that's all."

"I like animals myself, but pet toads . . . What if one of the toads spots the Magic Fly before I do?"

"I'll assume full responsibility for their good behavior. They're very quiet and clean. They have the manners of a prince and a princess."

"All right, Master Kedrigern, if you'll vouch for them. I take it we're agreed, and you're joining us?"

"I am. When do we leave?"

"You're the last one I need. I'll be ready to leave in the morning, if that suits you."

"Excellent. No point in dawdling. Is there any chance of meeting the others before departure?"

Conrad scratched his close-cropped head. "Well, Rospax is right here. Not much for talking, Rospax, but you won't find a mightier swordsman. And Gylorel and Anlorel are over there at the corner table. I'll take you over and introduce you.

And you've already met me. That leaves Ponttry, Maheen, and
Smeak. I'll need Ponttry to get my things in order, and
Smeak will be seeing to the supplies. . . . I'll send Maheen to
give you a hand with your baggage. How's that?''

"Very generous, but we're traveling light. There's really
no need.''

"Whatever you say. But I'll be glad to send him if you
should think of something. Just get word to me,'' Conrad
said, rising. "Come and meet Rospax.''

At Conrad's command, the swordsman who had been standing guard turned to face them. With thick, scarred arms
folded across his broad chest, he looked at the wizard with
objective professional antagonism. His eyes were as cold,
hard, and emotionless as stones, and Kedrigern felt a chill at
contact.

"Rospax, this is Kedrigern, the great wizard of Silent
Thunder Mountain. He's coming with us on the quest. He's a
friend,'' said Conrad slowly.

"Friend,'' Rospax repeated in a low growl, nodding his
scarred, shaven head.

"I've taught him not to shake hands. Had to, really. He
kept crushing people's fingers,'' Conrad explained.

At Conrad's words, a momentary glimmer of nostalgia lit
up the swordsman's icy eyes, but it died at once. To Kedrigern,
he said, "If anyone hurt my friend, I smite him a great
blow.''

"Thank you, Rospax. I'll remember that, in case a smiting
situation should arise,'' Kedrigern said, smiling.

"Pleasure all mine,'' Rospax growled.

As Conrad led the way to the corner table, he said over his
shoulder, "I think Rospax likes you. He generally has to
know someone for a while before he offers to smite people
for him.''

"Fortunate. I don't get on that well with swordsmen, as a
rule.''

"Just don't show fear, and you'll be all right. Here we
are,'' Conrad said, stopping before a table in the corner
where the green-bearded giant sat with the sprite perched on
his shoulder. "Gylorel and Anlorel, meet Kedrigern the great
wizard. He's joined our quest.''

Since the giant was at eye-level with them while seated, he
did not rise. The sprite rose from her perch and circled them,

leaving the men haloed in glittering motes of light. Returning to her place, she said in a sweet tinkling voice, "We are pleased to meet the wizard Kedrigern."

"And I'm happy to meet you, my lady."

At his words, she gave a little silvery laugh, and the giant shifted in his seat with a soft rustling sound and smiled at them. "This is no lady, this is my sprite. Call her Anlorel," he said in a deep voice. "I am Gylorel. I take it you are to be the quest's sorcerer."

"I am. I'm a wizard, actually, but for purposes of this quest I count as a sorcerer." There was an awkward silence as the four looked at one another, politely smiling, and Kedrigern broke it by asking, "What's become of the two gentlemen you were with last evening, if I may ask?"

"They've gone on a quest for elvish gold. We tried to talk them out of it, but it's no use talking to a skeleton. And a burning man is even worse. They think they know everything, those burning men," said Gylorel.

"Blue ones, especially," Anlorel added.

"I avoid elvish gold, myself. It's tricky stuff," said Kedrigern.

"Exactly what we tried to tell those two. But would they listen?" Gylorel said with mild annoyance.

"Might as well teach good manners to a troll," said Anlorel.

Briskly rubbing his hands together, Conrad said, "Well, we have our questers, so there's no need to hang about here any longer. We leave tomorrow. We'll assemble in the courtyard at dawn."

"Good. This place is too small," Gylorel said.

Conrad and Kedrigern left the room together. As they passed the bar, the wizard observed Harry still busy filling piggin after piggin and having them vanish out the window as soon as he put them on the ledge.

"You were fortunate to get Gylorel. He's a nice size of giant," the wizard said to Conrad.

"Oh, yes. Those other fellows are much too big. Just imagine keeping them fed! And they insist on working as a group—they wanted me to hire all seven. Well, I can't have that. And hiring Gylorel, I got my sprite, too, without a lot of searching."

"A stroke of luck," Kedrigern said.

Conrad frowned. He gripped the wizard's arm and shook

his head sharply. "Please, Master Kedrigern—never use that word if there's a chance of their overhearing. Words like 'stroke' or 'chop' upset them terribly. So does the sight of an axe. When they're not traveling, Gylorel is a tree, and Anlorel is his dryad."

"I see. Thank you for the warning, Conrad. I'll be careful."

"Sst! Master Kedrigern!" said the innkeeper in a strained whisper. He gestured for the wizard to come to the bar.

With a parting salute to Conrad, Kedrigern went to Harry, who was still putting piggins of ale on the window ledge, from which they disappeared as fast as he replaced them. He looked harrassed and anxious.

"Is everything all right?" Kedrigern asked.

"It's these giants, Master Kedrigern," Harry answered in a hushed voice. "I'm beginning to worry. They're drinking a terrible lot of ale."

"I imagine giants have a greater capacity than most people, Harry."

"What if they turn mean? Or get sick? Imagine seven sick giants staggering about here, Master Kedrigern!"

"Oh dear. Yes, I see what you mean."

"Can you do anything to help? I'm not a rich man, but I'll pay you a fair price."

Kedrigern nodded tolerantly. He was by now accustomed to the convention that when it comes to discussing payment, there are no rich men.

"I can do something for you, Harry. All I want in return is a couple of good heavy quilts and a pair of pillows for Lalloree. Clean ones, mind you."

"Done, Master Kedrigern."

"I'll just go to the wagon and mix something up, and I'll be right back."

As he crossed the innyard, Kedrigern heard a loud thud from behind the stables and felt the ground shudder under him. The giants were further along than Harry had expected. Dismayed by the thought of one of them collapsing onto the wagon in which his companions waited, he stepped out briskly. The potion he had in mind was a simple one, and he could have thrown it together easily at the bar, but he preferred to work in privacy. In his profession, it did not do to demystify.

The interior of the wagon looked like the aftermath of a hurricane in a clothes press. Lalloree stood in the middle of a chaos of shoes, gowns, cloaks, and linens, wearing a simple blue gown that accented her youthful figure and fairly illuminated the gold of her hair. She smiled radiantly upon the wizard.

"Isn't it *lovely*, Uncle Keddie? Don't I look absolutely *gorgeous*?" she exclaimed.

"It's her color, Keddie," Princess said. "I wish I could wear blue."

"You look very nice, Lalloree. Listen, everyone—I have some very good news," said the wizard.

"I can *keep* it! That's the good news, isn't it, Uncle Keddie? I can keep this beautiful gown, and the black slippers, and—"

"My news is of somewhat more immediate relevance to our original purpose, Lalloree. I've become acquainted with a gentleman named Conrad Coeur du Fer de la Tour Brisée, who knows where to find Arlebar. I've joined this fellow's quest, and he's agreed to provide all our supplies, plus a wagon for you and a horse for me. It's an excellent proposition. We leave in the morning."

"What about us?" Princess asked.

"I informed Conrad that Princess Lalloree would wish to keep her pet toads safely in the wagon, and they were not to be disturbed."

"*Pet toad?* I'm a princess!" Princess cried.

"And I, wise master—though I'm certain you had excellent reasons for doing as you did—am a handsome prince," added Handsome.

"You both told me to say nothing about you. I distinctly remember that," said the wizard.

In a mild pique, Princess replied, "Well, I certainly didn't tell you to refer to me as someone's pet toad. *I* distinctly remember *that*."

"My dear, we must be realistic about the dangers that surround us on all sides. Surely you—and you, too, Handsome—are aware of how valuable you are. Certain powerful spells require an enchanted toad as a key ingredient, and there are sorcerers and necromancers who would go to any lengths to acquire one."

"What spells, learned master?" Handsome asked after a brief apprehensive pause.

"Chiefly spells for reanimating the dead."

"And what role does the toad . . . play?"

Kedrigern averted his eyes and looked uncomfortable. "A very nasty one. It is always fatal, and quite unpleasantly so."

There was a moment of solemn silence, and then Princess asked, "How is a pet toad expected to act, Keddie?"

"Just be a toad. Sit on your damp moss, go 'brereep' every once in a while, and don't call attention to yourself. Above all, don't say a word to anyone. That would give it all away."

"How long would this go on, Keddie? It's bad enough looking like a toad, but having to act like one as well . . ."

"With good horses, and barring mischance, we could be at Arlebar's in about ten days. If he can tell me the spell those characters at Wizcon used, I'll have you back in proper form the day we meet him."

"And then, kindly wizard . . . if you would spare a moment . . . ?" Handsome asked.

"Oh, yes, Uncle Keddie, please make Handsome a handsome prince again, *please*!" Lalloree cried.

"If I can, I will, but I make no promises and I don't want to hear anything more about it until we reach Arlebar's. Right now, I have a bit of work to do, and you'd better start putting things back in place. We leave at dawn."

"Uncle Keddie, I'm a *princess*. I don't know *how* to put things back in place," Lalloree said plaintively.

"Now's your chance to learn."

"But I don't *want* to learn! It's so *boring*!"

Kedrigern closed his eyes, took a deep breath, and then said in a calm, quiet voice, "Lalloree, this wagon and everything in it are the property of a young lady who was carried off by an afreet. Afreets are mean, ugly demons whose only saving quality is a devotion to their spouses bordering on uxoriousness. If either the young lady or the afreet should return to a scene of such disorder, I doubt that all my magic could save us from severe inconvenience. Get to work, Lalloree," he concluded, fixing her with a cold glare.

"But Uncle Keddie, you could do it so *easily*, and it's so *hard* for me. All you have to do is work a little spell, but I'll be at it all *day*!"

"Lalloree, my misguided child, magic is not something to be used casually, as a substitute for work or study. This is why wizards require servants and libraries. Magic has a special purpose, and to use it indiscriminately has brought many a foolish wizard to grief. I myself, when I was young, very nearly . . . well, no need to go into that. You'll just have to do it yourself,'' said the wizard. Seeing her lip start to tremble and her blue eyes brim over, he added gently, ''And I'll see about getting that blue dress for you if you do a good job.''

"And the slippers, too, the black slippers? Oh, *please*, Uncle Keddie!'' she cried, clapping her hands together in an outburst of anticipation.

"The slippers, too. But the place has to be in perfect shape.''

"It will be, I promise,'' said Lalloree, gathering up an armful of cloaks and heading for the closet.

Kedrigern cleared a workspace on the little dressing table, drew pouches and vials from various pockets, and proceeded to mix a potion for Harry to use on the bibulous giants. Despite the size and number of the intended recipients, the amount he prepared was quite small; Kedrigern used only the best ingredients, and was a firm believer in quality over mere quantity.

The potion required only a few minutes, but by the time Kedrigern was ready to leave, Lalloree had made great headway in restoring order to the wagon. As he left, she reminded him of his promise. His reassurance spurred her to new efforts.

Crossing the innyard, he was assailed by loud voices singing a maudlin song, all out of key and in total disharmony. Just over the rooftop of the farthest outbuilding was a huddle of shaggy heads, and the singing came from that direction. At least the giants were not reeling about and crashing into things, he told himself; although that stage could not be far off.

Harry greeted him like a castaway sighting a sail. His face lit up and his eyes glittered as Kedrigern held out a small vial. Harry took it gingerly and cradled it in his dripping hands.

"It's a homesickness potion, Harry,'' the wizard explained in a lowered voice. ''Five drops in each piggin, and they'll be out of here by afternoon, all seven of them.''

"Bless you, Master Kedrigern,'' said the innkeeper fervidly. ''You've saved the establishment, and no mistake. Now, if only I can get this into them before they collapse on one of the buildings. . . .''

"Empty the whole vial into a barrel and wheel it out to them."

"I'll do it directly! But here—help yourself while I'm gone," said Harry, placing a pitcher and a mug before the wizard.

Harry trundled the barrel, properly doctored, out to the singing giants. In his absence, Kedrigern sipped Harry's very good ale and thought of his own cozy cottage, far away on Silent Thunder Mountain. He longed to be there. He needed no potion to make him homesick. He loved his cottage; his dark, dusty, cozy study; the stormy winter evenings spent *à deux*, just Princess and himself before a crackling fire; afternoon naps in the sunny shelter of his front yard; he missed all these things. He even missed Spot—grotesque, ear-splitting Spot with its flapping ears and one-word vocabulary and knack of sudden and inopportune appearances.

He wondered if Spot were really capable of caring for the cottage in his protracted absence. He weighed the wisdom of a very small magic to allow himself a glimpse of the building and grounds; just a safety check, no more. He thought of the days of travel still ahead, days that might stretch into months, and he sighed gloomily. Travel was a wretched business.

Still, home is not much fun when one's wife is a toad. If Princess was to be herself again, truly and fully, voice and form and all, they had to find Arlebar. He could only hope that Arlebar would be the end of their search, and not just the beginning. This business was hard on Princess. Not much fun for me, either, Kedrigern thought sourly. Lalloree was getting to be an infernal nuisance, and Handsome was going to be one more drain on the reserves of magic. There was really no question about helping poor Handsome. The fellow had apparently learned his lesson; though it was hard to tell with a toad.

Problems, always problems. Never should have gone to Wizcon. Or trusted Memanesha. Never should have left home in the first place. Nothing but problems once you leave home. Should have stayed on Silent Thunder Mountain and worked it out by myself, he brooded, instead of dragging about in these dreary wastes, collecting other people's troubles. People see a wizard and right away they expect him to work a bit of magic and make everything just right for them. Nobody stops to think that wizards have problems, too. Lots of them.

He was frowning into his empty mug when Harry returned, fairly bouncing with relief. "All done, Master Kedrigern, and well done, too. They hadn't finished the second round before they started sniveling about home and hearth."

"Don't demean honest sentiment, Harry," Kedrigern said crustily.

"Not my intention at all. It's just that the sight of a giant blubbering . . . It's not what you expect of them."

"Show a little sympathy, Harry."

"I do sympathize, Master Kedrigern, but I don't want them around the inn. They're dangerous, they are. And now that they don't have anyone doing their washing, they're getting a bit nasty to be near, if you take my meaning."

"I know," Kedrigern said. "I caught a whiff as I crossed the courtyard. They need a housekeeper badly."

"It won't be easy to get one. I can't think of anyone I'd wish the job on," Harry said.

Kedrigern looked up thoughtfully, and a slow smile spread across his face at the image of Memanesha hip deep in the dirty linen of giants. "I can," he said softly. "In fact, when this business is over, I may do something about it."

"You'd be doing them and us a great service, Master Kedrigern. Not that you haven't done a great service for us already. I'm almost ashamed to be paying you in quilts and pillows."

"There's something else you can do, Harry. I'd like a gown and a pair of slippers from the wagon for Princess Lalloree."

"From the wagon? Well, now, that's something of a tricky situation," said Harry, looking suddenly uncomfortable. "It's not my wagon, you see, and if that afreet comes hunting for it . . ." He shook his head and looked pained.

"Afreets are not methodical. He won't know anything is missing," Kedrigern said confidently.

"What if the princess is with him?"

"Princesses are even less methodical than afreets. You won't have any problems. Besides, you deserve compensation for storing the wagon and keeping it in condition."

Harry's face lit up. "I do, don't I? I've been so fearful of that big afreet that I clean forgot my rights. Giving up space in one of my best sheds . . . cleaning and dusting . . . the

constant worry and concern . . . that ought to be worth more
than a gown and a pair of slippers. A lot more.''

"Don't be greedy, Harry. Not with an afreet.''

"It could be my big chance, Master Kedrigern.''

The wizard nodded. "Your big chance to end up sealed in
a brass bottle in an iron chest at the bottom of the sea.''

Harry's eyes widened and his jaw dropped. In the sudden
profound silence, a deep rumbling voice from outside howled,
"I want to go home!" Other cries of similar import and even
greater volume soon joined the first. The jugs and mugs and
tankards on the bar began to dance, and tables and chairs to
jiggle, under the earth-shaking tread of determined giant feet
heading homeward over the border to Other Places.

Harry rushed to the doorway, where he stood until the
footsteps faded and all withindoors had settled back into
place. He turned to the wizard, shaking his head in wonder-
ment, vigorously rubbing the tip of his nose.

"They're gone, Master Kedrigern. It worked. Your charm
worked!" he said happily.

Kedrigern shrugged and smiled with idle, casual grace.
"Sometimes the magic works like magic, Harry,'' he said.

·⊰ᴥ Nine ᴥ⊱·

the quest for the magic fly

BY THE MURKY light of dawn and the feeble help of a few smoky torches, Kedrigern and his companions had their first look at their fellows on the quest. Princess and Handsome, who would risk only stealthy peeks from the hoods of Kedrigern and Lalloree, respectively, withheld comment until they could speak in private. The wizard observed and appraised the other questers, but kept his opinions to himself. Lalloree stared, did elaborate double-takes, muffled her laughter behind a delicate hand, and guided her palfrey to the side of the wizard's gray mare, where she began to delivery her assessments in a stage whisper.

"Is that the wagon I'm supposed to sleep in? It's so *klunky*, Uncle Keddie!" she said with a wry expression.

"You needn't ride in it. It's just a place to sleep."

"It needs painting."

"There's no time to paint it now, Lalloree."

"Look at those *wheels*," she said unhappily. Kedrigern obligingly looked, but even close scrutiny revealed no peculiarities. When he told this to Lalloree, she merely sighed and was silent for nearly a full minute before directing her critical faculties elsewhere.

"The big one with the scar is so *ugly*, Uncle Keddie! I've never seen anyone so ugly. My father has swordsmen, but they're not ugly. And the *scars*! He's practically covered with scars, and they're all so *ugly*!" she said of Rospax.

"Swordsmen do acquire the occasional scar," Kedrigern reminded her. "They're none of them perfect."

"But these are such *ugly* scars. And the minstrel and the cook are *sick*, Uncle Keddie. Have you noticed how they keep groaning and falling off their horses? They can't even *walk* straight. They could have some terrible *disease*, and we could all get it and *die*!"

"It's a temporary condition, my child. They contracted it last night, at the bar. It isn't catching."

"Are you sure? That weasely little squire seems to have a touch of it. He's practically *green*."

"The young feel it more, but he'll get over it, too. Don't worry about him. And please keep your voice down."

"The big fellow is very pleasant, Uncle Keddie," she went on, lowering her voice very slightly, "but he's so *strange* looking! His hair is green, and his skin is all brown and rough. He looks like a tree that's decided to pull up its roots and go walking!"

"He is, Lalloree. He's a tree. A real tree."

"But trees don't go on *quests*! Why would he go on a quest?"

"I don't know the whole story. Perhaps it's just a tradition in his part of the forest. Or he may be relocating."

After a judicious pause, Lalloree said, "He seems nice enough. He's very polite and easygoing."

"Trees are generally good-natured."

"The little lady who sits on his shoulder and flies around his head is *cute*, isn't she? I like the way she sheds little flecks of light wherever she goes. I wish I could do that. Could you help me do that, Uncle Keddie?"

"You have to be a dryad to do that," the wizard said. Lalloree fell silent, pouting at this bit of information, and he took the opportunity to excuse himself and check the situation with Conrad.

"Ready or not, we're leaving in three minutes," Conrad said, scowling more fiercely than ever, not at Kedrigern but at the world in general. "If Smeak and Maheen fall off their horses, they'll just have to walk. The giant's walking—if he can do it, they can do it."

"Gylorel has longer legs than they do," Kedrigern pointed out.

Conrad stared at him bemusedly for a moment, then said, "Of course he does. He's a giant."

"My point exactly. He's a giant. The other two aren't."

"Well, that's their problem. They knew we were leaving early." Conrad bestowed a scowl on the assembled questers and added, "At least they got the baggage wagon tidied up before they went out and got themselves besotted. Has your princess had a look at it?"

"Only from the outside. It's not the kind of accommodations she's used to, but it will do."

Conrad made an unhappy noise in his throat, something between a snarl and a groan, as the gaunt cook, Smeak, began to slide from his mount, saving himself from a nasty fall by a wild grab at the saddle horn. Ponttry, the shifty-eyed little squire, slouched back from being sick beside one of the outbuildings and dragged himself into the saddle. Maheen swayed a bit, but kept his bulky form upright. Rospax stood like a vandalized statue beside a great bay stallion, his thick arms folded across his broad chest, awaiting Conrad's command. Gylorel, with Anlorel glittering on his shoulder, looked on the scene impassively.

Conrad, with another grunting noise, vaulted into the saddle of the white warhorse. Just as he was about to give the order to start, the innkeeper dashed out, waving his arms wildly and calling to him.

"What is it, Harry?" Conrad demanded with visible annoyance. "You've been well paid, and we've broken nothing. What's the shouting about?"

Rospax stepped to his master's side. In a cold voice, he warned the innkeeper, "Speak with respect or I will smite you a great blow."

"No disrespect at all, my dear Sir Conrad," Harry said, bowing low. "Merely an idea that came to me at the sight of this goodly company—a way to make the quest more enjoyable."

"We're not on this quest for pleasure," Conrad growled.

"A little harmless diversion never hurt anyone, my lord. Hear my suggestion: on the way out, and again on the way back, let each quester tell two stories. They might be tales of chivalry and adventure, of courtly romance, legends and fables, merry tales of wit and bawdry—whatever they wish. The one who tells the best tale will be guest of honor at a great dinner here upon our return.''

"Who's to pay?'' Conrad asked suspiciously.

"All will contribute equally, except the one who tells the best tale.''

"And who's to decide which tale is best?''

"I will, my lord!'' Harry announced, flinging his arms wide and beaming at the company. "I'll travel along, at my own expense, and be the judge.''

Conrad glared down at him. "That's the dumbest idea I've ever heard of. Do you think we're going to ride all bunched up, so we can hear each other tell stories?''

"I don't know any stories,'' said squire Ponttry in a thin, whiny voice.

Maheen, the minstrel, edged his mount forward and focused his red-rimmed eyes on the innkeeper. "Dog of a tapster, you insult the honor of my calling!'' he thundered in an Olympian voice. "Am I to bawl out my finest tales in hopes of a free meal?''

"I'd rather sing,'' said Lalloree to no one in particular. "I don't want to hear a lot of boring old stories, I want to *sing*.''

"Shall I smite him a great blow?'' Rospax asked, looking up at Conrad hopefully.

"Get him out of here!'' cried the cook in a slurred voice.

"A good kick will suffice, Rospax,'' said Conrad.

The innkeeper was gone before the swordsman could draw back his foot. The loud slamming of the inn door echoed around the yard. Servants ducked out of sight as the questers exchanged ill-natured remarks about the innkeeper's proposal. Conrad, glowering in all directions, abruptly dismounted and walked to Lalloree's side. He bowed, and his voice and manner softened as he raised his eyes and smiled at her.

"My lady has expressed a wish to sing. Would it please my lady to ride at my side, and lead us on our quest with a song?'' he asked. His manner was almost charming.

She turned to Kedrigern with a hauteur that astonished the wizard, and in a cool and elegant voice replied, "If my guardian and protector permits, I will ride with you. You must ask Master Kedrigern, my lord.''

With a bow and a flourish to Kedrigern, Conrad said, "I will protect her with my life, honored mage.''

"No need for that, I hope. Lalloree may ride with you if she so desires, and sing to her heart's content."

Conrad bowed once again, and Lalloree flashed the wizard a placid smile.

Kedrigern waited while Conrad remounted and gave the command, and when the last wagon trundled by, he fell in behind it. The wheels creaked; the morning breeze fluttered the canvas; the sound of hooves on the hard-packed ground settled into a regular drumming; but even so, Kedrigern could hear Lalloree's voice, clear and sweet in the distance, singing:

> "Ninety-nine knights went a-riding;
> They spied a lady fair. . . ."

With wagons to conceal them from the others, and no one riding behind them, Kedrigern and Princess were free to talk, albeit with caution. She slipped from his hood and sat on his shoulder, ready to pop back into the hood at the first sign of company.

"What do you think of the quest so far?" she asked.

After a reflective pause, Kedrigern answered, "I'm not impressed. With our horses and supplies gone, we were lucky to be able to join up with someone, but I do wish Conrad had chosen his company more carefully."

"They don't exactly inspire confidence, do they?" said Princess with little enthusiasm. "I had a few quick glimpses of them, and I wish I hadn't. Is that cook really a master chef?"

"So Conrad said."

She gave a little disbelieving sniff. "He looks like something that died in the last famine. A cook should be fat."

"That's stereotyped thinking, my dear."

"It is not, it's plain good sense. If a cook isn't fat, he's not eating his own cooking, and if he doesn't, why should I? Smeak ought to look like the minstrel. He's the fattest minstrel I've ever seen."

"Probably good for his resonance."

With another little sniff, Princess said, "Or his thirst. He and the cook and that sniveling squire . . . heavens, what a crew! Three drunks, a brute—two brutes, if you count Conrad—a giant and a sprite."

"Anlorel and Gylorel seem pretty decent."

"Yes, they're all right. Lalloree approves of them, at any rate," said Princess, and they laughed quietly at the memory of Lalloree's observations on her fellow travelers. After a time, Princess asked, "Speaking of Lalloree, what do you think of her and Conrad?"

Kedrigern looked sharply around at her. "What about them?"

"Oh, really, Keddie, for a wizard you're not very observant. I only heard their voices, but I could tell right away that he likes her."

"Aside from her singing, she's a pleasant child."

"She's a young woman, Keddie. A very pretty one."

"And you think that Conrad . . . ? Oh, the rogue! The scoundrel!"

"He hasn't done anything to her," Princess said coolly. "He'll probably be on his best behavior now, and see to it that everyone else is, too. It may turn out that Lalloree will make this quest tolerable."

"Yes, but she's under my protection. I gave my word to bring her safely to her father's kingdom. I'm not going to let some swaggering warlord . . . some fly-questing adventurer . . ."

"Oh, Keddie, relax. Just relax," said Princess impatiently. "Her father bundled her off to marry Panglunder, didn't he? Even Conrad's a better-looking man than Panglunder. Especially when he's not scowling."

"Well, yes . . . but what do we know about Conrad?"

"He dresses nicely. He's generous. Accustomed to command. Firm, but not tyrannical."

"And possibly married," Kedrigern added.

"Certainly not."

"What makes you so sure?"

"I may be a toad for the moment, Keddie, but I'm a woman, and women know these things. Conrad is not married, and I suspect that Lalloree's father would look upon him as a good match."

Kedrigern weighed the possibility for a moment and then said, "I suppose he might at that. But where does all this leave Handsome? He and Lalloree seemed to be getting on so well."

"I'd forgotten all about Handsome!" Princess confessed with sudden alarm. "That could make for unpleasantness. I hope he doesn't fly into a jealous rage and challenge Conrad. That wouldn't help things at all."

"Do you think Conrad will try anything? If he lays a hand on that poor child, I'll turn him—"

"I wouldn't worry about Conrad. It's Lalloree who may upset Handsome. She's a dear little thing, Keddie, and I've grown fond of her, but she's a bit of a flirt."

"I never noticed."

"Well, she doesn't flirt with *you*," said Princess, as if the very notion of anyone's wishing to flirt with Kedrigern were absurd and outrageous, "but she started flirting with Handsome as soon as she learned he was a handsome prince. And you saw how she behaved when Conrad asked her to ride with him."

"Yes, that's true . . . but Conrad's not a handsome prince."

"He's not a toad, either. Women appreciate such things."

"I'll take your word for that, my dear."

"Lalloree's just beginning to realize that she's going to be a very beautiful woman. I could see it dawning on her in the wagon, when she was trying on all those lovely clothes. It's a very heady experience. I remember when I was her age . . . back at my father's castle . . ." Princess fell silent, and then, with a great sob, cried, "Oh, Keddie, it was so nice being a beautiful princess! I'll never be a beautiful princess again, never, I just know it!"

"There, there, my dear," said the wizard softly, reaching up to stroke her. "We're on our way in earnest now. We'll find Arlebar and learn exactly what spell is on you. It may be only a matter of days until you're quite yourself again."

"But it might be years!"

"My dear, my dear, you know I'll leave no stone unturned, no avenue unexplored, no spell unwoven to bring my lovely princess back. Trust in me— and get back in the hood, quick! Someone's coming!" Kedrigern whispered urgently.

Princess made a graceful twisting dive into the hood of the traveling cloak. Moments later a horseman appeared, his mount waiting by the road for the wagon to pass. It was Maheen, the minstrel, and he smiled and raised a pudgy hand in greeting.

"May I ride with you for a time, sorcerer?" he asked.

"I'm a wizard, actually. But yes, you may."

The minstrel guided his horse to Kedrigern's side and confided, "Everyone's listening to that little girl of yours. I thought I'd slip away and take it easy until her voice gives out.''

"It doesn't," said Kedrigern.

Maheen grunted and shrugged his portly shoulders. "All the less work for me, then. Ordinarily, I'd ride alone and observe the scenery. I appreciate scenery. But this is the worst countryside I've ever seen. I passed this way once before, in my youth. It was ugly then, and it hasn't changed."

Kedrigern looked off to the side, and was forced to agree with Maheen's evaluation of the landscape. Flat, treeless, with only a tumble of broken stone here and there to vary the desolation, it was a sight to dampen the most exuberant sensibility. Low jagged hills ringed the horizon and the questers rode in a shallow bowl between them.

"It is rather uninteresting," the wizard said.

"Besides, I'd like a bit of intelligent conversation. The others are a dreary lot. Anything but a bawdy song or a racy story, and they're yawning in your face."

Kedrigern nodded sympathetically. "It must be trying."

"It is. But it was not always so. Is this your first quest, wizard?"

"I went on quite a few in my early years. Hard to avoid it in my field. Things were different in those days, though."

Maheen raised a hand. "No need to say more. This is a sorry quest for those of us who have known the real thing. Oh, wizard, I could tell a tale . . ."

The minstrel shook his head sadly and rode on in silence for a time. His expression was troubled. He looked like a man engaged in a difficult interior struggle. At last he turned to Kedrigern and began to speak in a solemn manner, and yet simply and straightforwardly.

"It was my destiny to join in a great quest. Having had the foresight to enroll in the Questers' League during my youth, I was permitted to take part in a journey the like of which had not been attempted since the days of legend and fable. Unfortunately, all who join the League are required to take an oath of secrecy about its activities, its membership, its books, and its journeys, and the man who dares break it is disgraced forever. He becomes an outcast and a traitor. His name is stricken fron the annals of the League for all time. I would suffer any punishment, endure any death, rather than betray

my vow and humiliate myself before my brothers," said
Maheen gravely.

"If you'd prefer to talk about something else . . . ."

"No. I must tell you of the League, and our great quest.
Perhaps the greatest difficulty facing me, aside from the
solemn vow of secrecy which I have taken, is the very nature
of the deeds and events which I hope to relate. They were of
so fantastic and wondrous a nature, so gossamer in texture
and subtle in substance, that anyone hearing my attempt at
describing the indescribable will surely find a great deal,
perhaps all of it, absurd and incomprehensible. The paradox
of the necessity to express and the simultaneous impossibility
of any real communication was long ago expressed in a verse
composed by an early historian of the League:

> "What has been apprehended
> but not fully understood
> May be uttered, but will never be clearly expressed;
> What is not grasped,
> And is only partially and confusedly perceived,
> Can, perhaps,
> Under certain unusual circumstances,
> Be vaguely articulated . . .
> But no one will understand.
> Those who have never felt or heard or seen the
> unfathomable
> Can never hope for illumination
> From those who have experienced the indescribable.

"That historian was a man misunderstood by almost everyone he spoke to," Maheen concluded thoughtfully.

"And no wonder," whispered Princess, just loudly enough
for Kedrigern to hear.

"Ah, wizard, well do I remember the day I was accepted
into the League as a novice, and the leader revealed to me the
threefold secret, the four great laws, the five-sided oath of
fidelity, the six indissoluble obligations of the sojourner, and
the seven unforgiveable transgressions. We set off that very
day, and in no time at all we were traveling in far lands and
visiting people and places I had long believed imaginary, or
lost, or abandoned." Maheen paused, nodding his head in
retrospection, then turned to Kedrigern and said, "I soon

witnessed the first of the many incredible, even miraculous sights that I was to see on this quest, and it left an indelible mark upon my consciousness.

"We had entered a small but dense forest and come to a fork in the road. The signpost offered us three alternatives, none of them pleasant. Our leaders differed among themselves as to which of the paths should be followed. One of them consulted the stars and advised that we take the uphill path. The second cast the yarrow sticks and found that the level path was the one that promised the fastest and safest progress. The third, studying the entrails of a chicken, urged the downhill road upon us, assuring us that the others would only lead us to confusion and long wandering in the trackless forest. As the leaders disputed in voices that grew louder and more acrimonious, a giant with a beard of ancient moss burst from the forest, tore the signpost from the ground, and used it to knock all three of them unconscious. He then disappeared into the woods, and was seen no more. We decided to retrace our steps so as to avoid this intersection entirely. So clear an omen could be ignored only at great peril."

A deep rumbling voice asked, "I beg your pardon—did someone speak of a giant with a beard of ancient moss?"

Kedrigern turned and found himself looking Gylorel in the eye. The giant had dropped back from his place behind Conrad to walk close beside them, matching the canter of the horses with his long strides. Absorbed in the minstrel's tale, neither rider had noticed him. Anlorel reclined on the top of Gylorel's head, glimmering through the thick green tangle like a crown of diamonds.

"I spoke of such a being," Maheen announced. "It was long ago, on my first quest, that I saw him, but I have never forgotten."

"May I inquire further—did the giant resemble me in any way?" Gylorel asked.

Maheen pursed his lips and inspected the giant from head to foot, stroking his short untidy beard thoughtfully. "He was taller, I believe, and very mossy. You are scarcely mossy at all."

"I am still young," said Gylorel. "In time I, too, will be mossy."

"I wish you luck. And now, if I may, I will return to my tale," said Maheen. When the others expressed their willingness for him to continue, he cleared his throat and said, "My task on the journey was the amusement and diversion of my fellow questers. The most appreciative of all my listeners, and the one of whom I have thought most often since the fateful day of the crossing of Monte Imbroglio, was our helpful porter and errand boy, Fleon. He was a cheerful lad who worked harder than any of the others and took all the unpleasant, burdensome, nasty jobs upon himself, performing them with zest and great cheer, seeking no thanks and happy to be of service. We were glad to have him along.

"On and on through time and space we traveled, moving now to the past, now to the far future, sometimes in the real world, sometimes in Laputa or Cockaigne, but always toward our abstruse, ineffable, and recondite goal. I particularly recall one beautiful summer evening in the picturesque little village of El Durado. It was a time of unsurpassed beauty and splendor. All the universe seemed poised and still, trembling in expectation, hushed, waiting. From far off under a great brooding oak tree came the soft sounds of Fleon's gentle sweet yodeling in a serenade to the nymphs of the wood, the pure melody broken only by the occasional snort of a restless centaur. Little did I dream in those golden days with their hazy, gauzy glow of otherworldly contentment that soon all would be lost, nearly forgotten, and in some cases, thought of, if at all, as a delusion. Often, as the evening faded, the Jabberwocky burbled from the nearby wood to play with me, and we romped, carefree as children, in the gathering dark. It was a time of great and quiet joy, peace, and companionship, and yet even as we enjoyed it, we could feel the sense of approaching calamity."

"Why didn't you try to do something?" Kedrigern asked.

Maheen did not respond. He paused for a moment, gazing moodily into the distance. Kedrigern and Gylorel looked expectantly at one another. Anlorel glittered excitedly, and deep in the wizard's hood, Princess gave an impatient little hop.

Maheen sighed, then sighed again, and went on, "At last the mighty Monte Imbroglio loomed before us. We made our way slowly up the mountain's sheer face, clutching at tiny crevices in the rock. All around us the wind howled. Bursts of snow and icy blasts tore at us, and wisps of tattered cloud and mist hid us from one another. But always there was the warm, inspiring yodel of Fleon to draw us on and keep us in good cheer. And then his yodel began to fade, to grow faint and distant, as if he were pulling away from us into another world, another sphere of being. We heard his yodel, fainter and fainter, more and more distant, until our ears strained for the last muted echo of a yodel and heard nothing but the bitter mocking wind. We clutched the rock fearfully, dreading the future.

"Somehow, we made it through the mists and the snow and the buffeting wind and found ourselves in the sunny countryside below. But already a malaise had come upon us. The future seemed a threat and the good memories of the past were soured and embittered. We soon fell to bickering and petty recriminations. We blamed our predicament on one another, and then on the leaders and the League itself. At last, since he was not there to defend himself, we turned on Fleon and placed all the blame for our confusion and discomfort on his shoulders. With his disappearance, the cohesive force that had held us together through our long journey in time and space seemed to dissolve, leaving us uncertain, suspicious, filled with doubts and hesitant to act.

"This single incident, so small and apparently insignificant in itself, has been the great calamity of my life. I have attempted to tell, simply and clearly, what happened to me and my companions, but I find myself strangely unable to continue," said Maheen, and bowing his head, he spoke no more.

They proceeded for a time, without a word being spoken. Kedrigern caught an inquisitive sidelong glance from Gylorel, to which he responded with a restrained shrug. At length, when the protracted silence had begun to wear on everyone's nerves, Kedrigern, with muted voice, asked, "What happened?"

"I have no idea," said the minstrel without looking at him.

"You mean that's it? That's the whole story?"

"Alas, yes."

"But it has no ending."

"Of course it has an ending," said Maheen. "It's over, isn't it? It must have had an ending, or I'd still be telling it."

"I mean a proper ending. An ending in the Aristotelian sense."

Maheen's eyebrows rose. In a voice dripping with mockery, he said, "Oh, you want an *Aristotelian* ending. Well,

I'm so dreadfully sorry I didn't provide an *Aristotelian* ending. I *do* beg your pardon. I suppose you want an Aristotelian beginning and middle, too. And the music of the spheres playing in the background.''

"That might help," said Kedrigern coolly.

The minstrel growled and muttered, "Critic!"

Kedrigern gave an irritable little grunt of impatience and said no more. In time, Gylorel broke the peevish silence.

"The mossy giant—do you recall where you encountered him?"

"I do indeed, sir. That part is very clear in my memory. The place is in fact not far from here. A road leads to the left, between two fens. About a day's ride along, you come to the forest, and another day or two brings you to the triple signpost. The giant came out of the forest to the left of the road."

"Do you know this giant, Gylorel?" Kedrigern asked.

"I think he is my father, whom I have long sought."

"Ah, then you may be leaving us."

"Yes. I must find him and bring him back to Dark Wood. He has been too long absent."

"What if he doesn't want to return?" the wizard asked.

Gylorel raised massive rough-skinned brown arms and in a voice like a high wind in the pines, cried, "Then I am the King of the Forest!" and Anlorel, with a shower of light, added, "And I am the queen!"

"I see. Well, I certainly hope things work out for you," said Kedrigern. Turning to Maheen, he said, "And you, I presume, are seeking your lost companion."

"I seek nothing. I have forsaken all goals. I drift aimlessly through life, an empty man."

"And a rotten storyteller," whispered Princess.

"Why did you seek service with Conrad?"

"I did not. I was looking for the kitchen, to offer the slaveys a few jokes in exchange for a meal, when Conrad saw me. As soon as he learned that I was a minstrel, he urged me to come on his quest." With a negligent little gesture, Maheen concluded, "I had nothing better to do, so I came along."

"I can't take it anymore!" cried a slurred voice. "I can't stand it, do you hear?!"

At the shoulder of the road, swaying from side to side on his patient, motionless horse, the cook Smeak stared at them with bleary unfocused eyes. They nodded a greeting and rode on, expecting him to join them. They had gone only a short way when Smeak howled, "I don't have to take this kind of treatment! I'm a master chef!" and toppled from his horse.

"Pay no attention," said Maheen.

They had not gone far before Smeak caught up to them, rubbing his bony hip and muttering to himself. Before long, he gave vent to another outburst.

"Exactly what's the problem, Smeak?" the wizard asked.

"That song! She's a pretty little child, and she has a sweet voice, but that *song*!" Smeak cried thickly. "She's gone all the way down to knight number one, and then she started to work her way back up, and when she reached ninety-nine and started back down again, that's when I broke and ran. I can't stand it anymore!"

"How is Conrad taking it?"

"He just gazes into her eyes and says, 'How lovely!' and 'How sweet!' and 'Pray continue, fair Princess Lalloral-lorall. . . .' "

"Lalloree," the wizard corrected him.

"Whatever you say. I can't stand it."

Maheen looked about gloomily and said, "Obviously, my services will not be in great demand."

"What are you going to do?" Kedrigern asked him.

"For the present, nothing. At least I have my meals, and a decent horse, and no demands on my time."

"There won't be any meals if she doesn't stop singing about those ninety-nine knights. I couldn't even boil water with that song going on," Smeak said.

"Perhaps I ought to speak to Lalloree," Kedrigern said. The others agreed unanimously with this suggestion, and he urged his horse forward. As he passed the baggage wagon, out of earshot of the others, he said, "An unfortunate turn of events, my dear. My own fault, actually. I should have fore-seen the reaction."

Peeping from his hood, Princess asked, "What are you going to say?"

"I'm not sure. It's rather a delicate situation. If Conrad is as love-struck as he seems to be, there might be an unpleas-ant scene."

"Keddie . . . I know a spell for laryngitis."

"You do?"

"It's only a twenty-four-hour spell, but at least it will give us time to think. And Smeak can get us our dinner."

"My dear, you're wonderful. Can you cast it from this distance?"

"I think so."

"Pray do."

There was silence, but considerable activity, in the wizard's hood, and eventually Princess, panting from her exertions, gasped, "Done."

Kedrigern proceeded to the head of the column. As he moved forward, he heard Lalloree's sweet voice crack and falter. She cleared her throat, tried again, and again failed.

"Uncle Keddie, my voice!" she said in a rasping squeak as he appeared. "It's gone!"

"Poor child, you've strained it," said Kedrigern. Turning to Conrad, his expression severe, he coldly asked, "Is this the way you care for my ward? You've let her sing herself hoarse, just for your amusement."

"But she sings so sweetly. . . . I never imagined. . . . She was fine until a moment ago, I swear it, Master Kedrigern," said Conrad earnestly.

"That's as may be. She's hoarse now."

Lalloree tried to speak. She emitted a noise like a rusty hinge, but no intelligible speech. Kedrigern patted her hand comfortingly.

"Not another word, Lalloree. You'll have to remain absolutely silent for . . . oh, for at least three days. After that, we'll see," he said. "Now I think you'd best retire to the wagon. We'll be stopping soon, I assume."

"I had hoped to get to the other side before stopping," said Conrad.

"The other side of what?"

"That." Conrad pointed to a sooty gray mist that lay well ahead of them, filling the shallow valley from side to side, obscuring the encircling mountains.

Without a word, Kedrigern drew out his medallion and sighted through the Aperture of True Vision. The mist took on a different aspect. Dense and thick, opaque as a blanket, it moved slowly, circling and folding in upon itself. In its upper reaches, it bubbled sluggishly, like a thick porridge, and from the bursting bubbles floated wisps of gray that drifted a short distance and then sank back into the viscid mass. Other things rose out of the mist that were unpleasant to see and disturbing to contemplate. Kedrigern replaced the medallion in his tunic and blinked, murmuring, "Oh dear. Oh dear me."

"What's the matter?" Conrad demanded.

"Stop the column immediately. We must go no farther."

"Why not? There's plenty of daylight left."

"Not for *that*. It might take days to get through. It might take forever."

Conrad, reddening, cried, "It's only a mist! What's there to fear in a mist?"

"It is not 'only a mist,'" Kedrigern replied, raising his voice to match Conrad's volume. "Give the order to stop, and give it *now*."

Rospax turned and cast a baleful eye on the wizard. His hand moved to his sword hilt, but at a gesture from Conrad, he relaxed. Conrad looked sulky for a moment, then said, "It's getting late. We'll stop here for the night. Tell the others, Rospax." The swordsman rode off to pass the word, and when he was out of earshot, Conrad said, "All right, we've stopped. Now, what's wrong with that mist?"

"That thing ahead of us is a cloud of residual magic. There must have been a considerable battle here during the wizards' wars."

"The last great battle was fought here. That's what my grandfather told me," Conrad said.

"That explains it. They must have thrown every magic they knew at each other. There are things in there . . ." Kedrigern swallowed loudly and shuddered.

"But that battle was long ago! My grandfather heard about it from *his* grandfather. Surely after all that time the magic has dissipated."

"*Surely* is not a word to use when speaking of magic. It has not dissipated. It seems to have undergone a very nasty metamorphosis. That thing—the mist, if you like—is alive, but not as we're alive. It's intelligent, but not in any way we can hope to understand. It's a jumble of entirely different things, and yet it's all one entity. I've heard of such things, but I've never seen one before."

"Is it friendly?" Conrad asked hopefully.

"Impossible to say, but I certainly wouldn't take any chances. Its concept of friendship may not be even remotely like ours.

We might be able to ride right through it unscathed, but on the other hand, we could be devoured or immolated or turned into little piles of barley at the first touch. Maybe worse. There's simply no telling. The only certain thing is that it's unpredictable,'' the wizard said. A peculiar creaking sound made him turn. he saw Lalloree, eyes wide, lips parted, pale with fear, trying fruitlessly to speak. "Go back to the wagon, please, Lalloree," he said softly, smiling to reassure her. "You'll be safe there."

"Can you do something?" Conrad asked.

"I'm a wizard, am I not? Of course I can do something," Kedrigern replied grandly. "First I must see to the comfort and well-being of my ward, and then, when we've dined, I'll concentrate on a solution. Cheer up, Conrad. Trust me."

The baggage wagon had been drawn apart from the others to afford Lalloree a measure of privacy. As they approached it, Princess said, "Keddie, I feel awful. That was a mean spell to put on Lalloree."

"No twinges of conscience, please, my dear. You did exactly the right thing."

"But she wasn't hurting anybody."

"She was distracting, and distraction is the last thing I need right now. What's up ahead is going to require some pretty fancy magic."

"Is it that bad?"

"Much worse than we can imagine, probably. I hope I can get us through without burning up every bit of magic I've got."

"You sounded confident with Conrad."

"Conrad is a client. One is always confident in the presence of clients," said the wizard. "But I don't expect to get much sleep tonight."

He did not. With Lalloree incapable of speech and Handsome sulking silent in a corner, there was an uncomfortable air of tension in the wagon. Leaving Princess to deal with them as arbiter and chaperone, the wizard slipped off behind a low rise to evaluate the situation.

He badly needed the resources of his library. With his books at hand, he would find a proper spell within minutes. But his books, and his cottage, were far away. Much too far, he thought glumly.

This was a great mistake. All travel was a mistake, a lot of rush and discomfort and bad food and enchantments and nasty strangers and trick spells and fleas. It always took longer and cost more than you had anticipated, and it always turned out, once you were home again, that you had missed the best things.

Of course, this particular trip could not have been avoided if Princess were to regain her proper form. But he had certainly chosen a poor route. Going north, through Pan-glunder's lands, and then across the bridge, had been a way of saving magic; fat lot of good it had done. Getting through that swirling stew of old rancid sorcerous by-products could take all the magic at his command, and even that might not be enough to protect them. Far better to have used a bit of his power right off to get them across the impassable River of Misery and direct to Arlebar's doorstep. Wouldn't be in this spot now if I hadn't been so stingy with my magic, he thought, sighing.

A soft rustling sound nearby brought him out of his reverie. He sprang to his feet, alert and on guard for whatever creature of this grisly waste might be stalking him. Before he spoke the first phrase of a protective spell, he recognized the outline of Gylorel as the giant stepped from the shadow of the rise and stood in the faint moonlight.

"I did not mean to alarm you, wizard," Gylorel said in a subdued voice.

"I'm just a bit tense, thinking about tomorrow."

"I understand. The mist is filled with danger. I can feel it even at this distance."

"The uncertainty is the worst part. We might conceivably come through it unharmed, or even be helped in some way. The thing is totally unpredictable," said Kedrigern.

"Not so for us. If we enter the mist, we will shrivel and die. That is why we are leaving."

"But we haven't come to the road between the fens. It must lie beyond the mist."

Gylorel gave a deep rumbling laugh, rich and drumlike, and Anlorel's laughter joined it in a crystalline chiming.

"We can find our way to a forest, wizard, as easily as you can sense an enchantment. Do not fear for us," Anlorel said.

"Can I assist you in any way? A spell of some kind?"

"You are generous, wizard, but we need no help. Before the third sunrise, our quest will be over. It will be good to get back to my roots," said Gylorel. With a farewell wave of his long brown arm, he turned and made his way into the wastes. Anlorel's light flickered for a time, ever fainter, and then passed from sight.

Kedrigern seated himself and leaned back against the slope, hands behind his head. There was always something sad about good-byes. In a purely selfish way it was all to the good to have two fewer to worry about, but he knew that he would worry about Gylorel and Anlorel all the same. They were far and away the nicest pair among this sorry lot of boozers, babblers, and brutes. The thought of Gylorel striding across that naked desolation with Anlorel perched in his hair and no friendly company for leagues around depressed his spirits.

But there was no time to dwell on that. He had to concentrate on a good solid protective spell that would bring them all through that mass of curdled magic: questers, horses, wagons, everything. And he had to keep power in reserve for the unexpected. He could guard against the usual magics, but that thing awaiting them was not usual, ordinary, or normal in any way.

Kedrigern was familiar with the sort of spells that had been used in that last great battle in the wastes. They were bad enough in themselves, but when one destructive spell is hurled against another, and magic of even greater potency is sent after them, the end result is certain to be a situation of consummate nastiness. Wizards and sorcerers, witches, warlocks, conjurers and necromancers had destroyed one another and everything east of the River of Misery to the Mournful Mountains, and from the near slopes of the Dragonbacks to the fog-enshrouded ice fields of the far north. But the magic endured. It charged the air, and poisoned the water, and sank its roots deep into the earth. In time, spell mingled with spell to form magics unforeseen by the frenzied enchanters who had cast their originals. As the magic simmered and stewed, commingling and interbreeding, new and ever stranger powers developed in the blasted land, and the dark mist that was at once alive and nonliving, insensate and intelligent, maleficent and benign, rose up to claim the sway over the territory its creators had ravaged.

The potential was simply awful, especially for someone like Princess, who had already been spelled and unspelled more times than was advisable. Handsome, too, had been through too much magic to face more in safety. The longer Kedrigern pondered over what might befall them if they entered the mist, the less confident he felt. There had to be a way to go around it. Even if it added days to their traveling time, they would have to find some alternate route to Arlebar's home, whether Conrad liked it or not.

He lay looking up at the stars. Not many could be seen in the moonlight, but a few were visible. Then, suddenly, they began to go out as blackness spread from east to west.

The wizard blinked. He raised himself on an elbow, drew out his medallion and peered through the aperture of True Vision. Looming high overhead and enfolding them on three sides was a great darkness, rolling slowly westward.

Kedrigern's skin tingled at the chill touch of magic. He scrambled to his feet, intoning a protective spell, and ran headlong for the campsite to give the warning.

The mist had not waited. It was closing in on them fast, and in a very short time they would be in its grip.

···⚜ *Ten* ⚜···

the quest interrupted

"THE MIST IS coming! The mist is coming!" Kedrigern cried as he raced through the silent camp.

Maheen and Smeak lay by the dying fire in sodden oblivion, rattling snores their only sign of life. Squire Ponttry was being noisily ill by the side of the road. None of them paid heed to Kedrigern's warning.

Reaching the wagon where Lalloree was quartered, the wizard found Rospax standing before him, arms folded, face expressionless. The wizard halted, panting from his exertions. Rospax did not move or speak, but when Kedrigern started for the wagon, the swordsman stepped forward to bar his way.

"I must see Lalloree," Kedrigern said.

"My master is with her. He is not to be disturbed."

"Your master, and all of us, are about to be very badly disturbed, Rospax. The mist is closing in. They must be warned."

"My master is not to be disturbed."

"Rospax, I must get into the wagon. Please step aside," the wizard said politely.

"If you come a step closer, I will be obliged to smite you a great blow," the swordsman said, reaching for the hilt of his mighty blade.

"There's no time for this sort of thing, Rospax, and I really don't want to squander magic on—" Kedrigern began.

139

With a soft *whitt*, Rospax drew his sword and cocked his thick arms for a sideward slash. His thews bulged and the corded forearms swelled. "Now I must smite you a great blow," he growled.

"Oh, shut up, Rospax," said the wizard with an impatient gesture.

The sword fell to the ground. A white kitten looked up at Kedrigern with wide astonished eyes and emitted a plaintive mew.

"Sorry, Rospax. I did try to reason with you," said Kedrigern.

He had his foot on the first step leading to the wagon when the door flew open. Conrad stood in the doorway, silhouetted by candlelight. The kitten bounded up the steps and scooted between his feet. Kedrigern was close behind him. He ran full tilt into Conrad, sending him stumbling back into the wagon, and then he shut and bolted the door. For a moment he stood with his head bowed, both hands flat against the door, speaking in an undertone, his words unintelligible. When he turned to face Conrad and Lalloree, his face was pale and strained.

"What's going on? What do you mean, bursting in here, pushing me about like a sack of meal?" Conrad demanded.

"The mist is moving in on us. It may be all around us even now," said Kedrigern wearily.

Lalloree made an inarticulate squeaking noise. Conrad cried, "Mist? What mist are you talking about?"

"That cloud of ancient magic that was down the road. It's come up the road. I've warned the others, and laid a protective spell on this wagon, but I don't know if it will be enough."

"Then do more!"

"I can't. I don't even know what I'm protecting against. I've used the strongest all-purpose spell I know. All we can do now is hope."

Conrad slammed a fist into his palm and snarled, "We'll fight! Where's Rospax?"

"He's beside the washstand, licking his paw."

"That's a kitten!"

"That's Rospax. I'm sorry I had to do it, Conrad, but he refused to let me enter the wagon. Listen, now, all of you. We have to be prepared for anything," the wizard said. He took a step to the washstand, upon which Princess sat. "Princess will get into my hood. She'll be safe there. Handsome, you get into Lalloree's hood."

"I won't," said Handsome sulkily from his corner.

"Do as he says, Handsome," said Princess sharply.

Conrad started back, pale. His jaw worked soundlessly for a moment, then he said faintly, "They talk."

"Of course we talk. What do you think we are, toads?" Handsome said with asperity.

"They *are* toads! Aren't they toads?" Conrad asked, looking nervously back and forth from Kedrigern to Lalloree. "Obviously they're toads!"

"Stop babbling, Conrad," Princess said. She hopped to Kedrigern's shoulder and went on, "You can't fight or bluster your way out of this. You have to do exactly as Keddie tells you, or you haven't a chance."

"She's absolutely right. Handsome, get into that hood!" Kedrigern ordered.

"All right," Handsome replied.

He hopped listlessly from the corner. Rospax froze in the midst of his paw washing, eyes fixed on Handsome. The kitten's head went down. His rump twitched with the eagerness of the stalk. Kedrigern noticed his interest and quickly snatched him up as Handsome sprang to the bed and thence into Lalloree's hood.

"Now you, Princess," the wizard said. Princess turned and dove gracefully into his hood. "The three of us must now join hands, and no matter—"

A tremendous blow shook the wagon, staggering the wizard. Conrad and Lalloree fell in a heap, clinging to one another in terror. "Take my hands!" Kedrigern cried, but another blow sent him sprawling.

One side of the wagon was wrenched away, and the top tore off with a grating screech. Kedrigern reached for Lalloree's wildly flailing hand, but he gripped something tepid and slimy that darted up his arm. He tried to say a spell, but an icy wind tore at his breath and left him gasping. He felt his power being sucked from him.

A greenish glow surrounded Conrad and Lalloree. It flared and sparkled with unknown magics, and Kedrigern could only look on helplessly. A blob of purple light appeared before him. It held steady for a moment, as if studying him, and then spread out to engulf him.

There was only one hope. Kedrigern grasped his medallion and silently invoked the last desperate spell of escape.

He found himself sitting on a grassy sward at twilight of a mild spring day. Not far away, huge brightly colored things swept by him at great speed with a rush of air and a whoosh of sound. Their number was beyond counting, and all were in headlong flight in the same direction. Kedrigern wondered if he had let Princess and himself in for something no better than the enchanted mist.

But the rushing things did not attack, or pay him any heed at all. They merely whooshed on to their unfathomable destination. He stood, brushed himself off, and saw that beyond them was another army of similar things rushing just as fast and noisily in the opposite direction. This puzzled him. Looking more closely, using the Aperture of True Vision, he saw to his surprise that the speeding things held people, and that the people seemed unafraid and unharmed.

"Keddie? Keddie, where are we?" Princess whispered, peeping from his hood.

"Elsewhere," he replied.

"Yes, but where?"

"I have no idea. I used the last-ditch escape spell. It's instantaneous, but unpredictable. I think we're in the future, but exactly when, and where, I can't begin to guess."

"Look, Keddie—centaurs!"

A small herd of dark centaurs whooshed noisily by, weaving their way in and out among the larger creatures. They moved too quickly for him to get a good look, but he took reassurance from their presence. Where there are centaurs, there may be magic.

"They're awfully loud for centaurs, aren't they?" Princess asked.

"Oh, you know centaurs. Noisy lot."

Another herd roared past, and this time Kedrigern had the medallion raised for an accurate look. He followed them for a moment, and as they droned out of sight, he murmured, "They have *wheels*."

"Wheels? Maybe they're a new breed."

"Maybe they are. Centaurs with wheels . . . a strange place this is," Kedrigern marveled, shaking his head.

"We can get back, can't we?"

"Oh, certainly. The spell is exactly reversible. But it takes a lot of magic, and I'm running very low. We may be here for a while."

"But we *will* get back, won't we?"

"Of course we will, my dear," Kedrigern said, with more assurance than he felt. This was a very tricky situation. If he had landed in a nonmagical age, or worse still, an antimagical time, he could be in for a long stay. At the very worst, he could be marooned here permanently, his magic dwindling steadily until it was entirely gone, and Princess would remain a toad for the rest of her days.

"What are you thinking about, Keddie?" Princess asked.

"Just wondering about . . . about Rospax, my dear. He was clinging to me when we . . . ah, there he is."

Rospax was a white blur in the grass, in darting ineffectual pursuit of a grasshopper. Kedrigern scooped him up, and the kitten began to purr contentedly.

"He's much nicer as a kitten," Princess observed.

"He must be hungry. I certainly am."

"I wouldn't say no to a few flies."

The wizard pointed to a gaudy, busy building on the horizon. "Let's head that way. There must be an inn somewhere near, along the roadside."

"Will you be able to speak to people?"

He nodded confidently. "The medallion takes care of that. Good thing, too. I don't think I have enough magic left for a comprehension spell."

"Do you have enough magic to get us some food?"

"Never fear, my dear."

Darkness was falling as they reached the bright building. The roaring things had all sprouted glaring eyes that alarmed Kedrigern when they first appeared, but which helped light his path. The creatures still showed no sign of hostility, or even mild interest, so he concentrated his attention on the building.

The roaring things, too, seemed to be heading for it; a few of them, in any case. As he drew nearer, Kedrigern was astonished to see the sides of the things open, and people get out. The people did not run, or shout, or act in any way like escapees; it occurred to Kedrigern that the roaring things were a kind of wagon that moved without the aid of a horse.

He breathed a sigh of relief and smiled. He had come to a

time of magic, after all. That brightened the picture considerably. Depositing the sleeping Rospax safely inside his tunic, Kedrigern entered this building.

The interior was something like an inn, but much brighter and busier. Children were everywhere. Unlike most inns, it smelled of nothing but food. Kedrigern considered that all to the good.

He loitered on the fringes of the crowd, observing their mode of behavior until he felt ready to proceed further. He had feared that his attire might set him apart and attract attention, but his fears were unfounded. The people around him were dressed in garments unlike any he had ever seen before. The younger ones—by far the majority—were mostly ragged and barefoot, yet they looked sleek and well fed, with the sun-baked skins of healthy primitives. All wore a similar upper garment, a kind of singlet. These garments were in an array of colors, and each bore words and symbols that appeared to be either a charm or a heraldic device. In his plain homespun tunic and trousers and his well-worn boots, Kedrigern was in fact one of the most conservatively attired within those glass walls. His traveling cloak drew a few glances, but they seemed to be of an admiring, rather than a critical nature.

He joined a line and shuffled forward until he reached a barrier. Behind it stood an auburn-haired girl about Lalloree's age, with astonishingly white teeth and large blue eyes.

"Hi, I'm Ronni! What would you like to order today?" she said in a chirpy voice.

"I am Kedrigern of Silent Thunder Mountain, and I wish to order a cheeseburger and a double-thick chocolate malted," he replied.

"Any french fries?"

The question took him by surprise. "If you think it advisable," he said cautiously.

Within moments, he was handed a tray containing assorted containers in vivid tropical hues. Speaking a brief phrase under his breath, he handed Ronni two pebbles he had picked up on the way. She took them and gave him coins in return, bidding him, "Have a nice day." He left the counter and sought out a booth in a remote corner.

The cheeseburger, despite its name, turned out to be mostly meat and very tasty, prepared with unfamiliar spices and dripping with rich, fatty juices. The french fries and double-thick chocolate malted he approached cautiously. He found them delicious.

Rospax began to stir inside his tunic, digging his tiny claws into Kedrigern's side. The wizard gave him a bit of cheeseburger, and the kitten was still.

"Can I come out now?" Princess whispered.

Kedrigern looked carefully around. No one could see him here. "Come on out," he said.

She hopped to his shoulder, then to the tabletop. Almost at once she caught a fly. A second quickly followed.

"Delicious," she said contentedly. "the service here is very good. Now, if only I could have a good soak. . . . Oh, Keddie, look at that! What a lovely traveling case it would make!"

Kedrigern glanced down at the little box in which his cheeseburger had been given him. It was made of a light pliable substance unfamiliar to him, of a size to fit comfortably in his hand or his hood.

"There's a bit of grease on the side here, my dear," he said.

"You can easily wipe it away. Oh, it's perfect, Keddie! You can put a little damp moss on the bottom, and then close the lid so I'll have my privacy."

"It's certainly a good size for you," Kedrigern said, covering a yawn.

"Keddie, you're looking tired."

"I'm feeling a bit tired. All this exertion . . . I haven't got much magic left. That foul mist drew it right out of me."

He felt eyes upon them. Turning, he saw three portly men in shiny suits, with shiny faces, and shiny rings on their clean pink hands, staring intently at Princess and himself. As soon as he looked up, they gave three very shiny smiles from under thin black moustaches and slid into the booth across from him.

"That's pretty good, mister, you know that? You're pretty good," said one, gesturing with a large green object that appeared to be a stubby wand.

"Yeah, the way you yawn and the frog keeps on talking, that's good," said another.

"What's so impressive about my talking while Keddie yawns? I can talk while he's whistling, or drinking wine, or when he's asleep," Princess said.

"She *can*? How do you do that, mister?" the first shiny-faced man asked.

"I have nothing to do with it. Princess can talk without my help."

"Yeah, sure, we know. A talking frog," the third man said scornfully.

"I'm not a frog, I'm a toad. Actually, I'm a beautiful princess. My present appearance is only temporary," Princess said.

"What happened? Wait—don't tell me—you got zapped by a bad fairy, right?" asked the third man.

"How else would I become a toad? You don't think it was *my* idea, do you?"

The three shiny men seemed very pleased by the outburst. They smiled shiny smiles and nodded their shiny heads and waved their green wands in glittering many-ringed hands. "That's good material. You write it yourself?" the first one asked Kedrigern.

"I don't approve of your attitude one bit," said Princess, snatching a fly out of the air.

"Okay, okay, play it straight," said the third man, raising his hands in a gesture of surrender. "But if you was really a talking frog, we could make you a star."

Kedrigern looked at him in awe. "You could? I know only one man who even attempted such a thing, and it nearly killed him."

"We do it all the time. Hey, listen, mister, you're talking to the Barry brothers. I'm Harry, this is Larry, and that's Gary. We're talent developers. How can you be in the business and not know the Barry brothers?"

"We're new around here. Just arrived today."

"Where you from?" asked Larry, or perhaps Gary.

"A long way from here."

"Who's handling you?" asked Gary, or perhaps Larry.

"We do not permit ourselves to be handled," said Princess coldly.

"Okay, okay. My mistake," said the one who had spoken. He exchanged a glance and a nod with his brothers. Turning to Kedrigern, he said, "Look, mister, I'd really appreciate seeing you do like she says, and drink something down while she's talking. Would you do that for us? Just a favor, like?"

"It's easy enough. But my double-thick chocolate malted is all gone."

Harry snapped his fingers and Gary—or perhaps Larry—handed Kedrigern a piece of paper covered with a fine design in green. "Get yourself another one, pal. My treat," said Harry.

"Thank you," Kedrigern said, rising.

"Get yourself another burger, too. Live it up," Harry called after him.

The line to the barrier was long. The green paper was a hundred dollar bill, which required a search for the proper change. When Kedrigern returned, the booth was empty.

He was thunderstruck. The enormity of his folly burst upon him. Harry, Larry, and Gary Barry were brigands, abductors, smooth-talking rogues who had taken advantage of his trusting nature and innocent good will to carry off Princess. What was a talent developer? What would they do to Princess? How could he find them? And more to the point, with his magic almost gone, what could he do if he did locate them?

He sat down in the booth and buried his face in his hands, cursing his own foolishness. His wits had failed him, as well as his magic. Perhaps he should have stayed put and tried to spell his way out of that foul mist. But that would have been suicidal. Princess would not have had a chance of survival.

The thing to do now was to build up his power. That was step one. With his magic at full strength, he could rescue Princess and then return to save the others. He yawned again, and stretched wearily. He felt very tired.

The second helping of food restored him somewhat, and he determined to set about his work at once. He knew exactly what he needed, and had only to learn where the ingredients might be found.

A slender black girl in livery identical to that worn by Ronni and the other serving wenches was wiping clean a nearby table. She noticed Kedrigern, smiled at him, and said, "Have a nice day, Pops."

Obviously this was the local greeting. Raising his hand in salutation, Kedrigern said, "Have a nice day, my child. Can you tell me where I might purchase simples?"

She stopped wiping, cocked her head to one side, and stared at him for a time. "Simple *whats*?" she asked.

"Just simples. Herbs. Mandrake, belladonna, henbane, thyme . . ."

"Thyme? Like you put in stuffing?"

"One might do that."

"You can buy all that at the supermarket. It's right in the shopping center. You can see it through that window."

Kedrigern followed her pointing finger and saw a bastion of glaring light. "It doesn't look like a long walk," he said.

She looked at him in momentary alarm, then said, "I suppose you *could* walk. I've never heard of anybody doing it, though. You feel all right, Pops?"

"I'm fine, my child, thank you."

Kedrigern rose and started for the exit. As he reached the glass door, he saw his reflected image and gave a soft gasp of dismay. His hair was streaked with white.

He left the building hurriedly, and walked with brisk steps toward the place of simples. Things were more serious than he had imagined. With his magic depleted and his normal sources of renewal far away, time was rapidly catching up with him.

Kedrigern was 166 years old, give or take a few years; he did not keep careful track anymore. For a wizard, this was no age at all. Wizards measured life expectancy in centuries, not decades. But a wizard of 166 cut off from his magic was another case altogether. He was a very old man, and he would soon look and feel like one. Princess had said something about that when they were crossing the Desolation . . . or was it on the way to . . . what *was* that fellow's name?

Hair turning white, memory failing; it would not be long, Kedrigern realized, until he was a doddering old stick, useless to Princess or anyone else. He had to act quickly.

The sight of the supermarket raised his spirits. Surely there was magic in a place like this. He traced his way to the herbs, and found rows and racks of them—all in jars or tiny canisters, all dried and powdery, all most probably worthless for his purposes. They had no aura of potency. They were dry and dead as ashes. With a sinking heart he picked out the basic ingredients of an elementary sustaining spell, paid for them with change from Larry's hundred dollar bill, and hurried outside.

Under a bright light in a far corner of the parking field he mixed the herbs, gobbled the concoction down, and waited for it to take effect. He felt like a man dying of thirst who has been given a single drop of water. These enfeebled herbs—if he devoured them by the bucketful—might enable him to hang on for a few extra days. They could not give him back his magic or his bodily strength.

He flung the useless containers aside and walked aimlessly into the dark woods beyond the parking field. That night he slept under a tree, rolled up in his traveling cloak. He awoke to the loud purring of Rospax, who was curled in a ball just under his chin. The kitten's serenity was not infectious. Kedrigern was scarcely awake before the desperation of his plight was fully upon him. To make matters worse, he was hopelessly lost, and very hungry.

He wandered all that day and the next, Rospax romping at his side. The kitten found food and water. Kedrigern shared the water, but not the moles and field mice. He grew weaker and hungrier, and ever more confused.

He stumbled on in a daze, unaware of his surroundings and uncertain anymore of how and why he had come there. His eyesight failed, and things became blurry. His hands began to tremble, and his legs could scarcely hold him up. At last, when he could go no farther, he lay down under a bush and sank into a coma.

He had strange dreams, from which he awoke in a narrow bed in a plain room. He had no idea where he was, or whether he was alive or dead. He felt very weak, but his mind was clear.

As he lay staring at the ceiling, someone entered. Kedrigern turned his head and saw a monk, carrying Rospax in the crook of his arm. He closed his eyes and despaired. This was truly the end. The monks, no friends to wizards, had taken him in to burn him.

"Am I disturbing you? I thought you might like to see your kitten. He led us to you."

It was cruel of the monks to gloat over a helpless victim. Kedrigern opened his eyes. The monk smiled and placed Roxpax at Kedrigern's side. The kitten at once began to reverberate with purring.

"He's happy to see you feeling better. May I bring you something? You must be very hungry," said the monk.

That was an unexpected offer. Perhaps the monks of this

time were different. "Haven't eaten for days. Lost," Kedrigern said weakly.

"We thought that was the case. We aren't far from the highway, but it's easy to lose one's way in the woods."

"Lost my way. Lost . . . everything."

"Perhaps we can help you. First, you must regain your strength. I'll bring you some soup."

This was not the talk of a man about to drag one to the stake. Kedrigern felt slightly hopeful. At least he might be allowed to wither away peacefully. And uselessly. What had become of Princess? He sighed miserably and scratched Rospax under the chin.

"One of us is happy, anyway," he said glumly.

The monk entered with a tray bearing a steaming bowl and a plate with two thick slices of dark, buttered bread. The soup smelled delicious and tasted even better than it smelled, and the bread was almost as good as Spot baked at home. Kedrigern finished the soup and asked for a second bowl, which he also finished.

"I'm glad you like it. Cream of sorrel is one of Brother Gregory's specialties. It's the chervil that adds the real flavor, I think. Nothing like good herbs for flavor, is there?"

"Nothing in the world. Can't get them now, though."

"Oh, my, no. That's why we're so lucky to grow our own."

"You grow your own?" Kedrigern said. He propped himself up on an elbow and looked eagerly at the friar.

"Yes. It's a very traditional garden, just like the ones in the old European monasteries, centuries ago. We use all the modern technology in making our wine and our preserves, because that's what people seem to want, but the herb garden is for our own use, so we're very old-fashioned in our methods."

"I wonder . . ."

"Yes?"

"I've always been a believer in herbal medicines. If I were to list a few herbs, would it be possible for you . . . to bring them to me?" Kedrigern asked.

"Why of course! I myself use anise regularly, for my digestion. And I find that sage truly does strengthen my memory."

"I'd like some sage. And a few others."

"I'll have them for you this afternoon. It's so good to see you improving!" said the monk.

"I'm feeling better every minute," Kedrigern said. His voice was a bit stronger, and there was a touch of color in his cheeks.

Kedrigern received a generous daily portion of herbs, and at the end of a week he was up and about. The infirmarer, Brother Alfred, was utterly astounded by the recovery.

"But you look as though you've lost decades, my dear Kedrigern!" he exclaimed as they strolled in the vineyard of an evening. "When you came here, your hair was white, your eyes were rheumy, you were almost a skeleton—I'd have said you were a hundred years old. And now there's scarcely a white hair to be seen. You're full of energy. Practically robust!"

"It's the good food and the rest. And plenty of fresh herbs."

"I'm amazed. We're all amazed. You're actually getting younger every day!"

"Stronger, too," Kedrigern said cheerfully. "The climate is a great help. All this sunshine."

"You *are* stronger," Brother Alfred marveled. "I can scarcely keep up with you."

"I think I'm back to my old strength. In another few days, I'll be ready."

"Ready?"

"Ready to leave. Tell me, Brother Alfred, have you ever heard of the Barry brothers? They call themselves 'talent developers.' "

"The name is unfamiliar to me. 'Talent developer' sounds like something to do with entertainment. Brother Donald might know of them. He was in show business before he joined us."

At Kedrigern's request they sought Brother Donald, and found him in the library. He was a husky young man, with the brilliant white teeth that seemed native to this time. He was indeed acquainted with the Barry brothers, and the sudden change in his expression at the mention of their name suggested a relationship less than cordial.

"They made me an unknown, Mr. Kedrigern," he said grimly, setting his square jaw. "They signed me to a rotten contract and swindled me out of the miserable salary I got."

"Do you know where I might find them?"

"I'll never forget their address. But if I were you, I'd have nothing to do with them."

"I'll have as little as possible to do with them, Brother Donald, I assure you. I only want to find out about someone I know."

"They'll probably lie."

"I'm prepared for that. Tell me, would you, just what a talent developer is. I've never encountered one before."

"I'm tempted to say 'a rotten swindler,' but that would be uncharitable. They may not all be like the Barry brothers. Supposedly, they're experienced managers who take talented amateurs and groom them for the big time. If they're good, they get you on 'The Jerry Fagin Show' or 'Have A Nice Day, America,' where millions of people can see you."

"And if they're not good?"

"Then they leave you stranded on the Interstate with $1.87 to your name," said Brother Donald grimly. "It brought me to my senses, so I suppose I should be grateful to them. But it was a very unpleasant experience at the time."

"I see. And do they really have the power to make someone into a star?"

Brother Donald gave a soft, sad laugh and shook his head. "You have to make yourself into a star, Mr. Kedrigern. No one can do it for you. It's a matter of inborn talent, and drive . . . of star quality. I don't deny that others can be very helpful, and smooth the way, but it's the individual who makes himself a star these days."

"Do many people become stars?" Kedrigern asked, fascinated.

"Very few. Star quality is a rare gift."

Kedrigern nodded. "It's probably better that way."

He spent the next few days alternating between the herb garden, the dispensary, and the kitchen, preparing ever more potent compounds. He extracted, pounded, and pulverized, blending simples skilfully so that their virtues would enrich and enhance one another. Some he ground to powders, to mix in wine; others he blended with honey, to form electuaries pleasant to the taste. Over each preparation he spoke words of power and made intricate and subtle gestures. He could feel the magic building within him until it fairly tingled in his blood and he was bursting with eagerness to confront the shiny perfidy of the Barry brothers and rescue Princess.

Brother Donald had given him their address. Kedrigern soon learned that Prior Martin traveled to the city every other Thursday. Accordingly, when the eve of the proper day arrived, he presented himself to the prior, thanked him for the generosity he and the others at the monastery had shown, and asked to be taken to the city in the morning.

"I'll be happy to oblige you, Mr. Kedrigern," said the prior with a broad smile. "I must say, you've made an amazing recovery. You look like the grandson—no, the great-grandson—of the man we carried in here only a few weeks ago."

"Brother Alfred was most conscientious in caring for me."

"I hear that you helped in your own recovery, with medications from the herb garden."

"I did, Prior Martin. And I've left my recipes with Brother Alfred. You may notice an improvement in the general well-being of the community in a very short time. It's the least I can do to repay your kindness."

Kedrigern said his farewells that evening, all but one. In the morning he sought out Brother Alfred and presented him with Rospax.

"Mr. Kedrigern, this is so generous of you! I've always wanted a white kitten, ever since I was a boy," said Brother Alfred, deeply moved.

"I could see how he took to you. Listen to him purr."

"We do get on well, Rospax and I. But he must mean a great deal to you. If it weren't for him, we might not have found you."

"Maybe he'll help you to find others. He's better off here than where he came from, Brother Alfred. Please accept him."

"Oh, I do, Mr. Kedrigern. I accept him gladly. Tell me—is he a mouser? We can use a good mouser."

"If Rospax sees a mouse, he will smite it a great blow. You can count on that," Kedrigern said confidently.

He left shortly after eight with Prior Martin and Brother Daniel in one of the wagons he had seen in such noisy and unnerving profusion upon his arrival. This wagon was not brightly colored. It was black.

Kedrigern hopped in jauntily and settled back in the soft

seat. He felt very much at home. From his conversations in the monastery, he had determined that magic was a significant force in this society, every bit as important as it was in his own. For some reason, these people referred to their magic as 'technology,' but the wizard was not deceived. Magic is magic, call it what you will, he thought complacently.

As their journey proceeded, and more and more of the wagons began to gather around them, Brother Daniel became visibly strained. His jaw was tightly set, and his knuckles were white. Prior Martin sat with his eyes closed, praying feverishly. He was very pale. The drain of magic, Kedrigern thought, must be enormous. He was glad they had not asked him to assist.

After hours of travel, with much stopping and starting and lurching short distances, the wagon came to rest. Brother Daniel gave a great sigh and lolled his head back like a wounded man. Prior Martin ceased his praying and smiled wanly upon Kedrigern.

"This is the address you wanted, Mr. Kedrigern. It's along our way, so I thought we'd take you to the door," he said.

"Thank you. You've been most kind to me."

"We could do no less. Tell me, Mr. Kedrigern, do you have enough money?"

"Money? Oh, the green paper! Yes, yes—in fact, I won't be needing it. Here, you take it," Kedrigern said, digging into his tunic and bringing out a wad of bills.

"Are you quite certain? There's more than eighty dollars here."

"I assure you, Prior Martin, I won't be needing it."

"Ah, I see. You're going to collect something from these gentlemen."

Grinning broadly, expectantly, Kedrigern said, "Indeed I am."

Accustomed to this world's magic by now, Kedrigern was able to enjoy the ascent to the fifteenth floor with a professional's aplomb. Flying boxes were certainly an improvement over a dragon's back when it came to protection from the elements, but the view was sacrificed. On the whole, he preferred Fingard for long trips, although these boxes seemed quite well suited to quick vertical jaunts.

Reaching the fifteenth floor he quickly deciphered the numbering system and made his way to 1522, where bold letters on the door proclaimed, "Barry Brothers, Talent Developers: We make the stars of tomorrow." He took a step toward the door, but paused, smiling at an idea that occurred to him. At a wave of his hand, everything but the Barry brothers' name vanished. A second wave, and the words "vile mendacious miscreants" appeared. Pausing only a second to check his handiwork, Kedrigern entered, closing the door behind him.

At a desk facing him sat a spectacularly beautiful young lady in a bright pink garment that seemed just about to fall from her superbly formed, sun-bronzed body. Her hair was a tumble of straw-colored curls; her wide-set bright eyes were a deep violet; her nose was exquisitely sculpted and her full pouting lips were a pale coral. She smiled to reveal the whitest teeth the wizard had yet seen in this land of dental splendor.

"Good morning," she said in a soft, breathy voice.

"Are the brothers Barry in their office?" Kedrigern asked.

"Yes, sir, they are. They're waiting for you. You *are* the man from UTM Enterprises about the Princess Froggy contract, aren't you?"

"I've come about Princess, my child, yes."

"Then you may go right in. Have a nice day," she aspirated sweetly.

"I plan to have a marvelous day," Kedrigern said, returning her smile.

He sealed the door behind him with a word, and looked at the shiny faces of the Barry brothers, seated behind a large table of gleaming metal with a glass top. On the table stood a golden cage, and in the cage sat Princess.

"Keddie, you've come at last!" she cried.

"Yes, my dear. It's all right now," he said. He stepped to the table, took up the cage, and released her. She hopped to his shoulder. "Did they treat you properly, my dear?" he asked.

"Hey! Hey, what is this?" a Barry brother demanded.

"They were very unpleasant, Keddie. They threatened me," said Princess.

"*Threatened* you?"

"You're not the UTM lawyer," another Barry brother said accusingly, and the third cried, "It's the creep from the fast food!"

"It is I, Kedrigern of Silent Thunder Mountain," the wizard announced.

"He's been out in the sun."

"He got a face lift."

"And a great hairpiece!"

"You have mistreated Princess. You threatened her," said the wizard.

"They said they'd feed me to a snake if I didn't sing, Keddie. They made me get up on a table with a lot of bright lights around me, and people shouting, and I had to *sing*," Princess said, her indignation growing.

"Now, look, creep, before you try to make any trouble here, remember something," said a Barry brother, rising and waving his green wand. It was glowing at one end, giving off a faint smoke, but Kedrigern sensed no magic. "You sold us that frog. I gave you a hundred bucks for it, in front of witnesses."

"That's right. We saw you take the money," said another Barry.

"You just took the money and walked away. We never saw you again," the third added.

"They called me 'Princess Froggy.' They were going to sell me to a lot of men who'd make me sing every week to strangers, and tell people to buy repulsive food."

"Sweetheart, you got it wrong. We wouldn't dream of selling you. We got you a beautiful contract—your own show, 'The Princess Froggy Hour.' We're making you into a star," the first Barry said.

"You've never made anyone into a star," said Kedrigern scornfully. "You couldn't even turn someone into a pile of stone."

"Now, listen, creep—"

"Wait a minute, wait a minute," another Barry cut in. "We don't want to lose our tempers. We can afford to be generous." Turning to Kedrigern, smiling a shiny smile, he went on, "We know what's bothering you, and we're going to set things right. We'll have Sue Anne type up a little agreement, just to make sure everything's perfectly legal, and when you sign it, we'll give you another five hundred. The Barry brothers are always willing to go the extra step to make everybody happy."

"Don't believe a word they say, Keddie. They're terrible men," Princess whispered.

"We don't have to give the creep nothing. All we got to do

for him is throw him out and make sure he don't come back and bother us no more," said the biggest of the brothers. The other two pondered that for a moment, then rose decisively from their chairs. "Yeah, that's a better idea," said one. "Just watch out for the frog, that's all."

"So now you threaten me, as well," Kedrigern said.

The big one laughed sharply. "This ain't a threat, creep. You're going to get it."

Kedrigern extended his hands before him, moved them in a smooth gesture, and uttered a sibilant phrase. The shiny Barry brothers vanished. In their places, three shiny garter snakes lay on the thick rug, hissing in astonished rage.

"Hiss off," Kedrigern said raising his foot menacingly.

They slithered in quick alarm to the farthest corner, where they piled into a tangled heap. Settling his hands on his hips, the wizard looked down on them with satisfaction.

"Thank you, Keddie. It's exactly what they deserve," Princess said.

"A pleasure, my dear. I'm sorry you had to wait so long. Was it very bad?"

"It was unpleasant. But I knew you'd come for me."

"I came as soon as I could."

"You look remarkably fit and well, Keddie. The last time I saw you, you seemed to be aging fast, but now you look younger than I've ever seen you. And your magic is working splendidly!" Princess said with considerable enthusiasm.

"I owe it all to herbs. You can always trust herbs—provided you can find nice fresh ones, grown in the traditional manner. I was fortunate to find a whole garden whose magic potential had never been tapped. It's been building for centuries. I've never felt so strong, my dear. I think I can face that filthy mist now."

"Are you quite certain?"

"With magic, one is never certain. I feel confident, though. I'm going to go back and hit it with everything I've got."

"Whatever you think best, Keddie," said Princess dubiously. Suddenly she cried, "Where's Rospax? You can't abandon him in this awful place!"

"I've found a good home for Rospax. He's among people who like him and will treat him well. I think he'll be very happy here. He was purring quite loudly when I left him."

"What if he turns back into Rospax, and wants to smite people?"

"He won't, my dear. He was subjected to so much magic in so short a time that he's frozen in his present form forever."

"What about me, then?" Princess asked, alarmed.

"Your situation is quite different. You've been under the influence of magic for much longer, and you've even worked a few spells yourself. You'll be far less susceptible. And I can protect you now, I think."

"Keddie, let's go home right now. If we wait, I'll lose heart."

"Hop into my hood and hold tight, my dear."

As soon as Princess was settled, Kedrigern laid the fingertips of both hands on his medallion and recited the spell of escape, this time in reverse. He felt himself whirled away. There was a great roar that shook the earth, then silence.

He was aware of something soft gently stroking his forehead and caressing his cheek. A hand. A woman's hand. He opened his eyes and looked into the loveliest face he had ever seen, the face he had so sorely missed these long months.

"Princess!" he cried.

"Oh, Keddie, I'm all right again! I can talk, and I feel better than ever!" she said, bending over to kiss him.

"You look better than ever to me," he said, pulling her close, returning her kiss enthusiastically.

"How do you feel, Keddie? You were unconscious for a time. I was beginning to worry."

"I'm fine, my dear. A little tired, that's all. I've worked a lot of magic in a very short time," he said, embracing her warmly. After a tender silence, he asked, "My dear, does your back feel all right to you?"

"Yes. No. It doesn't *hurt*, Keddie. But it does feel as though something is pulling at my shoulders."

"Something is. You seem to have wings. They're very nice little wings," he quickly assured her. "Gauzy. Iridescent. Quite lovely, actually. They're rather like Anlorel's."

"*Wings?!*"

"Wings. Do they work?"

"I didn't even know I had them, Keddie."

"We came back right smack into that mist and completely scattered it. A lot of odd things happen when you do something like that. Magic goes flying in all directions. I imagine that's how you got your form back, and wings besides. Why don't you give them a try?"

"I don't know how."

"Just concentrate."

Princess rose, clenched her delicate fists, furrowed her smooth brow, shut her eyes tightly, compressed her lips, and concentrated. The wings gave a twitch, then a flutter, and then settled into a graceful regular motion. Slowly but steadily, with a faint hum, Princess rose from the ground. Kedrigern looked on, much impressed, until her feet were just above his head.

"Perhaps you'd better not go too high until you're a bit more experienced, my dear," he suggested.

She opened her eyes, gave a little startled cry, and dropped slightly, but recovered almost at once, and rose to a higher altitude. She seemed quite at home in the air.

"Keddie, it's wonderful!" she exclaimed. "What a delightful surprise—it's much nicer than being a toad!"

She rose a bit higher. Her posture became more relaxed as she leaned forward, reclining on the air.

"Don't tire yourself, my dear."

"It's no effort at all. It's easier than walking," she called down to him. "Keddie, it's fun!"

"Can you see any sign of the others?"

She climbed still higher and then hovered, peering in all directions. Suddenly, excitedly, she cried, "Keddie, the camp! The wagon! They're just over this hill! Come on!"

...⅜ *Eleven* ⅜...

the quest completed

KEDRIGERN ARRIVED ON foot just as Princess touched gently down, looking very pleased with her first aerial excursion. The scene itself, though, offered little scope for pleasure. They reached instinctively for one another's hands as they surveyed the devastation wrought by the magic mist.

Lalloree's wagon had been smashed flat, as if giant feet had trampled it into the ground. Nearby, gleaming white under the early morning sun, stood the cook's wagon. It had been turned to alabaster: food, pots, pans, everything was now lifeless alabaster.

They heard a low snort of breath, turned quickly, and saw three of the horses looking at them curiously. They returned the looks with equal curiosity, for the horses, too, had been transmogrified. One had grown a long blue trunk, with which he was picking up bits of food from the wreckage and inserting them in his mouth. His coat was a dizzying pattern of green and yellow checks. The second was a nightmare apparition: glossy black, with eyes red as blown coals, silver hooves and a spiral silver horn jutting an arm's length from his forehead. The third had become transparent. He moved about in a vague shimmer, sometimes—as when he passed before the alabaster wagon—disappearing from sight completely.

"At least we won't have to walk," Kedrigern said.

"That big black one is perfect for you. That's a wizard's mount if I ever saw one," said Princess appreciatively.

160

"He's certainly an imposing beast," the wizard said, stroking the black's muzzle and eying the long shining horn. "I've always been uneasy about riding anything with horns. I keep remembering poor King Yunarian."

"I don't recall your mentioning the name before."

"Yunarian had a nice little kingdom off to the west. A decent man, but too fond of spectacle. He always wanted to impress his neighbors. He got the notion of having a crack cavalry troop mounted on unicorns, and spent a small fortune acquiring the beasts and outfitting his finest horsemen. When they were all ready, he invited the neighboring kings to come and see his wonderful unicorn riders. They must have looked splendid . . . pennants flying, horns gleaming in the sun, lavish saddles. . . ." Kedrigern paused, then turned to Princess and said, "I wonder if there are any saddles lying about. We have a long way to go."

"Keddie, what about Yunarian?"

"Ah, yes. He had his unicorn riders do a feat he'd heard of from some Eastern potentate: a headlong charge at the reviewing stand that comes to a dead stop just a handsbreadth short of trampling everyone. Very dramatic effect it is, too. They'd practiced and practiced, and had it all down pat. But what no one realized was that when unicorns get excited, they run faster and stop more abruptly than anything else on earth. And, of course, with the trumpets, and the flags, and the crowds, the unicorns were very excited that day." Kedrigern shook his head. "Impaled, to a man. It was a terrible embarrassment to poor Yunarian. Worse still, his neighbors took advantage of the situation to invade his kingdom and carve it up among themselves."

"As long as you don't make any sudden stops, you should be all right," Princess said.

"Yes. And I'll try not to get him excited. Which one would you like, my dear?"

"The transparent one. He matches my wings."

Kedrigern dug in the debris until he found enough rope to tie up the horses. Further rummaging rewarded him with saddles and bridles. There was no trace whatsoever of the other members of the quest, except for three curiously shaped vessels by the remains of the fire. They were sort of jugs, or pots, and if one held them properly to the light, they each bore a suggestion of a human face.

"This long skinny one looks very much like Smeak," said Princess, setting the vessel down carefully.

"The round one is a good likeness of Maheen. It's hard to make out the features on the tiny one, but I'm almost certain it's Ponttry," Kedrigern said.

They looked down on the three jugs for a moment, thoughtfully silent. At length Princess asked, "Can you bring them back?"

"I wouldn't dare try. There's no telling what kind of magic they were exposed to in that mist." The wizard smiled reluctantly, and shaking his head, said, "Whatever its negative attributes, the mist seems to have had a wry sense of humor."

"Perhaps Arlebar can do something. I don't require his services anymore, but his house is on our way."

"That's true, my dear. We still have to deliver Lalloree."

"And you promised Handsome . . ." Princess began, but her voice faltered. She turned to Kedrigern with brimming eyes and said, "Oh, Keddie, just thinking of them . . . of what may have become of them . . . and Conrad, too."

Kedrigern's expression became severe. "I have a few things to say to Conrad when we do find him. Forcing his attentions on Lalloree like that, and posting Rospax outside the wagon to make sure he wouldn't be interrupted! He won't behave like that toward my ward and get away with it, I promise you."

"Keddie, she invited him in, just as soon as you were out of sight."

"But she couldn't talk."

"She could smile, and wink, and ogle. Speech was quite unnecessary."

Kedrigern grunted thoughtfully. "How did Conrad behave?"

"Like a lovesick boy. And Handsome just hopped into a corner and sulked. It was all very uncomfortable."

"Perhaps I'd better speak to Lalloree, too."

"If we ever see either of them again," Princess added in a subdued voice.

"I'm sure we'll see them, my dear. Unfortunately, there's no telling what they'll look like. I only hope we recognize them."

"Poor little things," said Princess. "They're so innocent, Keddie. Even Conrad, for all his bluster. It's sad to think of them caught up in something like this."

Kedrigern took her in his arms, and they clung close to one

another for a time without speaking. "I'll do all I can to help them," he said softly, "and what I can't do, Arlebar will. He's been around far longer than I have, and he has enormous power."

"But you don't even *know* him, Keddie."

"Well, no. But I'm sure he's heard of me. Of us both. And wizards do help one another out. We're a kindly lot, for all that people say about us."

"*You* can be kindly. Arlebar might be a mean old buzzard."

"Fraigus and Bess would never send us to a mean old buzzard, would they, my dear?"

"Memanesha would."

"Ah, but Memanesha didn't expect us to reach Arlebar. She probably doesn't even know him. I think she was lying right from the beginning. We'd be wise, I think, not to mention her name. Don't worry yourself, my dear. I'll saddle up these horses, and we'll start looking for the others."

With Princess mounted on the transparent horse, Kedrigern on the horned black, and the motley creature with the blue trunk trotting behind them, they set off in a southerly direction. The land was generally flat, with an occasional shallow dip or low rise that served to accentuate rather than break the monotony. As they rode on, Princess got into the practice of taking flight at the base of each rise to scout out the way, and delivering a brief description of the topography ahead. Toward evening, as she rose on one of her reconnaissance missions, she gave an excited cry.

"Keddie, there's a man up ahead!"

"Is it Conrad? Where's Lalloree?"

"It's not Conrad. Conrad was wearing a maroon cloak, and this fellow's cloak is green. He's all alone," Princess called down.

Groping for his medallion, Kedrigern galloped to the top of the rise and reined his mount in. Peering through the Aperture of True Vision, he saw a solitary figure trudging across the wastes, his head bowed in a posture of dejection. His dark green cloak was lined in white. He wore pale green tights and close-fitting white boots. As the wizard watched, the wayfarer paused and looked around, and Kedrigern had a glimpse of his profile. It was magnificent. It was, in truth, Handsome, and Kedrigern called his name, waved to him wildly, and urged the black horse to his side.

"You look wonderful, my boy! You're quite yourself again. What happened? Where are the others?" the wizard greeted him as he sprang from his horse.

"Where's Lalloree? Is Lalloree all right? Who are you, anyway?" Princess asked, alighting beside Kedrigern.

"I am Handsome," said the young man in a rich, resonant voice, bowing deeply. Brushing back the wayward golden locks from his splendid forehead, he added, "And you, I assume, are Princess."

"I am. Did the mist change you back, too?"

"It did indeed, fair lady."

"And give you wings?"

"Alas, no wings. Not even a mirror."

"You look as good as ever, Handsome," Kedrigern assured him. "What happened?"

"I have no idea," Handsome confessed. "The last thing I recall was the wagon being torn to pieces. I awoke in the night as you see me. The wagon was in ruins, and another wagon stood nearby, turned to alabaster. Flight seemed the safest course, so I fled."

"And what about the others? What of Lalloree?"

"Alas, poor Lalloree," said the handsome prince, lowering his head. His long lashes drooped, and he wiped a tear from his cheek. He held out his hand. Seated on it was a tiny toad.

"Lalloree?" Kedrigern asked faintly.

"Yes, Uncle Keddie," the little toad replied.

"Conrad is in my hood," Handsome said.

Kedrigern looked at the creature in the prince's hand, sighed, and slowly nodded his head. "Well, well," he said. "Dear me. Oh dear me."

"You'll change me back now, won't you, Uncle Keddie? And Conrad, too?" Lalloree asked.

"I dare not, poor child. There's no telling what magic you've been exposed to. I'm going to wait and seek Arlebar's advice."

"Then hurry!" cried a wee voice from Handsome's hood.

Kedrigern reached in and drew forth a toad slightly larger than the one Handsome held. This toad was a bit darker, and appeared angry. "I think you'd better ride with me, Conrad," said the wizard. "And Lalloree can travel with Princess."

"I'd like a nice splash. Is there a puddle anywhere near?" Conrad asked. "It's dry in that hood, you know."

"Right by the rock over there. Be very careful. You're the only one who knows the way to Arlebar's house."

As Conrad hopped off, Handsome sank to the ground and sat with his head buried in the crook of his elbow. Princess took Lalloree to the puddle for a quick dip, and when the two men were alone, Kedrigern said, "Cheer up, Handsome. Your ordeal is over."

"Alas, good wizard, all is over for me. . . . Life, and love, and all hope of happiness."

"But you're a handsome prince again."

"And Lalloree—Lalloree the fair, the sweet-voiced, Lalloree the lovely—is a toad!"

Kedrigern laid a consoling hand on the prince's shoulder. "Don't give up hope. Arlebar may know something about such cases."

Handsome looked up, and the pain of loss was in his deep-set dark eyes. "I know your intentions are kindly, good mage, but you forget that I have some personal experience with spells of this kind. I can tell when I'm in the presence of irrevocable enchantment."

Kedrigern dropped his consoling hand. He was silent for a moment, then he said, "Irrevocable, eh? Are you sure?"

"Positive," said Handsome in an emotion-choked voice.

Kedrigern sat at his side and put his arm around Handsome's shoulder. "This is tough, I know, but it might be saving you from worse later on. You're a prince. You have responsibilities. Your family probably has a wife all picked out for you."

"I had no responsibilities at all, Master Kedrigern."

"You didn't?"

"I was the youngest of twelve sons. No one cared whom I married. I did as I pleased. I was spoiled rotten. It was wonderful."

"But surely this experience has changed you, Handsome."

"I am a new prince. You have taught me to be humble and grateful, and Lalloree has taught me the meaning of true love. I intend to return to my father, the King, and dedicate my life to quiet suffering and the service of others. Hence, vain deluding joys! Farewell, vanity! Oh, hollow, hollow, hollow all delight!"

Kedrigern was moved by the speech. "Good man. But try to keep up a brave front when the others are around. There's a chance that Arlebar might be able to do something."

"You have great faith in this man. Do you know him well?"

"Never met him in my life, but he's been highly praised by people I trust. He's very old, and he's said to be a very great wizard. So perhaps there's some hope after all," Kedrigern said, clapping the prince on the back and climbing to his feet. "Now let's mount up and get out of this place. There shouldn't be any danger from magic. That mist used it all up."

"What became of the mist?"

"I took care of it," the wizard said coolly. "I also managed to find a few horses. The one with the long blue trunk is yours."

Handsome gave a start at his first sight of the trunked and parti-colored horse, but when he saw the others he accepted without question the one assigned him. With Lalloree and Conrad properly stored, the little party mounted and set off to the west, toward the looming Dragonback Mountains.

As Kedrigern had predicted, they had no further encounters with magic. The Desolation of the Loser Kings was purged at last, and their main struggle along the way was against boredom at the monotony of the surroundings. A solid day and night of fine steady rain came almost as a relief, and greatly raised the spirits of Lalloree and Conrad, who frisked and hopped and splashed merrily about at every pause in the journey. By the time they reached the foothills, faint traces of green could be seen where they had passed. The Desolation was desolate no more.

Kedrigern felt rather proud of himself. It was difficult not to feel a touch of arrogance riding that great fire-eyed, silver-horned black stallion, and even though there were no crowds to see him, he sat erect, cloak thrown back, head high, one hand aristocratically on his hip while he held the reins loosely in the other.

Guided by Conrad, they followed an intricate path through the mountain passes, with Princess doing scouting flights where the going was especially complicated. She returned from one of these flights at great speed, breathless with haste and excitement.

"Keddie . . . someone ahead . . . a man, I think," she said even before touching down.

"Is he alone?"

"Yes. Carrying some kind of spear . . . bent at the end . . . his horse is a bag of bones."

"Poor fellow may be lost. I'll ride ahead and see if he needs help," said the wizard. "You wait here with Handsome."

"What about me?" piped Conrad.

"You'd better wait here, too," Kedrigern said, removing him from his hood and placing him in Handsome's hand. "I won't be long."

"Be careful, Keddie. That spear . . . it looked dangerous."

"All spears are dangerous, my dear. Don't worry. I'll put on a protective spell."

With a jaunty wave of farewell, Kedrigern urged his black steed ahead at a good pace. As he rounded a turn in the path, he saw the horseman blocking his way, and reined in hastily.

The horse was a pale and sickly white, thin as a skeleton. The rider was cloaked in black, with his hood pulled forward to conceal his face. In one pale hand he clutched a scythe. With the other, he pointed at Kedrigern. In a hollow toneless voice, he said, "I have come for you, wizard."

"Just a minute, now. I think there may be some mistake," said Kedrigern, working a quick back-up for his protective spell.

"Your magic is of no avail against me, wizard."

"Who are you, anyway?"

"All men know my name, though few dare speak it," said the other, hefting his scythe.

"Oh dear. You're not Death, are you?"

"I am. And your allotted time is over, wizard," said the pale rider, raising an hourglass in his other hand. There was scarcely a trace of sand in the upper half. "You have enjoyed many centuries of power. Now it must end."

"What are you talking about? I haven't lived centuries, I'm only 166. Maybe 167, but no more."

"Do not mock me, Arlebar! Your time has come!" Death roared, drawing back his scythe.

"I'm not Arlebar! I'm Kedrigern of Silent Thunder Mountain—you've stopped the wrong wizard!"

Death lowered his scythe. "I have?" he asked nervously.

"You certainly have. You ought to check more carefully. You gave me quite a start."

"I'm terribly sorry, Master Kedrigern. I really am."

"You should show a little consideration. Popping up in front of a man like that, and waving that scythe around. Really, Death, it's too much."

"Oh, I *am* sorry. I haven't made a mistake like this in centuries. I simply had no idea that there was another wizard about," Death fretted.

Kedrigern was in no mood to be pleasant. He disliked sloppy workmanship and carelessness in all forms, but particularly those forms that threatened to shorten his life. "Well, there *is* another wizard about, and he's very angry," he said huffily.

"Oh, this is so embarrassing," said Death. "You see, I tried at Arlebar's house—it's only a few minutes from here—and he was out. So when I sensed a wizard coming this way, naturally I assumed it was he."

"You should have asked before you started waving that scythe around."

"Please accept my apologies. To my certain knowledge, you're the first full-fledged wizard to visit Arlebar in sixteen years. It's sheer coincidence that you happened to arrive today, of all days."

Kedrigern grunted. His expression did not soften, and he sat a bit taller in the saddle.

"You will forgive me, won't you, Master Kedrigern?" Death wheedled.

"Well . . ."

"And you won't mention this to anyone, will you? If it should get around . . . My work is difficult as it is, and if people even *suspect* that I'm not completely dependable . . . I'm sure you understand."

"I think I do."

"I'd be very grateful."

Kedrigern smiled faintly. "How grateful?"

"Anything within reason—one thing excepted, of course."

"Of course. I don't want to live forever, anyway. All I want is the chance to speak to Arlebar before you take him off."

"How long do you want?"

"Ten minutes should do it."

Death held his hourglass up to the light and examined it closely. "Arlebar doesn't have ten minutes left. I'd really *love* to oblige you, but I'm afraid—"

"Whose fault is it that his time is up?" Kedrigern demanded. "Who missed him at his house and then stopped the wrong wizard? I've been traveling over hard country for a long time, and to miss seeing Arlebar because of your silly clumsiness is really insupportable. Believe me, Death," he went on, wagging his finger at the sepulchral form, "if I don't get to speak to Arlebar, every wizard, sorcerer, innkeeper—"

"All right, ten minutes," Death blurted. "But not a second more."

"Ten minutes from the time he returns to his house. Ten *full* minutes, uninterrupted."

"Agreed," Death said hurriedly.

"Good. Now, if you'll just give me directions to Arlebar's house, I'll go back for my companions and meet you there."

It took all Kedrigern's persuasive powers and more eloquence then he knew he possessed, but he finally got the others to ride with him to Arlebar's house. The sight of the pale horse and its pale rider waiting in the dooryard put them off anew, but Death took the initiative, introducing himself and assuring them that his business was with Arlebar alone. Death had regained his composure by this time, and was actually quite gracious to his new acquaintances. At his suggestion they dismounted and sat in the garden to await the master's return.

Handsome quietly slipped away to pine and mope in a shadowy corner, while Lalloree and Conrad hopped directly into the fountain. Only Princess and Kedrigern remained with Death, seated under an apple tree.

"So this is Princess," Death said. "How lovely you are, my dear lady. What an enchanting couple you two make!"

"Sometimes you enchant, sometimes you disenchant," said Kedrigern with a shrug. "It's a living."

"How very nice it is to be among healthy people for a change, and not hear a lot of moaning and groaning. My dears, you wouldn't *believe* the things I'm forced to put up with," Death said. "It's just rush, rush, rush, and never a minute to myself."

"You're looking very fit," Princess observed, smiling pleasantly at Death. "I expected you to be much thinner."

"Do you know, Princess, a great many people say that. I don't believe there's a single decent picture of me to be found. And the *statues* . . . Well, the less said about them, the better."

"Most of the time they portray you as a skeleton," said Princess, looking very sympathetic.

"Isn't that the silliest thing? I do try to keep trim, but I ask you, could a skeleton carry this heavy scythe around? It's ridiculous. And yet everywhere you go, there I am, bony old Death on his bony old nag. Sometimes I feel like giving it all up," Death said with a petulant little toss of his head.

"On the other hand, you wouldn't want them to picture you as fat," Kedrigern pointed out.

"Oh, no fear of that, not the way I have to dash about. If it isn't a plague, it's a famine, and then there's *always* war. And you wouldn't *believe* the accidents. . . . I do wish people would learn to look after themselves better. It would make—ah, the master of the house has returned," said Death, rising and straightening his dark cloak, and taking up his scythe and hourglass. "Back to work for me. You have ten minutes," he added, *sotto voce*, to Kedrigern.

A very tall, very thin, very old man with a very long white beard was walking slowly toward them, sighing as if each step were a great and painful ordeal. He stopped, peered at Death, then at Princess and Kedrigern, then back at Death, slowly chewing on his empty gums all the while.

"So you finally got here. Took your sweet time about it, didn't you?" he said in a thin, raspy treble.

Lowering his voice a few octaves, Death said, "I have come for you, Arlebar."

"About time, too. Who are all these people? I thought you worked alone."

"They are visitors, Arlebar."

"Visitors," the old wizard muttered in disgust. "No time for that now. Let's go, Death. How do we work this? Do you carry me? Do we have to ride double on that bony old nag of yours?"

"Before we go, I will allow you time to speak to these people. They have traveled far to see you," said Death. Aside, to Kedrigern, he added, "Nine minutes."

"Well, they can turn right back. Come on, Death, get a move on," said Arlebar.

"Please, master—I'm Kedrigern of Silent Thunder Mountain, and this is my wife, Princess. I'm a brother wizard, and she's a student of our art. We seek your help, but not for ourselves."

"Not for yourselves?"

"No," they both said.

"Who needs my help, then, lad? Be quick about it."

"We're on a quest for a magic fly. Originally, she was a young lady named Lazica, and we set out with her cousin and a picked group of questers—"

"Lazica? She's inside. I think she's good and sick of being a fly by this time. I'll turn her back before I go, if she's willing. Anything else?"

"Yes. Her cousin Conrad, and a young Princess, Lalloree—they've been turned into toads."

"Eight minutes," Death announced.

"Toads? You don't need my help for that, lad. Turn them back yourself."

"But it happened in the magic mist, in the Desolation of the Loser Kings."

Arlebar's thick white eyebrows went up and he looked at Kedrigern with dawning respect. "You came through *that* just to see me?"

"We didn't just come through it, we overcame it!" Princess blurted. "Keddie scattered the mist with his magic. The Desolation is starting to bloom again."

"You *overcame* the mist?" Arlebar's thin voice was faint with awe.

"Yes. It nearly got us at first, though. I could feel myself slipping, and I used the escape spell. Princess and I landed far in the future. She was a toad at the time, but when we came back, she became herself, and even got a nice pair of wings."

"See?" Princess said, fluttering her wings and rising a few inches from the ground.

"Handsome was a toad, too, but he stayed behind in the mist," Kedrigern continued. "When we returned, we came right back into the mist at full power, and we just blew it apart. All the magic went off at once. Handsome became handsome again, but Lalloree and Conrad, who had been people, were turned into toads. And the others became jars. And I guess you noticed the horses."

Arlebar stared at him, nodding slowly. "Maybe it would be best if you just told me what you'd like me to do. I know about Lazica. What about the toads?"

"Lalloree and Conrad were transformed when the mist was coming apart. I didn't dare try a spell on them because I didn't know what had been done to them. That mist was a jumble of all sorts of old magic, and some new stuff I'd never seen before. I was hoping you'd be able to suggest something."

"Six minutes," said Death.

"Be quiet, you. I'm trying to think," Arlebar snapped.

Death gave a little sniff. Mumbling, "Well, the manners of *some* people . . . ," he walked off to take a seat under the apple tree.

Arlebar stroked his beard, frowning and shaking his head all the while. He finally gave a deep sigh and said, "There's nothing to be done for them, lad. I had a brush with that mist myself, about a century ago, when it wasn't half as bad as it became, but it was full of tricks even then. If the mist made your companions into toads with its last strength, then toads they'll stay. On the other hand," he added, his expression brightening, "Princess and Handsome won't have to worry about transformation spells anymore. They'll be immune. And Princess will keep those nice little wings."

"Poor Handsome. He was so fond of Lalloree," said Princess.

Kedrigern nodded. "We were bringing Lalloree back to her parents, Brindom of the Bright Plain and the kindly Lady Toomeera. They had sent her off to marry, but it fell through. We thought perhaps they'd agree to a marriage with Handsome—if he wasn't a toad. But now . . ."

"Let her marry the other toad. They seem to get on well enough," said Arlebar, pointing to the fountain where Lalloree and Conrad were frisking and splashing like happy children.

"That doesn't help poor Handsome, though."

Arlebar smiled a wise old smile. "I may be able to do something for him, Princess. Did you say that other toad's name was Conrad? Conrad Coeur du Fer de la Tour Brisée, by any chance?"

"Yes, it is! How did you know?"

Arlebar chuckled. It was a thin, wheezing chuckle, but it bespoke genuine amusement. "Lucky guess, dear lady. Just follow me inside, both of you, and I'll see if I can't fix something that will make everyone happy. One last little bit of magic as a farewell gesture."

"Five minutes!" Death called to them.

They ignored him and walked a few steps to Arlebar's tiny sway-backed cottage, with its sagging shutters and tilting chimney and general air of dilapidation. Stooping to pass through the low door, they entered a spacious gallery from which rooms and corridors went off in all directions. The old wizard led them to his study, rolling back the sleeves of his robe as he walked. Once inside, he closed the door and extended his hand before his face.

"Lazica!" he called in a reedy voice.

With a flash of light and a soft buzz of sound, a fly came from the high shadows and landed on his fingertip. It was a thing of gold and ruby and sapphire, with wings like etched crystal. Arlebar raised his hand close to his face and spoke softly to the fly, who groomed herself while listening.

"Lazica, it's time to lift the spell. You're safe now, and I have to go away. These people are friends. You can trust them. Are you ready?"

The fly stopped grooming and took off, landing on the floor in front of Arlebar. The old wizard extended his hands, murmured a brief spell, and gestured gently, and a lovely young woman appeared before him. She reminded Kedrigern of Lalloree, but a Lalloree no longer on the brink of womanhood. In Lazica, the promise of beauty had been richly fulfilled. Hair the color of sunstruck honey hung to her waist, swaying as she turned to cast her deep amber eyes on Princess and Kedrigern, and finally rest them on Arlebar.

"Am I truly safe? Has he ceased to pursue me?" she asked in a soft melodious voice.

"He will never bother you again, child. Now I must ask you to go outside and find a young man with golden hair. Bring him here at once. Hurry, child, our time is short!" As soon as she was gone, he took up a decanter and filled two small crystal cups. "When they return, have them drink this. It's a love potion. Never fails."

"Who was after the poor girl?" Princess asked.

"She'll explain everything. What else do you want me to do?"

"The vessels!" Princess cried. "Three of the questers were lying by the fire drunk when the mist closed in. They were turned into empty clay vessels."

"Fill them with wine. That'll keep them happy. Anything else?"

"That's all, Arlebar. Thank you for everything," Kedrigern said.

"It's been a pleasure. Took a lot out of me, all this excitement, but it was worth it." The aged wizard gummed silently and thoughtfully for a time, then went on, "Listen, now—this place will hold together for an hour or two once I'm gone, but after that it will start to disappear. If there's anything here you can use, take it. I've got some fine old books of spells, and I think a bright young couple like yourselves could do a bit of good with them. And there's a very old book on flight that might interest you, Princess. Take them, and take anything else you want, only get out of here before it all goes, understand? Otherwise, you'll go with it."

"Where, Master?" Princess asked.

"Where the flame on the candle goes when you blow it out," said Arlebar.

"We'll be gone. Thank you, master. You're very kind," Kedrigern said.

"I'm glad I met you, sonny. I had just about given up on the young wizards. I've seen too many sorry specimens lately. But you've got the stuff. Overcoming that mist . . ." Arlebar shook his head slowly and appreciatively. "Didn't think there were any good ones left. Thought it was all over for the profession."

"I've felt that way myself once or twice, Master, but I feel a lot better now that we've had a glimpse of the future."

"Does it look good, lad?"

Death appeared in the doorway, his scythe at the ready. He looked very businesslike.

"One minute," he said in a deep booming voice.

"All right, all right," said Arlebar impatiently. "What about it, lad?"

"Well, in the future it will be possible to become a star. Isn't that wonderful?"

"Incredible, my boy!" Arlebar said, his voice hushed. "I heard once of a wizard who almost turned herself into a comet . . . but a *star* . . .!"

"Some people even become superstars. There are great days coming, Master."

"Are you ready?" Death asked.

"Don't have to bring anything, do I?"

"Nothing at all. Come as you are."

"Good. Let's go," said Arlebar. At the doorway, he turned,

waved, and said, "Remember—get out before it all disappears." Then, spurning Death's offered arm, he shuffled slowly off at the dark figure's side.

"What a sweet old man," Princess said. "He called you 'sonny.' "

"I guess I look like a boy to him. He must be close to six hundred."

"He liked you. He was really impressed by the way you conquered the magic mist."

"So was I. But I wouldn't want to try it again."

Lazica returned, leading a dazed and silent Handsome by the hand. "Is this the man I was to bring? I didn't see anyone else," she said.

"He's the one," said Princess.

"Are you friends of Arlebar? Who are you? Where has he gone?"

"I am Kedrigern of Silent Thunder Mountain, and this is Princess, my wife."

"He's a very prominent wizard. I do a bit of magic too. And I fly," said Princess, rising gracefully and circling the little group.

"I used to do that," said Lazica. "I was a fly for ever so long."

"I used to be a toad, myself. This is much nicer," said Princess, coming lightly to ground at Kedrigern's side.

"I'm glad we didn't meet when I was a fly and you were a toad," Lazica said with a merry little laugh.

Princess, too, laughed at this sally, and Kedrigern smiled along with them. Handsome merely stood silent and pale, his eyes fixed adoringly on Lazica. While the ladies chatted like old friends, Kedrigern drew Handsome aside.

"Still planning to lead a life of quiet suffering and service to others?" he asked.

As if he had not heard, Handsome said, "What a wonderful woman! Magnificent! Those eyes . . . that figure . . . that soft sweet voice . . ."

"Beginning to think you can live without Lalloree?"

Handsome turned on the wizard indignantly. "That silly girl? Lalloree is a mere child. Lazica is a woman. A very beautiful woman."

"I noticed. Do you like her?"

"Oh, good mage, you must help me to win her heart. I cannot live without the fair Lazica. Help me, I implore you!"

"All right, Handsome. You do exactly as I say, and I think there's a good chance that you and Lazica may live happily ever after . . . for a while, anyway."

As the two men conferred by the doorway, Princess and Lazica exchanged memories of their time as toad and fly, respectively. Princess told of the spell placed on her, and of the complicated and frustrating series of events that had followed, ending with their final meeting with Arlebar. When her tale was done, she asked Lazica what kind of spell, curse, or enchantment had caused her to be a fly.

"Dear me, Princess, it was nothing like that. It was my own idea."

"You *wanted* to be a fly?"

"Well, not specifically a fly. I wanted to be something that my dreadful cousin would never think of marrying. He hounded me unmercifully—kept sending me jewels, and dwarfs, and captured enemies to do me tribute, and he wrote me awful poems, and sang beneath my window. I was always finding love notes in my food. He simply would not leave me alone. And my sisters were all after me to marry him, because I was the oldest and had to marry first. And my parents never stopped telling me how lucky I was to have a man like Conrad Coeur du Fer de la Tour Brisée panting after me, and all in all—"

"Conrad? Your cousin is Conrad?" Princess broke in.

"Yes. Have you met him?"

"We've traveled together. Do go on, Lazica."

"In desperation, I sought the help of Arlebar, and he promised me I need flee from Conrad no longer. What's happened to him? I didn't want Arlebar to hurt him or anything like that, I just wanted to be left alone."

"Conrad has found another."

"Well, that's a relief." Lazica smiled nostalgically and said, "Poor old Conrad. He wasn't a bad sort, really, under all that brag and bluster, but he had the clammiest hands I've ever touched."

"He still does. He's a toad," Princess informed her.

"He is? What sort of woman would marry a toad?"

"She's a toad, too. It's a perfect match."

"How sweet. Well, I'm glad for Conrad. And I'm glad I

don't have to be a fly anymore. But I suppose as soon as I return home, my sisters will be after me to marry someone else," Lazica said resignedly.

"How about him?" Princess asked, indicating Handsome by a twitch of her left wing.

"He's very ornamental," Lazica conceded, without enthusiasm.

"He's a prince."

"Everyone's a prince these days. He's not very talkative, is he?" said Lazica dubiously.

"Handsome has been through some very difficult magic. You have a lot in common."

Lazica looked thoughtfully across the room at Handsome. "His hands aren't the least bit clammy. I noticed that right away."

"Well, there you are, Lazica. He's handsome, he's a prince, and he has nice dry hands. And obviously he's mad about you. What more could you ask?"

"I was hoping to fall wildly and passionately in love just once in my life, before I settle down. I don't think there's much chance of that with him," said Lazica wistfully.

"You never know," said Princess, patting her hand in a sisterly fashion. "I'll get him over here. You can have a little sip of cordial together and get better acquainted. I'm sure you'll feel different about him in no time."

At Princess's summons, Kedrigern led Handsome to Lazica's side, where the prince stood blushing and looking fixedly at the floor. Princess took up the cups that Arlebar had filled, and held them out to the young couple. The ruby liquid contents glowed hotly through the facets of the crystal.

"Drink this. It will warm you up," she said, with a surreptitious wink at Kedrigern.

They took the cups and sipped politely. Their eyes met and held. Their breathing became audible. They emptied the potion simultaneously, let the cups fall from their hands, and extended their arms to each other.

"Lazica, my love, my angel . . . my beautiful one!"

"Handsome, my rescuer . . . my hero . . . my love!"

They flew to one another and locked in a passionate embrace. Amid panting and heavy breathing and deep shuddering sighs, in the intervals between lingering hungry kisses, could be heard murmurs of "Away together . . . eternal love

. . . your slave forever . . . Princess of Kallopane . . . lord and master . . . queen of my heart," and similar highly charged phrases.

"Good stuff, that," Kedrigern said appreciatively, eyeing the decanter.

"Fast, too," Princess added.

Handsome swept Lazica up in his arms and carried her through the doorway. Outside, he turned and said, "I ride to Kallopane with the fairest of all women. There shall we be wed, and there shall we live in ever-growing love and happiness, with the blessings and good wishes of my father, the King!"

"My prince, my life, my Handsome, let us away!" cried Lazica.

"Have a pleasant trip," said Princess, waving.

Kedrigern stepped to the doorway, whispered a few words, and gestured toward the departing couple, who had halted for a torrid embrace under the apple tree. He stood watching until they had mounted the gaudy, blue-trunked horse, then turned to Princess, smiling benevolently.

"I put a little spell on them. They'll be invisible to all enemies along the way and find friends by sunset every day. It's my wedding present," he said.

"They seemed very preoccupied. I hope they remember to invite all the right fairies to the wedding."

"Apparently Handsome's family are good that way. I only hope his father behaves himself. That's how Handsome's troubles started, you know."

They turned their attention to Arlebar's bookshelves, and emerged from the house a bit later with several volumes under their arms, looking quite pleased with their acquisitions. Conrad and Lalloree were perched on the rim of the fountain, awaiting them.

Conrad at once asked, "What about us?"

"Yes, Uncle Keddie—when are you going to make *us* human again?" Lalloree asked.

"How about right now?" Conrad demanded.

The wizard put his books down, folded his arms, and said, "I'm afraid I have some bad news. Perhaps you'd better sit down."

"We *are* sitting down. We're *always* sitting down," said Conrad irritably.

"So you are. Sorry. I've spoken to Arlebar, and he verified my suspicions. It would be deadly to tamper with any magic worked by that mist."

"I thought you were a wizard. Some wizard, if you're afraid to undo a spell."

"I work magic, not miracles."

Conrad gave a contemptuous little sniff and hopped back into the fountain. Lalloree looked sadly at Kedrigern.

"Can't you do *anything*, Uncle Keddie?"

"I'm afraid not."

"What will we *do*?"

"I'll bring you home to your parents. I'm sure they'll approve of your marrying Conrad . . . under the circumstances."

"They'll just nag and say that they warned me something like this would happen to me."

"Did they?"

"All the time," she admitted with a sigh.

Princess sat on the edge of the fountain at Lalloree's side and said gently, "It isn't really such a bad life, once you get used to it. You can be outdoors in the moat all summer, and spend the winter in the castle. And you can have all the children you want. Thousands, if you like. Toads have ever so many children, and they're no bother at all."

"Are you sure?"

"Absolutely."

"It really isn't so bad . . . but to think of the rest of my life . . . a toad. . . ." Lalloree said thoughtfully. "It could be so awfully *boring*."

"But you have someone to share it with, Lalloree. That's the secret."

Lalloree was silent for a time, and then she hopped into Princess's lap. "Take us home," she said.

·⚜· *Twelve* ⚜·

perfect matches

THEY STOPPED ON the nearest peak to watch as Arlebar's house and grounds, the gardens, fountain, arbor, pond and all, slowly faded and vanished from sight, leaving not a rack behind. When the shimmering air was once more still, and the site was a grassy dell sprinkled with clusters of daisies, they urged their horses southward, toward the pass that led to Brindom's realm.

The way was smooth, and free of vile enchantments. The air was warm and fragrant with early summer. Once they left the mountains, flowers and bright butterflies were everywhere, and they awoke each morning to birdsong. The journey became almost pleasant. Best of all, they knew that after delivering Lalloree they would turn their steps toward home.

The Kingdom of the Bright Plain was a very large kingdom with a very small population, all of it crowded together at the geographical center. That was where the good land lay, and where Brindom's forebears had built their castle. Their subjects had settled nearby and left the forests and rocky hills of the outlands to such unsociable souls as chose to dwell there. Here in the rich green midlands they produced all the necessities of life, and enough extra to trade for the luxuries so essential to the happiness and well-being of a respectable ruling family.

The defenders of the kingdom were twelve plump, slow-moving, good-natured guardsmen. They carried swords and shining pikes, but had only a vague notion of their proper use and no wish to increase their knowledge. The real defense of the kingdom was its borders.

To the east was forest, dense, dark, and impenetrable. To the south and west was the impassable River of Misery and the Terrible Falls, whose ceaseless thunder could be heard from the turrets of Brindom's own palace when the wind was right. To the north, beyond the Dragonback Mountains, lay the Desolation of the Loser Kings. Nothing and no one had come that way in living memory, and it was believed that anything or anyone that might come from the north would not be deterred by mere pikemen.

Thus it was that when Kedrigern and Princess were seen on the north road, they were first shunned, and then greeted with stupefied stares. The sight of their horses did not do much to encourage a hearty welcome. It was a guardsman, pale and displaying much white of eye, who first spoke to them. He approached at a slow, reluctant pace, trailing his pike in the dust, waving furiously and smiling a ghastly smile.

"Hail, friends! Greetings! Welcome to the Kingdom of the Bright Plain!" the guardsman cried. "We greet you in peace. We are a friendly people. Really, we are. We love to have visitors. We mean no harm."

"Neither do we," Kedrigern replied. "We wish to see Brindom. We bring news of his daughter."

"Yes, yes, of course. I'll take you to His Majesty at once. Have you come from . . . from . . . the north?"

"Obviously we have."

"Across the Desolation?" the guardsman asked, his voice hushed. The peasants at the roadside inched closer to hear the reply.

"We have crossed the Desolation of the Loser Kings," Kedrigern said with cool indifference. His black horse snorted and flashed its silver horn in a menacing gesture.

"Then you must be great wizards!" cried the guardsman, dropping his pike and stepping back.

"We are," Princess said. "This is Kedrigern of Silent Thunder Mountain. There is no wizard greater."

"And this is my wife, Princess, herself a wizard of no small accomplishment."

"I fly, too," Princess cheerfully announced, rising from

the saddle of the transparent horse to circle the guardsman
and wave to the dumbstruck crowd. A few children returned
her salute enthusiastically, but the main body simply stood
with their heads back and their mouths open.

When the guardsman had collected his wits and his pike,
he led the newcomers to the palace. The road widened, and
the crowds grew, and by the time they reached the palace
gates, most of the population was gathered to see the mighty
wizards from the north.

Brindom had been advised of their coming, and was at the
gate to greet them. He was as round as his guardsmen,
white-haired, rather short, and red of cheek. He was smiling
bravely. What he expected, they did not know. His relief
when the fearsome pair turned out to be a beautiful dark-
haired lady in a close-fitting green and yellow robe, with a
circlet on her brows, and a slender clean-shaven man in plain
homespun garments and worn boots, was unmistakeable. He
beamed at them, took their hands warmly, and placed his
palace and servants at their pleasure.

"But please, my honored guests," he said as they entered
the castle arm in arm, "I am told you have word of my
daughter. Forgive me my eagerness, but Lalloree has been
long away from us and we hunger for news of her."

A tiny giggle escaped from Princess's hood. She and
Kedrigern exchanged a quick glance over Brindom's head and
said nothing of it.

"Perhaps it would be best to deliver our news to you and
your gracious queen together," Kedrigern suggested.

"Yes, yes, of course, it would indeed," said Brindom,
rubbing his pudgy hands together briskly. "You are thoughtful, wizard. In my eagerness I forgot my beloved Toomeera's
anxiety. She awaits us even now."

Smothered laughter erupted in Princess's hood. To cover
the sound, she had a coughing fit, which sent Brindom into a
flutter of solicitude, eliciting more smothered laughter and
louder coughing. In this way they walked the length of the
throne room and passed through a door behind the two imposing thrones.

They entered a cheery sunlit chamber holding six plump
cushioned chairs, all with footstools. The woodwork was
painted in bright colors, and the walls held pictures of dogs
and cats and children cutely posing. A pitcher of milk and a

plate of cookies rested on the low table around which the chairs were grouped.

"I've brought the wizards, Momma!" Brindom called, explaining, "We prefer to conduct business of state here. It's so much more comfortable than the throne room. We can all relax. Take some milk and cookies, please. Take all you want." He took up the pitcher and proceeded to fill four mugs that stood beside it on the table. As he was filling the fourth mug, a plump and very sweet-looking woman bustled into the room, drying her red hands on her apron and making anxious little clucking sounds.

"Here you are, Momma! Just in time to join us for some nice milk and cookies," Brindom said. "These are the wizards from the north, Princess and Kedrigern."

"I must look a fright," said the queen, untying her apron and folding it neatly, patting her hair into place, smiling nervously at the visitors. "Daddy didn't say you were coming until just a little while ago, and I thought to myself, well, mercy me, they'll be starved to death after all that travel, so I went right into the kitchen to put a nice little supper on."

"Your Majesty is too kind," said Kedrigern with a bow.

"Oh, I know all about you wizards. Always on the go. A bite here, and a sip there, and never a decent meal two days running. That's why you're all so thin. And there's no call to be fancy. Just call me 'Auntie Toomie,' same as everyone else does," said the queen.

"Momma! Daddy!" cried Lalloree, her wee voice charged with feeling. As Brindom and Toomeera looked about the room in bewilderment, Lalloree struggled from her place of concealment and hopped to the tabletop, narrowly missing the plate of cookies. "It's Lalloree! I've come home again! Aren't you glad to see me?"

"That's a toad, Momma," Brindom said warily.

"It's our Lalloree's voice, Daddy."

"I'll grant you that, Momma, but I'd know our Lalloree anywhere, and that's a toad."

"But I am Lalloree, Daddy, I really *am*!" the toad cried, hopping up and down anxiously.

"Our Lalloree is safely married to Panglunder the Unyielding. She's somewhere way up north, across the river. You're a toad," Brindom said flatly, folding his plump little arms and looking grave.

"She *sounds* like our Lalloree, Daddy," Toomeera said.

"I *am*, I *am*! Panglunder was funny looking, and there was an awful old lady in his castle and they put me to sleep but Uncle Keddie promised to bring me back to you and then we met Handsome and joined a quest but the mist came and turned Conrad and me into toads and even Arlebar couldn't help us but it doesn't matter because we love each other. Can't we get married, please? *Please*, Daddy! Momma, *please* let Conrad marry me!" the little toad blurted, then sat panting for breath.

"Who's Conrad?" Toomeera asked, bewildered.

"She's in trouble, Momma. I was afraid of something like this."

"Now, daddy, it was all your idea to marry our little girl to a warlord. I was all set—"

From the recesses of Kedrigern's hood a small voice rang out. "It is I, Conrad Coeur du Fer de la Tour Brisée, Count of Elberance and Morfoi, Earl of Bexxforde, Heseldown, and Tarncrofts, Grand Marshal to Almorac Goldenbeard of Gossinghans, who seek the hand of your fair daughter!" Climbing to the wizard's shoulder, Conrad made a great leap directly into the cookie dish, scattering bits of broken cookie in all directions. He extricated himself, muttering peevishly, and took his place at Lalloree's side.

"Another toad," Brindom said dimly.

"He has a lovely name, Daddy. And a nice clear voice. And he wants to marry our little girl," Toomeera said, her interest quickening.

Brindom sighed. "I was sort of hoping she'd marry a warlord, or a petty tyrant, or maybe a nice prince."

"This little fellow has all sorts of titles, Daddy."

"Don't suppose a prince would be much interested in a toad," Brindom said glumly.

Conrad puffed up. "Hear me, Your Majesties. I was born to a noble family, and won great honor in the service of my king. When I first laid eyes on your fair daughter, I knew I could love no other, and vowed that I would make myself worthy of her hand. But then . . ." He paused and sighed before going on, "I fell victim to magic so powerful that even the greatest wizard in all the world cannot disenchant me."

Brindom sat down heavily and drummed on the arm of the

chair with his plump fingers. "Is that so, Kedrigern?" he asked.

"It is, Your Majesty."

"Lalloree, too?"

"I'm afraid so."

"Oh, let's give them our permission, Daddy," Toomeera said, patting her husband's hand. "We can have a nice little wedding right here in the castle. You can bake one of your special cakes."

"We could live in the moat!" Lalloree cried excitedly.

"Wouldn't last very long. There's pike in the moat," said Brindom.

"We have that lovely fountain in the garden, Daddy. They could set up housekeeping there."

"Please, Daddy, *please*!"

"I implore you, Your Majesty!"

"Oh, all right, you have our permission," Brindom said wearily.

Kedrigern and Princess smiled at the rejoicing toads and the beaming Toomeera. Brindom snatched up a handful of the broken cookies and munched on them noisily. Toomeera unfolded the apron she had been carrying since her entrance, tied it on, and took up the pitcher and cookie dish.

"I'm just going to get some more milk and cookies. Supper won't be ready for another hour, and you must all be simply starved," she said.

"May we have a few flies, Momma?" Lalloree asked.

"Gracious sakes alive, child, whatever do you . . . ? Oh . . . Well, I'll see if I can rustle up a few nice flies for the two of you."

"Thank you, Your Majesty," said Conrad.

"Call us Momma and Daddy, son. You'd better get used to it."

Supper was a heaping dish of chicken and dumplings in a rich gravy, with Toomeera's own honey-glazed spice cake for dessert. The wizards and the royal couple ate in the small dining alcove off the kitchen. Lalloree and Conrad took supper at the fountain.

Kedrigern and Princess spent the night in the castle's guest room, where everything seemed to be smothered under pink ruffles. They departed the next morning. Brindom and

Toomeera thanked them profusely and presented them with a thousand gold pieces and a dozen sweet buns still warm from the oven.

They rode in silence, enjoying the bright summer morning and each other's company, and when the last house was out of sight and the sun directly overhead they stopped to rest. Kedrigern took two of the buns and gave one to Princess. They reclined in the shade of a maple and slowly ate.

"Very tasty, isn't it, my dear?" said Kedrigern.

"Delicious. So was that spice cake last night."

"And the cookies. Excellent cookies. Well, I'm not surprised."

Princess looked at him curiously. "I am. I've been in palaces where the breads and pastries were practically inedible."

"No danger of that in Brindom and Toomeera's palace."

"And why not?"

"Before they became king and queen, they ran a little pastry shop just a short walk from the castle."

"Is that the custom in this kingdom? I've never heard of heirs to a throne running a pastry shop."

"It's quite unusual, actually. The last ruler here, Jarantra, was 122 when she died, and had outlived all her known descendents. It took months of searching to discover that Toomeera, on her mother's side, was a distant cousin of Jarantra's great-grandfather's aunt. She and Brindom didn't want to give up the pastry shop. They had built a lot of good will, and business was thriving. They only did it for Lalloree's sake, so she could marry someone of station."

"Pity it didn't work out," said Princess sadly.

"Well, Conrad's not all that bad."

"Do you think they'll be happy, Keddie?"

"I'm certain they will, my dear," said the wizard, smiling serenely. "Before we left this morning, I poured a cupful of Arlebar's love potion into the fountain."

Some days later, from the foothills of the Dragonback Mountains, they looked down on the lush green expanse that had once been the Desolation of the Loser Kings. Tall grass and berry bushes and trees newly leaved waved in the breeze, and lakes and ponds formed by the reawakened springs glittered under the morning sun.

"It's quite lovely, isn't it?" Kedrigern called up to Princess.

"It's even more beautiful from up here. You must be very proud of yourself," she said, lazily circling the horses in a slow descent.

"Those good monks and their herbs deserve a lot of the credit, my dear."

"But it was you who came back here and despelled the place. Just think, Keddie . . . people will come and settle here and be happy and prosper, and they'll never know that they owe it all to you."

He raised a hand in a benign gesture. "I don't seek praise, my dear. Just the satisfaction of good work well done, and the occasional fat purse of gold."

"Still, it seems hard," she said, settling lightly down on the transparent horse's saddle. "This place should be called 'Kedrigern's Bounty' and not 'The Desolation of the Loser Kings.' You really ought to get the credit you deserve."

"I'll pass it up. Getting a place named after you is a sure way of being dragged into politics. I prefer to stick to magic."

Princess reached out to pat his hand. "Whatever you like, Keddie," she said sweetly.

"I'll name it after you, my dear. Would that please you?"

"No, thanks. I prefer to stick to magic, too."

The earth so long held barren by magic now thrust forth its pent-up fecundity. Even at this early point in summer, the bushes, and the tiny pear and apple trees, were bowed under their weight of fruit. The horses feasted on juicy sweet grass. The air was heavy with the scent of flowers and somnolent with the drone of bees. Bright birds flashed and swooped around the princess and the wizard as they passed, adding their song to the ground bass of the insects and the burble and plash of ever-swelling streams.

They camped for one night by the alabaster sculpture that once had been a cook's wagon. Already its outlines were softened by climbing vines, brightened by flowers. Birds nested in every cranny, and field mice dwelt beneath its unmoving wheels. There was barely a trace of the other wagon, and no sign at all of their passing only a short time earlier. The scene was lovely, but fraught with melancholy memories, and they did not linger but resumed their travels at first light, moving north without a backward look.

At the Inn on the Outer Edge, Harry came out to greet the wizard with unfeigned joy. The host, inured to peculiar sights, scarcely noticed their horses. He offered Kedrigern and Princess his finest sleeping chamber all to themselves, and promised a dinner of welcome that very night. As the trembling stable boy, having been cuffed and kicked and cursed into motion by his master, fearfully led their horses off, Harry shook the wizard's hand vigorously.

"It's grand to see you again, Master Kedrigern—and this lovely lady you've brought with you. Ah, when we saw the mist gathering over the Desolation, we all thought that was the end of you, but here you are, looking better than ever, and in the company of the loveliest lady who's ever graced these halls."

"This is Princess, my wife," said the wizard.

Harry bowed low. "Honored to meet you, my lady." He straightened and looked at Kedrigern. "What's become of the others? Is there any hope for them? Here, Master Kedrigern, let me carry them vessels for you."

"Careful, Harry. You're carrying three of our companions."

Harry started, nearly dropping the long, slender vessel. "Companions? From the quest? These jars?" he asked, gaping.

"This little one is Ponttry, the squire. The round one is Maheen."

"And . . . I nearly dropped one," Harry said in a numbed undertone.

"That was Smeak," Princess informed him.

"If you look very closely, you can just make out their faces," Kedrigern said, taking Smeak and holding him to the light, allowing the host to inspect him.

"He's smiling!" Harry cried.

"Well, I filled him with wine. I imagine he'll keep smiling as long as he's full. Shall we go in? I'm sure Princess would like to freshen up, and we could both use a good rest in a real bed."

Refreshed and rested, they came down to dinner that evening and found the inn unusually quiet, but filled with an undercurrent of joyous anticipation, like a city on the eve of some great festival. The air shimmered, as desert air does under the unabated sun, and faint shadows seemed to pass to and fro around them, formless and colorless, often no more than the faintest flicker at the corner of the eye, but all radiating an unmistakeable aura of happiness and good will. Kedrigern did not remark on the phenomenon, but as they took their places at the table Harry had laid for them, Princess gave a little flirt of her wings, rose slightly from the floor and turned about, smiling beatifically and clasping her hands on her breast.

"Keddie, it's all the lost travelers—they're free from the spells that held them, and they're so *happy*! Can't you feel the happiness?" she said.

"I can, my dear. Very pleasant it is, too."

"And they know they owe it to you. They can sense it."

As Princess descended to take her seat, Kedrigern felt the circumambient spirits press closer around him. It was an odd sensation, not at all unpleasant or confining, rather like having a garment of gossamer laid over one's shoulders against a mild breeze; he felt enfolded in a cloak of thanksgiving.

"You look very comfortable, Keddie," Princess observed.

"It's quite cozy. It appears that we'll be having company for dinner, my dear. Do you mind?"

"Not at all. They're very friendly."

Maheen rested on the table, replenished with Harry's best wine. A peaceful smile suffused his diminished ceramic features.

"Do you have qualms about using an acquaintance as a decanter?" Kedrigern asked.

"None whatsoever, Keddie. You may pour."

The wine was rich and robust, a perfect accompaniment to the juicy tender slabs of beef that Harry served them and they consumed with gusto. As they sat sighing with repletion over their last bits of cheese and fresh fruit, Princess rose.

"Are you all right, my dear?" Kedrigern asked.

"Just a bit warm. Don't get up, Keddie. I'm going over to the window for a breath of air."

"Now that you mention it, the atmosphere is a bit close."

Kedrigern pushed back his chair, preparatory to rising and joining Princess at the window. He was full and comfortable and surrounded by grateful spirits, and was in no hurry at all to move, so he was still at the table when Princess sat in a chair by the window and with a great whoosh and crackle of air, an afreet appeared in the room.

It was a very large afreet. Its flattened green head nearly touched the ceiling beams and its bloated body splintered a table and thrust benches aside. Its left arm was brilliant red, its right gleamed black, and its hands were pale blue with long curving silver talons. The walls shook and the plates danced as its deep malevolent laughter reverberated through the room. It pointed a long silver-taloned finger at Princess.

"Pretty princess set off spell. Afreet take her away!" he cried, laughing even more wickedly than before.

Coming to her feet with a quick gesture, Princess said, "You will do nothing of the kind."

The afreet lunged forward. There was a loud *clong*, like the sound of a spoon tapped against a crystal bowl, and the afreet leapt back, wringing his hands and making little pained noises. Glowering with his red-rimmed yellow eyes, he hurled himself forward a second time, emitting a shrill howl, and again rebounded to the sound of a deep-toned crystalline knell.

"That will be enough of that, I think," Kedrigern said, rising to face the afreet.

"You make spell?" the afreet demanded in a rage, his eyes dilating and darting flame.

"Not yet. That spell was entirely my wife's," Kedrigern said proudly. "But if you don't disappear right away . . ."

At that moment, all around them, the air began to tingle eagerly. He felt the pent-up anger and the wish to pay old debts. Laughing loudly, he said, "Go right ahead, my friends. He's all yours."

A slight breeze brushed past him, and at once the afreet was enveloped in ghostly presences. As Kedrigern looked on, arms folded, chewing the last morsel of apricot, the afreet winced under a blow, then another, and in no time at all was rolling and writhing on the floor, giving off great cries and groans and caterwauls of pain as an invisible mob pounded, pinched, poked, and pummeled him from all sides. He begged for mercy; he shouted apologies; he implored Princess to intercede for him and Kedrigern to rescue him; he began to shrink. When he was down to just under human size, Kedrigern raised his hands. The pummeling stopped.

"What do you think, my dear? Has he had enough?" the wizard asked.

"He deserves everything he gets," Princess replied angrily. "The colossal nerve of these afreets! Take *me* away, indeed!'

The afreet clambered to his knees, blubbering huge pink-and-orange tears that rolled around the floor like melon balls.

"Please, pretty princess, forgive afreet! Him was beside self for grieving!"

"What have you got to grieve about? All you do is cause grief to others. Just last fall, you carried off a poor little princess from this very room, you heartless wretch."

The afreet gave a wail of anguish and sent forth a volley of dichromatic tears. "Little princess gone away!" he howled. "One day, all gone away—little princess, other people afreet catch, all nice magics hidden everywhere, all go away quick sudden. Afreet come back here to look for new pretty."

"I'm not the least bit interested in being your pretty," Princess said.

The afreet let out a fresh wail. Kedrigern snapped, "Be quiet, you. You're lucky to get off with a thrashing, after all the trouble you've given people these last few centuries."

"Afreet just try to do job right."

"That's what they always say."

"Afreet *supposed* to carry people off, do nasty things," said the afreet self-righteously.

"That will be quite enough of that kind of talk. The evil magic is gone from this region now, and there's no more place for you. Do you understand?" Kedrigern demanded sternly. "In a little while there'll be decent people coming here to settle, and I won't have the likes of you bursting in on them and getting everyone upset."

Leering, the afreet said, "You give afreet pretty princess, him go."

With an accuracy and force that Kedrigern found as impressive as it was unexpected, Princess hurled a joint-stool that caught the afreet just behind his pointed, long-lobed purple ear and sent him sprawling. He crouched on the floor, arms over his head, blubbering, "Afreet must carry off pretty. *Any* pretty be fine, then afreet go away and be good."

Kedrigern looked at Princess and smiled. "Nice work. That was a very neat shield you raised, too."

"Thank you, Keddie. It's good to know that I haven't lost the touch."

"What about this big crybaby? We can't just let him go, or he'll grab the first woman he sees."

"We can't allow that. Do you think Harry . . . ?"

"No."

They stood looking at the weeping, wailing afreet, each of

them deep in thought. After a time, Kedrigern said, "Actually, it would be all to the good if we could find a woman willing to put up with him. Once he has a good sensible wife to keep him in check, an afreet can behave almost decently. This fellow's problem is that the little princess was too young and inexperienced to manage him. What he really needs is someone like . . ."

He glanced aside, smiling faintly, and his eyes met Princess's. She was smiling the same quiet, knowing smile, and they nodded in unison. They stepped closer to the sniveling heap. The pale light of the liberated spirits hung all about the afreet.

"By your leave, friends," Kedrigern said softly. "I think there's a constructive way to deal with this fellow."

The cloud of spirits moved, some parts of it becoming very agitated, sparking and crackling, while other portions swirled slowly and placidly, like peripatetic philosophers deep in meditation. After some minutes it settled, was still, and then slowly faded, and Kedrigern knew that the matter of the afreet had been placed in his hands. He murmured his thanks to the departing wisps, and prodded the afreet with the toe of his boot.

"Swear by the ring of Solomon, Lord of the Djinn and Afreet, that you will obey me and behave yourself, and you may rise in safety," he said.

A yellow eye peeked cautiously through blue fingers. "Afreet no more be thumped?"

"Not if you do as I say. Swear."

"Afreet swear by ring of Solomon. Afreet will obey wizard and behave self," said the creature abjectly.

"You may rise."

Bouncing to his feet, leering, the afreet said, "Now you give afreet pretty, and him go, yes? Where his pretty?"

"He's incorrigible," said Princess with distaste.

"Afreets will be afreets, my dear. It's a matter of training. All this chap needs is a sensible woman who can teach him civilized manners, and in a very short time he can be a suave, polished afreet about town. I can see the potential."

Princess cupped her chin in her hand and studied the gaudy figure. "An ordinary woman couldn't do it," she said thoughtfully. "She'd have to be very special."

"Extraordinarily gifted. Ideally, a sorceress."

Eagerly, the afreet said, "She be pretty, too, yes? You find afreet nice pretty?"

"She'd have to be beautiful. That goes without saying."

"A mature, voluptuous kind of beauty, I'd say."

"A mixture of passion and melting tenderness."

"Where this nice pretty? Where her be?" the afreet cried excitedly, rubbing his hands together with a loud clattering of talons.

"Ah, there's the problem, my motley fellow," said Kedrigern gravely.

"You don't find a woman like that in your typical peasant hovel," Princess pointed out.

"Nor in your ordinary manor house."

"Nor in most palaces, for that matter."

"In fact, I doubt that one could find a score of such women in the whole world."

"A score?" Princess repeated dubiously. "There can't be more than three, at most."

"Three? I can only think of one, and she . . . No, it's impossible," said Kedrigern, shaking his head.

"Where this pretty? You tell afreet, him go get her. Afreet want to be suave and polished. You tell, afreet promise to behave all time forever," the creature begged.

"Well . . . it's a few days' journey from here," Kedrigern said reluctantly.

"She's living in a very nice castle. She may not want to go with you," Princess added.

"And if she doesn't want to go, it will be hard to force her. She's a powerful sorceress. Besides being a voluptuous beauty."

"Afreet fix. You show afreet castle."

"That's another problem. I don't have a map, and I'm terrible at giving directions. Wait a minute, now . . . afreets can fly, can't they?"

"Afreet fly like bird, only faster."

"Could you carry the two of us, and our horses?"

"We don't have much baggage," Princess said.

"You wouldn't have to carry us all the way there. You could drop us off a few miles from the place and go on ahead."

"Afreet take you and horses. Also baggage. You ready?"

"Not now, my impetuous fellow. I couldn't find the way in the dark. We'll leave after breakfast. Meanwhile—as earnest of your good intentions—you might tidy up the dining room. You've made an awful mess of things."

"Afreet fix, make tidy. You be ready, we leave after breakfast, horses and all," the afreet said, rubbing his hands together with a great jangling.

"We'll be ready," said Kedrigern, taking Princess's arm and turning toward the door. Just as they were leaving the dining room, the afreet called to them.

"You tell afreet name of nice pretty in castle?" he asked.

"All in good time. We'll tell you before we arrive there," Kedrigern replied.

"Pretty lady have pretty name? Afreet like pretty name."

"You'll adore her, and her name," Princess said, smiling her most radiant smile. "You were made for each other."

···⟨ *Epilogue* ⟩···

homecoming

PANGLUNDER STOOD AT the main gate of Mon Chagrin in his nightshirt, looking bewildered. In one hand he held a wicked-looking battle-ax. He was blinking at a phenomenal rate, and his words came with difficulty.

"I say, Kedrigern . . . the most extraordinary . . . the most amazing . . . I don't expect you to believe . . . hardly believe it myself . . . most extraordinary," he jabbered, accompanying his words with vague gestures of his free hand.

"Is something wrong?" Kedrigern asked, dismounting.

"Oh, yes, extremely wrong. Most outrageously wrong. Great apparition, right in the middle of . . . oh, I say!" Panglunder cried, dropping his battle-ax, as Princess rose from her transparent mount and lighted softly at Kedrigern's side, her little wings humming merrily. He noticed the horses for the first time, and shut his eyes tightly.

"It's all right, Panglunder. The horses are real," Kedrigern assured him. "This is Princess, my wife. You've met."

"I was a toad at the time," Princess explained.

"Yes, of course. You're . . . looking much better, I must say."

"And how is everything at Mon Chagrin? You seem a bit ill at ease, if I may say so. Been beseiged by someone? Any enchantments I should know about? How's dear Memanesha these days?" Kedrigern asked, clapping the blinking warlord on the shoulder.

195

"It's Memanesha. She's gone . . . carried off . . . snatched from my side . . . only moments ago!"

"We saw no army, Panglunder. Surely such a daring raid would— "

"It was no army, it was an apparition. A great blubbery yellow-eyed thing, skin all red and black and blue, with great talons . . . ghastly-looking thing to have pop into one's bedroom of a morning."

"Sounds like an afreet to me," Princess said, looking somber.

"I'm afraid so," Kedrigern said. They exchanged a glance, and shook their heads gravely.

"The most extraordinary thing was, it *knew* her *name*! It burst into the room shouting her name. 'Memanesha! Where my pretty?' it cried, and then it scooped her up, and they both vanished."

"Definitely an afreet," said Princess. "They're very quick."

"Very possessive, too. I'm afraid you've seen the last of Memanesha, my friend. Buck up," said Kedrigern.

Panglunder drew a deep breath, threw his shoulders back, raised his head high, set his jaw, and gazed off to the east with narrowed eyes. Except for the fact that he was in his nightshirt, the effect was quite heroic. "Then I've found my quest," he said, his voice steely. "A long and perilous road lies before me, but I will rise up, and arm, and go forth. I shall not sleep under a roof, nor drink wine, until I have my beloved back."

"You're being rash. You'll never see Memanesha again," Kedrigern told him firmly.

"That's marvelous news, old chap. I was referring to Lalloree," Panglunder said cheerily.

"Lalloree?"

"Of course. Dear little thing, Lalloree. A man could spend a lifetime with Lalloree and never once have to worry about having her lose her temper and turn him into . . . into something loathsome."

"Like a toad?" Princess said tartly. "I thought your arrangement with Lalloree was purely political."

"That's how it started. But the moment I saw the dear creature . . ." Panglunder paused and heaved a great sigh. "Memanesha noticed at once, and enveloped her in flame. I had to pretend indifference, for Lalloree's sake. But now . . ."

Princess slipped her arm through Panglunder's and gave his hand a comforting pat. Kedrigern, on his other side, put his arm around the warlord's shoulder.

"I think we ought to go inside, Panglunder, so we can tell you our whole story before you do anything rash," he said.

"It would be best if you were seated," Princess added.

It was with a warm inner feeling of accomplishment that Kedrigern and Princess ascended the last steep slope of Silent Thunder Mountain leading to their cottage. They had done what they set out to do, and a great deal besides.

Princess was a lovely woman once again, and certain to remain so. She had gained an attractive and useful pair of wings. Handsome, too, was permanently liberated from toadhood, and passionately in love with Lazica, herself a fly no longer. Lalloree and Conrad, though toads, at least had each other, a pleasant fountain to live in, the sympathy and understanding of her parents, and the valuable assistance of Arlebar's love potion. Arlebar had his rest at last, and Death had Arlebar. Rospax had a good home, and was being useful.

Even Smeak, Maheen, and Ponttry seemed to have a tolerable future. Harry had kindly offered to retain them at the Inn on the Outer Edge as decanters. Their expressions, when filled and stoppered, suggested complete satisfaction with this arrangement. The Desolation of the Loser Kings was bursting with life and purged of its heritage of vile enchantments. All had indeed turned out well.

Kedrigern picked his way through the maze of false trails and blind byways in the silence of concentrated attention. He and Princess exchanged words only when he shouted up questions and she called down directions. When they reached the last long curving stretch before the cottage, Princess swooped gracefully down and settled on her limpid steed.

"I feel sorry for poor Panglunder," she said after a time. "I'm not the least bit sorry for Memanesha or the afreet, but I hate to think of Panglunder all alone in that gloomy castle."

"He'll get over the loss, my dear. All for the best, actually."

"That sounds a bit callous, Keddie, I must say."

"Well, you saw what a flirt Lalloree was with Conrad. And she flirted with Handsome even when he was a toad. Think what might have happened if she'd become chatelaine of Mon Chagrin and a handsome prince had stayed for the night. Wars have started over less,'' said the wizard soberly.

Princess rode in thoughtful silence for a bit longer, then said, ''Perhaps you're right. Still, poor Panglunder . . . I hope he doesn't take to drink.''

''He won't, my dear. I gave him my flask of Old Fenny Snake just before we left. One sip of that will cure him of any desire for further imbibing. Ever.''

They decided to walk the rest of the way home. At the end of the long curve they stopped, hand in hand, to gaze upon their cottage. It was a warm and welcome sight. The evening sun struck gold from the western windows. Long shadows deepened on the lawn and fell on the little dooryard where Kedrigern took his nap on sunny afternoons in the cool weather. To the east rose the sun-flooded peak of Silent Thunder Mountain, still crowned in white. Off to the west of the house stood the arbor, shaded by two majestic oaks that spread like great green mushrooms over the space beneath. And that was very odd, for when they had left, in early spring, only one oak had stood in the arbor.

''My dear . . . does everything look right?'' the wizard asked.

''It's lovely, Keddie. I'm so happy to be back home.''

''But does it look *right?*'' he persisted.

''The garden could stand weeding.''

''How about the arbor?''

''It looks lovely and cool. Those oaks . . .'' She paused and furrowed her brow. ''Keddie, wasn't there *one* oak when we left?''

''There was, my dear.''

''And we've only been gone a few months; not enough time for an acorn to grow *that* size. Oh, I hope this isn't an enchantment, Keddie. Really, I'm in no mood to cope with an enchantment after all the traveling we've done. I just want to take a nice bath, and have a light supper, and get to bed early. I don't want to have to deal with an enchanted tree; not until I've rested up, at any rate,'' Princess said impatiently.

''Well, let's just see what we have to deal with,'' Kedrigern said, reaching in his tunic for the medallion and raising it to his eye to peer through the Aperture of True Vision. He gazed for a moment, then turned to her, smiling. ''Nothing to worry about, my dear. It's someone we know.''

"I don't know any trees."

"It's Anlorel and Gylorel. It would appear that their quest was successful."

He waved to the oaks. Though the evening was still, the top of the larger tree swayed in response. A corona of sparkling lights encircled both, winking like a legion of fireflies in the upper branches.

"Welcome home, good wizard!" a deep voice boomed, to the accompaniment of mellow chiming.

"This is a pleasant surprise. Allow me to present Princess, my wife. She was with us on the quest, but she remained concealed."

"We are honored," said the voice, and the chimes rang merrily while pinpoints of light flickered overhead.

"But what are you doing here? I thought that once your quest was over, you'd return to Dark Wood. How did your quest turn out, anyway?"

"We found our father. The evil mist had petrified him," said Gylorel, while Anlorel tolled a slow knell.

Princess patted the trunk of the oak gently in sympathy, murmuring, "We're sorry to hear that . . . after all the searching and the journeying. . . ."

"The mist disappeared the day after we left you. We had great hopes of finding him. But when we did, he had already been turned to stone," said Gylorel.

"If it's any consolation, the mist is gone forever. Keddie destroyed it," Princess announced, taking the wizard's arm and beaming at the trees.

With much rumbling and ringing, the air was filled with the response, "Then he is a great wizard indeed, and we did right to come to him."

"Just why *did* you come?" Kedrigern asked.

"We seek wisdom."

"I don't teach, I do magic."

"But you are a wise and good man, and know much about the world. We would learn from you."

"You do me honor. But even the wisest man can't teach you how to be a good tree."

With an agitated rustle of his upper branches, Gylorel said, "We must learn to rule over the forest. Our father cannot teach us. We ask only that you allow us to remain here to listen and observe until we feel ready to return to Dark Wood."

"We will not trouble you," Anlorel chimed in. "Let us stay, and we will shade you from the afternoon sun and shelter you from the wind. Birds will nest in our branches and fill the air with sweet sound and glorious color."

"It would be nice to have someone to talk to if you're called away. It does get lonely here with no one around but Spot," Princess said.

"You're welcome to stay as long as you wish, and listen and observe and learn whatever you can," Kedrigern announced, looking up into the green mass looming over him.

"We thank you, kindly wizard, and ask one further boon: may we have your permission to wed this lovely oak that stands at our side?"

"Isn't this charming, Keddie? What a wonderful homecoming!" Princess exclaimed.

"Indeed it is, my dear. Of course you may, my friends, and I wish you great happiness," the wizard said.

Scarcely had he spoken when the evening was filled with soft rustling and chiming and the creak of branches gently rubbing one another in tender arboreal caresses. With a farewell wave, Princess and Kedrigern turned and made their way arm in arm toward the cottage, quite content. Their horses grazed placidly on the twilit lawn, and they paused to look upon the peaceful scene.

"Keddie . . . do you hear the voices?" Princess asked.

"Voices? What sort of voices?"

"Little happy voices. Like children playing far away," she said, cupping a hand beside her ear.

Kedrigern followed her example. Sure enough, he heard faint cries and tiny shouts of glee. "Of course, my dear—how silly of me to forget—it's Midsummer Night!" he exclaimed.

"The fairy ring!"

Hand in hand they hurried to the eastern slope. There, bent forward, alert, they made their way slowly, scanning the ground, closing in on the source of the merry wee voices.

"There it is, Keddie!" Princess cried.

No sooner had she spoken than the fairy voices were stilled. But in an instant, a chorus called out, "It's Princess and the wizard! They're home again!" and a small circular patch of the lawn at their feet came aglow with the light of scores of tiny lanterns. In twos and threes, diminutive figures stepped forward to offer greeting.

"Welcome home, sweet Princess and wise Kedrigern!"

"Thank you, Peasblossom and Mustardseed," said Princess.

"Well met by twilight, good wizard and lovely lady!"

"We thank you, Tansy and Samphire, and you, Zingiber and Coltsfoot," said the wizard, bowing low.

"Our blessings on your home and hearth, kind folk!"

"Thank you, Coriander and Lovage. Thank you, Cobweb," said Princess, seating herself on the grass and smiling down on the little people. Kedrigern took his place at her side, and together they received and gratefully acknowledged the welcomes and good wishes of the fairy band. When all the rest had greeted them, their chief stepped forward and with a flourish of his glittering wings and a spray of tiny motes of light, bowed profoundly and announced:

> "We are happy, every one,
> That your anxious quest is done,
> And Princess, whom all adore,
> Is a little toad no more."

"Why, thank you, Puck. That's very sweet of you," said Princess.

> "Our relief is most profound:
> Seeing you home safe and sound
> Much increases our delight
> On this sweet Midsummer Night.
> As we gaily dance and sing
> Here within our fairy ring
> We will pause, from time to time,
> To pronounce a grateful rhyme
> For the fortunate return
> Of Princess and Kedrigern."

"You're more than gracious, Puck, and we appreciate this kind welcome," said the wizard, rising and assisting his wife to her feet. "If you'll excuse us, we'll go inside now and let you resume the revelry."

"Good night, Puck. Good night, everyone," Princess said, waving to the assembly.

A chorus of tiny voices echoed her farewell, and then at once, with cries of "Over here, Cobweb!" and "Come on,

Moth, dance with Scammery and Mustardseed!" and "Melilot and Mistletoe are going to sing a comic song!" the little folk returned to their festivities.

"Dear little things," said Princess as they started for the cottage. "That was thoughtful of them."

"Woodland fairies are a decent sort. Mischievous now and then, but there's not a bit of malice in them. It's the water fairies you have to watch out for."

"I know," said Princess. "And bog-fairies are the worst of all."

"No need to think of such things ever again, my dear. Bertha's spell is broken forever."

"Yes. It was a successful trip, Keddie, in every way. But I'm glad to be home."

While they were still some distance away, the front door swung wide and a small, grotesque figure appeared in the doorway. It stood transfixed for a moment, then it began to bounce up and down on its great flat feet, clapping its huge hands and wiggling its saillike ears ecstatically. "Yah, yah!" it cried joyously, a smile splitting its knobbed and warty face.

"We're home, Spot!" Princess called, waving to it.

It raced to them in great bounds, shouting, "Yah! Yah!" at each bound. When it reached them, it skidded to a halt and began to bounce up and down eagerly. At the sight of Princess rising into the air with a soft hum of her dainty wings, Spot fell to the ground astonished and lay supine, its tiny eyes agape.

"That's right, Spot. Princess can fly now," said Kedrigern.

"Yah?" the house-troll inquired faintly.

"She won't go far. We're home to stay," the wizard assured it.